The Dragon's Child

The Dragon's Child

Six Short Stories

J. Kathleen Cheney

1st Print Edition, 2017, cover by J. Kathleen Cheney.

NEWSLETTER INFORMATION:

If you would like to get the latest publication information, please consider signing up for the newsletter. Your email and personal information will not be shared.

Sign up for the newsletter by visiting
www.jkathleencheney.com

Please consider leaving an honest review of this book to help other readers find it.

Contents

About These Stories:

The Dragon's Child was originally published in **Beneath Ceaseless Skies** in December of 2008. **Early Winter, Near Jenli Village** was originally published in **Fantasy Magazine** in 2009, and was placed on the *Locus Recommended Reading List for 2009*.

The Dragon's Child

The Dragon's Child

The ground trembled and the mountains shook, bringing all motion in the great courtyard of the wizard's complex to a halt—guards and servants alike stilled in fright. Jia-li clung to Kseniya's arm until the tremor passed, her dark eyes wide.

Breath steaming in the frigid air, Kseniya glanced down at the girl and squeezed her hand. "It's over now."

Jia-li's brows drew together. "I can feel the dragons under the mountain, and they are angry," she whispered.

The dragons' fury had become more evident the last few months, the quakes growing more frequent, making Kseniya wonder if the wizard's control over them had grown lax.

Jia-li shivered. "They don't want to be there. I told my father so. I told him he should let them go, but he just says I don't understand."

A thing he often told her. The wizard kept Jia-li at lessons most of the day, a hard thing for any child to endure. That the child was also his daughter made no difference to him. He showed no love for the girl, nor any interest in her beyond her general health and what talents she demonstrated. And with her mother dead, only Kseniya remained to care for her.

Kseniya knelt in the snow and straightened the collar of the girl's quilted jacket. Even after eight years, she still found it disconcerting that Jia-li had her father's eyes, dark brown with a distinctive hooded shape. Only the lighter hue of the girl's hair gave hint of her foreign mother's blood. "Come, you don't want to be late. He would be angry."

Jia-li nodded dutifully. Two guards stood at the outer gate, so Kseniya stopped there while Jia-li walked up the wide red-painted stairs of the wizard's grand house without looking back.

It would have to be soon, Kseniya decided as she watched Jia-li disappear within those walls. Now that the girl was old enough to make the trek through the mountains, Kseniya had to find a way to steal her away before the wizard broke the girl's spirit and corrupted her soul.

In the pale afternoon light that slipped through the high windows of the storeroom, the fine silk of a red veil slid through Kseniya's fingers, and she wondered when a bride had ever come to this bleak mountaintop. Underneath folded lengths of more mundane fabrics, she'd found an old wooden chest, and secreted inside lay a fortune in embroidered silks—tunics and jackets and trousers—the answer to her prayers.

She had always known that if she were to steal away with her niece, it must be in winter when the dragons preferred to sleep. These long-forgotten silks would provide warmth during their passage, and when they escaped the mountains she could sell them for food.

She shut the lid and quickly rearranged the fabrics over the chest, only regretful she'd not found any weapon within. She took a deep breath and forced down her excitement. She could not risk giving away her intentions.

Calmed, she gathered up the length of plain ramie Bao-yu had sent her to fetch and hurried back to the inner hall of the women's house. The old woman took the cloth in her wrinkled fingers, then smiled and patted Kseniya's hand in thanks.

Unable to speak, Bao-yu was still the closest thing Kseniya had to an ally atop this mountain, the only one of the servant women willing to associate with the outlander held among them. Bao-yu didn't seem to mind her foreign style of dress or strange accent. Nor did she look away from Kseniya's scar-lined face, as most of the women did.

The mountain froze in the winter and no rain fell in the summer, making it inhospitable, so servants never stayed long, neither the men who guarded the wizard's complex nor the women who did the cooking and washing. Only Bao-yu had lived there longer than Kseniya, and she supposed the old woman simply had no place else to go.

Bao-yu resumed her work, embroidering a hidden luck-token on the inside of the collar of one of Jia-li's tunics. It was one of the dragons native to this country, Kseniya realized, not the fiery creatures the wizard held captive. The servants told tales of the dragon the wizard had driven away with his horde ages before—one who brought the spring and rain—but Kseniya thought that creature a myth. Even so, Bao-yu's furtive rebellion against their master warmed her.

When a knock sounded on the outer door, Kseniya went to open it, expecting her niece returned from the wizard's house. Indeed she found Jia-li there, the wizard's bodyguard with one hand on the girl's shoulder.

Her eyes properly downcast, Kseniya didn't catch his movement in time to retreat. He laid a hand upon her arm.

Startled, she slammed his hand into the doorframe and trapped it there, her fingers clamped about his wrist. A knife lay concealed under his jacket's sleeve, stiff against her palm. His fingers stayed relaxed, though, not resisting her hold.

Aghast at her actions, Kseniya grasped Jia-li's jacket with her free hand and dragged the girl into the warmth of the hall. Then she stepped back and let go of the man's wrist. She kept her eyes on the ground, desperately wishing she could look at his face to gauge his reaction.

To her surprise, he didn't strike her in return. "I need to speak with you," was all he said, the words delivered in a whisper. Then his dark-booted feet moved out of her range of vision.

Kseniya raised her face and stared after him, her heart pounding, but he was long gone. What had she done?

There would be trouble later due to her rashness, threatening all her planning. Letting loose a shaky sigh, Kseniya closed the door.

Jia-li stood in the foyer, her pale face worried. "What happened?"

"He startled me, dearest. That's all." Kseniya didn't think she'd heard the man's voice once since his arrival on the wizard's mountain late in the fall. She didn't know what it meant that he'd spoken to her. In all her time on the mountain, none of the guards had ever come near her, repulsed by the scars that mapped her skin. She bit her lip. "Does he ever talk to you?"

Jia-li shook her head. "He just watches."

Easy to believe, for the man had alarmingly sharp eyes. Kseniya had tried to avoid him, reckoning him more of a threat than the old bodyguard he'd replaced. It would have to be tonight, she decided then, even though the moon was not full. She would have preferred more light.

Sighing, she leaned down and turned Jia-li's hands upward so that she could see the girl's palms. The skin showed red and blistered. "Let's go back to your room so I can take care of these."

In the winter the house felt chilly, but Jia-li's ornate bedroom in the rear of the building retained its warmth. The girl settled cross-legged on her silk-draped bed, her light-brown hair streaming over one shoulder. With her back to the lamp, the flame outlined her small form with a flickering glow.

"It is worse every day," Jia-li said, her eyes glistening. "He keeps asking me things I can't do."

Kseniya knelt and took the girl's hands in her own. The blisters lay under Jia-li's skin, not atop it, as if the skin burned from the inside, the fire inherent in the girl burning its way out of her body.

Kseniya concentrated her will into her hands, and where they touched Jia-li's, she set the damaged flesh to rights, thieving away the pain. She felt grateful for the winter's cold—it eased the fire that prickled along her skin. She let it flow throughout her body, spreading the dull ache thinly so that it did little harm beyond discomfort. She breathed slowly, her eyes shut, not wanting to worry the girl.

Jia-li's small hand touched her cheek, tracing along one of the old scars. "I wish you would teach me to heal."

"When you are older, dearest. You're not ready yet." Kseniya opened her eyes and smiled at her.

"I wish he weren't my father," Jia-li said.

"I know," Kseniya whispered. The women's house had ears, and ill-spoken words might find their way back to the wizard. Whether by magic or some mundane method, it mattered not. Better to give the man nothing to use against them.

For a second, she suspected Jia-li would cry, but the girl squared her small shoulders, determination on her face. "Will you tell me about my mother again?"

Kseniya refused to let her sister's memory die. As one of their father's bastards, Kseniya had been raised by Anushka's side—to guard her more royal sibling. But Anushka's will to live had faded after giving birth to Jia-li, and she slipped away to a different freedom.

Kseniya tucked an errant strand of Jia-li's hair behind her ear and resettled herself on the floor. "Your mother was a princess of the Cholodio Mountains, and her people were known far and wide for their healers. When the Emperor heard of them, he decided he must have them. He took all his soldiers there but couldn't conquer the mountains. So he set his wizard at the task, and *he* unleashed his dragons upon their lands, destroying their villages and farms."

It sounded only like a child's story now, even to her own ears—and she had lived through it. "The princess escaped and hid among her people, but the wizard sent men to hunt her. Long before, a seer had prophesied that the wizard would only be defeated by a child of his own blood. So, to save her people, Anushka gave herself up. When you were born, she hoped you would be the one to free them."

"And then we can leave?" Jia-li asked in a wistful voice.

She had chosen not to burden the girl with hopes of escape, and even now thought it best to hold them secret. "Yes, dearest. Then we will go home."

It was no small matter, waking the girl in the dead of the night, but the moon would rise soon, and Kseniya wanted them off the mountaintop before the light gave away their escape. She stole into the storeroom and retrieved the satchel hidden there, filled now with hoarded food and the finest of the bridal silks.

Jia-li dressed without argument, drawing on layer after layer for warmth. Once satisfied, Kseniya carried the girl through the women's house and out to the courtyard. They slipped through the side door onto the platform where the washer women rinsed their laundry in a spring that emerged from under the foundations of the house.

A gate led out on the back of the mountain, the path the guards watched least in the winter as it led only down a steep, icy trail. "We must stay in the shadows," she whispered.

Jia-li nodded fervently, and Kseniya set the girl on her feet. But when they stepped toward the distant gate, it swung inward.

One of the guards, Kseniya realized, sneaking into the women's house. Heart pounding, she shoved Jia-li behind her. The guard couldn't help but see her there, but she hoped he might not notice the child cringing behind her.

He stopped twenty paces from them. The rising moon's pale light crossed his face—the wizard's bodyguard.

Kseniya didn't know how he'd guessed they would flee this night, but it was over, her attempt to steal Jia-li away ruined before they even escaped the house. Biting back tears of frustration, Kseniya cursed herself silently. Her aggressive reaction to his touch must have warned the man that she'd been trained to arms, and made him suspicious of her.

The man came no closer, though, holding his hands wide. It seemed an odd gesture, one perhaps meant to lull her suspicions.

"Go," she whispered to Jia-li and pushed the girl toward the courtyard. She heard the girl's footsteps patter away, too soft for the man to notice. And once a moment had passed, Kseniya fled the platform as well, her heart like lead.

Kseniya sat in the inner hall of the women's house, where the morning light from the courtyard served best for mending. Bao-yu sat nearby, completing the embroidery she'd begun the day before.

In the quiet before dawn, Kseniya had returned the silks to the chest and thrown the food out past the gate where the birds could squabble over it. She hoped the wizard might believe she'd merely stood on that platform in the night to look at the stars. The bodyguard might not even have seen the girl behind her. And Jia-li had not known her plan, which should protect the girl should her father question her.

When the groan of the outer gate alerted Kseniya, she went to greet her niece, but it wasn't Jia-li in the courtyard. Two of the wizard's guards stood there.

"Come," one ordered.

Kseniya hadn't been inside the wizard's house for years. Large braziers burned on the edges of the room, keeping it over-warm. It reeked of incense, a heavy cloying musk meant to mask the burning smell of the wizard himself. That remembered scent triggered a wave of nausea, and Kseniya paused. Then she lifted her head and walked to the carpet before the dais where the wizard held his court.

He sat on a heavily-carved chair of dark rosewood—a copy of the emperor's throne, one of the other servants had once told her. The wizard's dark hair showed far grayer than when Kseniya had last seen him. His handsome face sagged about his hooded eyes, age and power wearing at his flesh.

His robes of blue silk were richly embroidered, dragons flying across them stitched in bronze and red and gold. Not the slender twisting dragons Kseniya had seen on the robes of envoys from the Emperor's court, but the wizard's own dreadful creatures, fire and smoke billowing from their jaws. They were carved into the beams of the sanctuary, painted on the red walls.

They looked out of the wizard's eyes at her.

The bodyguard stood some distance behind the dais, his somber tunic and trousers letting him blend into the shadows. Even so, Kseniya could feel his eyes on her. Her two encounters with him had surely led to this pass.

One of the guards pressed a hand on her shoulder, and Kseniya sank to her knees.

"Why did you bring her?" Jia-li asked from somewhere beyond her line of vision. The girl must be several feet behind her, and to the left. The bodyguard's dark eyes flicked in Jia-li's direction, confirming that.

"Quiet, girl," the wizard said. He raised a hand, his long, pointed nails painted with blue lacquer. With one finger, he drew a slashing arc through the air.

Pain seared like fire along Kseniya's cheek, a line cutting across one of the old scars. She clenched her jaw to keep from crying out. She remembered that pain all too well.

Jia-li screamed. She turned to her father and cried, "Stop it! Stop it!"

The first flare of pain passed, leaving a low burning in Kseniya's skin like poison. She could sense blood, hot and sticky, flowing down her cheek, but didn't dare heal herself. Should the wizard witness it, she feared he might learn the way of healing from her.

And there would be more to come; she knew that from experience. A drop of blood fell to her chest, bright against the drab ramie of her over-robe.

"Now, you will heal her," the wizard said to his daughter.

"I can't!" Jia-li protested. "I don't know how."

The wizard stroked the air again, and the dragon's fire cut through Kseniya's skin, a trail of red blossoming across her left sleeve. Kseniya bit down on her tongue.

"Heal her," he said. "You heal your hands at night, so I know you have the power in you."

The girl cast a horrified glance at Kseniya.

The bodyguard hadn't precipitated this after all, she realized. "No," she mouthed at the girl.

That defiance earned another stripe, this time running from shoulder to shoulder.

"Heal her," the wizard ordered, his voice louder.

It had been the same with Anushka—the constant demands that she demonstrate her ability to heal. The wizard had only kept Kseniya alive to provide a victim for his game. *I should have warned the girl before*, she thought. *I knew this day would come.*

Jia-li drew herself up to her full height, crossed her arms over her chest, and lifted her chin. "She's only a servant," she said in a disdainful tone.

It was a valiant attempt, but the wizard ignored her ploy. He raised his hand, and fire traced across Kseniya's forehead. Blood seeped into the corner of her eye, and she shook her head, trying to dash it out. One of the guards put his hand atop her head to keep her still.

It went on until Jia-li lay sobbing at her father's feet.

"Heal her," the wizard insisted.

Kseniya had no recollection of how she got back to the women's house. She lay on the cold tiles of her tiny room, the smell of her own blood going stale about her. It must be night, she decided, for only a dim sliver of light showed under her door.

The wizard would do it again, she knew, once she had recovered enough. His talent let him cut flesh, even from a distance, but nothing else. He couldn't cut her clothes or put out her eyes. His guards, however, could easily do that for him. Little else held much horror for her any longer, but Kseniya feared the day she would lose her eyes.

And there was no hope of escape now. Weakened so, she could never make it through the frozen mountains alone, much less with a child. She pressed one hand over her mouth to quiet the sound of her sobs.

Someone leaned over her in the darkened room, and Kseniya jerked away in sudden fright.

"Hush. I will not harm you." Light flared about a man's form as he uncovered one pane of a lantern. The wizard's bodyguard fetched the pitcher of water and basin from her table and picked up a towel. "I do not think you should lie on your bed yet," he said. "Can you sit here?"

The wooden chair by the door seemed too far. "I am too weak to walk," she whispered.

"I will help." He half-carried her to the chair. Her headscarf slid to the floor and her braid came loose. It fell over her shoulder, looking like a stream of blood in the darkness. "I have an unguent to help these heal," he said. "I must clean them first."

She felt too weak to fight him, no matter what he did.

"These are narrow cuts and should knit well." He dabbed at her face, cleaning away dried blood. "I confess I suspected how you earned all those scars. I regret that I cannot protest."

The thin lines crisscrossing her face represented hours of pain under the wizard's phantom touch. "He would not heed you in any case. He is not kind."

A short, dry laugh greeted that statement. "No. Kindness does not run in his blood. Do you understand what he wants of her?"

Kseniya forced herself to focus. "I believe he wishes to learn to heal himself."

"But healing is an inborn talent, is it not?" The bodyguard wet the towel again and wrung it out over her basin. "There is a great difference. Save for the dragon's fire, his own inborn talent, all the arts he practices are learned ones. He cannot *learn* to heal."

Kseniya hissed as he caught the edge of a cut.

"I'm sorry," he said. "She is too young, anyway, is she not?"

Jia-li would not be able to heal for years, not until she

reached her full growth. "How do you know that?"

"My mother is of the Condara, who know much of your people."

Nearly a century before, the wizard had sent his fire-dragons to hunt down the nomadic peoples of the steppes in the name of his emperor. The Condara were one of the few surviving clans. They had lived quietly in the valley south of her own people's mountains until the day the dragons returned to stamp them out.

Yet this man's hair and dress proclaimed him one of the Manchu, the Emperor's clan. With his dark hair and dark eyes, he looked like he might be of the Emperor's own family. "I wouldn't have thought you one of the Condara," she finally said.

"And you should not tell, either. But you have shown you can hold your tongue." His dark eyes looked inky black in the dimness of the room. "He wants to be certain that healing is an inborn gift, rather than an art."

"Why?"

"For that reason, he *bred* her. To bear a healer's gift as well as the dragon's fire, so that when he places his spirit into her body, he will possess both."

Kseniya stared, uncertain if she'd heard him aright. "He will place his spirit in her body?"

The bodyguard nodded his head and produced from a satchel a small tin, an unguent that smelled strongly of herbs. He patted some against the freshly bleeding cut on her cheek and the pain fled. "You didn't know?"

"No. What would become of Jia-li?"

The bodyguard dabbed more of the unguent on the cut across her forehead. "He lives on by taking over the body of another—to cheat death and hold onto his power. In time, *she* will become the Emperor's wizard, only it will not be her living in that body any longer."

She had feared his breaking Jia-li's spirit, but this was far more horrifying. "I cannot let that happen."

"*You* cannot stop him. His magics protect him. None can come near him unless they share his blood."

She shook her head, but the motion made her dizzy.

"You need to rest. We can discuss this later." He lifted a small bowl from her shelf and poured water into it. Then he pulled a slip of paper out of the satchel, folded to hold herbs, and poured them into the water. "Let this steep for a few minutes, then drink it all. It will help build up your strength."

Kseniya felt her eyes drifting closed. The bodyguard shook her shoulder. "Do not fall asleep until you have cleaned all the cuts. Can you do so yourself?"

"Yes," she whispered. "Why are you helping me?"

But he was gone. Kseniya eased off her blood-stained robes and tended the cuts across her chest and arms. She hoped the man had good intentions, for though he chose to help her, he could have killed her just as easily.

Kseniya woke, stiff and sore in every part. She'd lain down atop her bed without even bothering to don a shift, allowing the cold to ease away the burn of the dragon's fire. Flecks of blood marked her fingers where she'd touched one of her cuts in the night. All told, she felt fortunate to be breathing still.

Her first attempt to rise failed, so she lay there and waited until her weakness receded. After a time, she used the chair as a crutch and heaved herself upright.

Her bloodstained garments were scattered about the floor where she had dropped them. The tin of unguent lay near the door, the overturned bowl next to it.

Recalling that she hadn't seen Jia-li since the afternoon before, Kseniya forced herself to dress, taking fresh garments from the chest next to her narrow bed. The stained ones she bundled together to take to Bao-yu. The old woman could get blood out of anything.

When Kseniya entered the inner hall in the center of the women's house, Jia-li threw her arms about her waist, sobbing.

"Hush, dearest," Kseniya whispered.

Jia-li drew away and wiped her streaming eyes. "They wouldn't let me see you."

"I expect not, dearest. I was very tired."

"I was so afraid."

Kseniya knelt on the floor, feeling better for not standing. She set her hands on the girl's shoulders and gazed into her dark eyes. "You were very brave. It's harder for you to watch me hurt than it is for me to endure it. I know. Your mother went through this many times."

"I don't want him to hurt you." Jia-li's small mouth turned down at the corners.

Kseniya managed a smile that didn't pull at the cuts on her face. "I don't either, but I prefer this to his hurting you. Explain to him that you don't know how to heal. If he doesn't believe you, then there is nothing more you can do."

Jia-li leaned closer. "He doesn't know that *you* can."

"He has always suspected."

"I wish he was dead."

Kseniya stroked the girl's pale cheek, wondering if that was the truth of the prophecy—that the girl must kill her own father. "Hush. We will survive this."

At least, she hoped they would.

The wizard didn't send for Kseniya that day. Instead he kept Jia-li working at her normal tasks: making fire between her hands and moving small things without touching them. Smaller parts of his talent, Kseniya believed, that would allow Jia-li to control the dragon's fire. The girl returned to the women's house with burned palms again.

"He didn't hurt you today," Jia-li said as Kseniya inspected her hands.

"He tries to make you dread it." She knew this game well. "He will wait until you don't expect it."

The girl nodded gravely. Kseniya gathered her faded strength to heal the girl's hands, but Jia-li jerked them away. "No, don't."

"Punishing yourself will not change what he's done, dearest."

Jia-li's lower lip slid out, a rare mulish expression. "You should heal yourself instead."

She had done so where it couldn't be seen, causing the cuts across her chest and arms to knit. Covered from the wizard's sight, he wouldn't know of it unless he had the guards strip her. If he did that, she would have greater worries than explaining healed cuts.

"Perhaps he will wait longer if he thinks I am unwell," she suggested.

Jia-li refused to let Kseniya heal her hands anyway, and Kseniya honored that decision. Instead, she went to her room and retrieved the tin of unguent. "We can rub this into your palms and wrap them so you don't hurt them in your sleep."

Jia-li acquiesced and went to her bed that night with her hands covered in a clean pair of summer stockings.

Kseniya returned to her room and blew out her candle. She lay awake on her pallet for some time, listening. Her patience was rewarded when she heard a quiet footfall in the hallway outside her door. A second later, the bodyguard slipped inside. He closed the door behind him and opened his lantern.

Kseniya caught the faint smell of burning about him, picked up from the wizard during the day, no doubt. Jia-li's skin bore that same scent.

"What is your name?" she asked as he settled on the floor.

His dark eyes laughed. "I am not going to tell you that, woman, not if there is a chance it could come to his ears."

"You think I would tell?"

"After yesterday, certainly not. But walls have ears. I am pleased that you seem better."

"I'm grateful for your aid," she said. "You know your herbs well."

He shrugged eloquently. "My mother taught me."

Kseniya sat back on her bed. "Why did you steal into the women's house that night, when I saw you in the courtyard?"

"To speak to one of the others. I would prefer you not give her away."

She gave him a sharper look in the dim light. He was a handsome man, perhaps only a few years older than herself. She should have expected he would, like the other guards, have a girl among the servants. "Of course not," she said. "Why have you helped me?"

"It is my place to do so," he said. "I told you what he wants of her. Most of his arts are nothing to him, but controlling the dragons—that saps his life. Soon he will need another one, so I need your help to get Jia-li safely away."

"Away?" She could hardly keep the incredulity from her voice. "That was my intention that night, to take her from the mountain. Only I thought you knew our plan, so I sent her back inside."

He laughed shortly. "Ah, I understand now. My apologies, but where did you intend to go?"

"I meant to follow the stars to the north and west—to take her to her mother's family."

"It is a dangerous time of year to cross the mountains," he said, shaking his head.

"But now you say we cannot wait."

"No, we cannot. I will take care of him, but I need you to get Jia-li away. There is a village halfway down the *eastern* slope. I know those there who would hide you until spring. You can cross the mountains safely then, if you will accept their help."

After so many years alone, the offer of aid surprised her, but she was not too proud to take it. It gave her hope again.

She kept her secret to herself, not wishing for Jia-li to have something more she must bear. Nor could the girl be forced to tell what she didn't know.

Kseniya had just begun to stitch on the tunic left behind two days before when she heard the outer door creak open. A shudder ran down her spine. She hadn't expected them to come for her so soon. She set the handwork aside and looked up to see two guardsmen enter the inner hall.

"Come," one of them said.

She rose stiffly. They hauled her out of the women's house and before the wizard, not bothering this time to make her kneel.

The wizard turned his dark eyes on Kseniya and snapped his fingers. Jia-li came to stand next to him. He grasped her small fingers in his and brought them near to his nose, all the while keeping his burning eyes fixed on Kseniya's face. "She tells me you used an unguent on her hands last night. Is that so?"

Kseniya bowed, perplexed by the unexpected question. "Yes, my lord."

The bodyguard stood several feet behind the dais, his dark brows drawn together.

"And where did you get this unguent?" the wizard asked. "Did you make it yourself?"

For a split-second, she considered saying yes, but she had no supplies with which to have made it. "No, my lord."

"Where did it come from? I have only smelled its like once before."

Kseniya forced herself not to look in the bodyguard's direction. "I found a tin of it in the women's house."

The wizard's eyes narrowed. "Foolish woman, this is fresh-made. I know the scent of it. Myrrh and comfrey, ginger and cloves. Where did it come from?"

Kseniya went still. She'd fallen into some sort of trap. "I found it only days ago. In the store room, in an old chest there that holds silk robes. A tin sealed with wax, I don't know how long, my lord."

"Hidden in the women's house?" the wizard said in a flat voice. "So it comes back disembodied to haunt me, the smell of the salve on her skin."

Her skin? Kseniya didn't believe he spoke of Anushka, and wondered who that other woman might be. And then an answer came to her. The bodyguard had said his mother taught him the making of the unguent. She must have lived on this mountain once. Kseniya trained her eyes on the floor, hoping that new awareness didn't show on her face, not when the bodyguard had risked himself for Jia-li's sake.

"You are not to use it again," the wizard snapped. "Throw the tin in the spring."

Kseniya waited for the pain to come. It didn't.

"Take the girl back to the women's house and clean her hands." He released Jia-li's fingers and shoved her toward the steps. She stumbled, and Kseniya leaped forward to catch her. When she reached the first step, though, a wall of power pushed her back. She fell to the floor, her breath stolen away. She'd forgotten the wizard's spell that kept others at a distance.

Jia-li ran to her and helped her up. Under the wizard's dark eyes, she and the girl walked slowly from his sanctuary.

The mountains rumbled as the sun set. From the platform by the side door of the women's house where the washer women worked, Kseniya and Jai-li stood and stared at the sky. The normal gurgle of the stream went unheard.

Woken from their restless slumber, the dragons rose into the night and flew to the west. They were huge and terrifying creatures, all leathery wings and fire. Hot gusts of wind swirled off their bronzy wing-tips, making the snow sizzle and melt.

Kseniya held her headscarf fast to her head with one hand, using the end of it to protect her face. She had seen this many times before, flights of dragons over her people's lands.

Frustration showed on Jia-li's features. "I tried to call them back, but they won't listen to me."

"Dearest, you don't have his power."

Jia-li sniffed and wiped her eyes with the back of a blistered hand. "I had to try."

"I know, dearest. Why don't you go to your room? I will come in a moment."

Jia-li nodded and made her way from the platform back into the house. Now that the dragons had gone, the cold returned on a bitter wind. The girl hugged her quilted jacket about herself, looking quite small and defeated.

Kseniya watched her go, and then went to where Bao-yu stood watching the dragons' flight. Her own people's lands lay in that direction. She could only pray that the wizard hadn't sent the dragons there to punish them because she'd not told him where she had found the cursed unguent. She glanced down at Bao-yu, reckoning that the old woman knew the wizard's mind better than any other. "Do you know were the dragons went?"

Bao-yu took Kseniya's hand and drew her back inside to the inner hall where she kept a tray of sand. The old woman drew in it with one gnarled finger, a simple drawing of a woman with a babe in her stomach, followed by another of a woman with a child.

"Anushka?" Kseniya asked.

The old woman shook her head. She drew a sword and pointed at it.

Kseniya met the old woman's eyes warily, wondering what the old woman knew of the wizard's bodyguard, and if he might not have come to the woman's house that first night to see Bao-yu. "Did he...?"

One of the servant girls walked into the inner hall then and Bao-yu wiped her hand across the sand, erasing her drawings. She walked away without a glance, as if she feared being caught there. Like Kseniya, Bao-yu evidently believed the walls of the women's house had ears, or in her case, *eyes*.

Kseniya stood there a moment, weighing possibilities, and then made her way to Jia-li's room. The girl sat on the edge of the platform of her bed, her hands cradled on her lap.

"Will you let me heal them today?" Kseniya asked.

"No." The girl shook her head. "He sent them hunting for someone. The dragons will kill people tonight because I didn't wash my hands well enough. It's not fair."

Kseniya sat down next to her and began to braid the girl's hair. "No, dearest. He is not fair."

Jia-li heaved a great sigh. "Will you tell me about my mother?"

The rattle of leathery wings woke Kseniya just before dawn, the dragons returning to their place under the mountains. The smell of burning floated on the air, the scent of the dragons.

She'd waited up late, thinking the bodyguard might return to the women's house, but he hadn't. She had questions for him, ones that Bao-yu's drawings had stirred in her mind.

Kseniya rose in the graying light and dressed. Her face ached less. She had cheated somewhat, healing the cuts from within so they didn't look as improved on the surface. She gingerly touched the torn skin. She and Anushka had once looked much alike, but she hadn't seen the reflection of her face since coming to the wizard's home. It could not be as she remembered–she would surely never be called beautiful again.

She combed out her hair and began to braid it, but a tap on her door startled her. She opened it quickly and found the bodyguard waiting there. He stepped inside and she shut the door behind him.

"I must thank you," he said, "for not revealing me yesterday."

"You are his son." She waited for his reaction. He didn't deny it, his dark eyes downcast. Now that she knew to look, she saw the resemblance. "When did you escape?"

"I was twelve when my mother took us away, near twenty years ago. She discovered what he truly wanted of me, and one of the bodyguards helped us and hid us. He raised me as his own son and took my mother as his wife. That was whom the dragons sought last night. My mother's household."

"How can you stand by and watch what he does? How many of your people died last night in the dragons' fire?"

"They are safe. He will not find them."

"And what of you?"

"I am changed enough that my father does not recognize me," he said with a short laugh.

No, she couldn't imagine him as a boy of twelve. "Can you do what he does? Did he train you as he does Jia-li?"

"Yes."

"Then why did you not call back his dragons last night?"

"I am sworn not to." He touched her scarred cheek. "He treated my mother as he does you, to force my compliance. So I swore never to use his arts again, not even the dragon's fire."

Which must be inherent in him, she realized. The faint sulfurous smell of his skin must be his own. "Then why did you come back here?"

"I received a message telling me of Jia-li. The Emperor no longer trusts his wizard. He suspects that should the wizard become young again, he might seek to seize the throne. So with the Emperor's blessing, I came here to keep her safe." He took the small knife from a sheath at his wrist. "Give this to her. He will be weaker today. I fear he might take her soon to save himself. I will not allow that to happen, but it would be better if she has some defense."

Kseniya slid the knife inside her dress. "What do you want us to do?"

"Act as normal. Once he becomes weak enough, I can take him myself. You must take Jia-li and flee." From inside his jacket he produced a second knife, single-bladed and as long as his forearm, and smiled wryly. "I have watched you. When you see the guards at their exercises, you look as if you want to join them, so I suspect you know how to use this."

Kseniya took the blade from him. The leather of the hilt

was worn and the balance unfamiliar, but it felt welcome in her hands. "My father had me trained to the sword to serve as my sister's guardian. Not one like this," she said, hefting the blade, "but it will suffice."

"Good. I will count on you to protect her, then."

Kseniya glanced at the early light slanting in through her high window. "Why did you come so late? The sun is already risen. You must go."

He took a strand of her hair between his fingers. "I wanted to see your hair. It is the color of fire in sunlight."

Kseniya simply stared at him, at a loss for words. He let himself out, his footsteps not even audible to her, despite the fact that she pressed her ear against the door to hear them.

Kseniya fixed the blade to her thigh using strips torn from an old shift. A careful fold of fabric under her belt hid a slit in the side of her over-robe. Jia-li secreted the little knife inside her jacket. Kseniya had never trained her to use such a thing, but agreed that the girl should have some chance to defend herself.

When the guards bore Kseniya into the wizard's presence later in the morning, the wizard sat slumped on his throne. He looked far older than the day before, as if he'd aged years overnight. His hair had gone mostly white, something Kseniya would not have thought possible—surely a result of his magics.

The guards shoved her to her knees. One laid his knife to her throat. Kseniya didn't move.

"Jia-li claims she did not ever heal her hands." The wizard's voice rattled in his throat. "I believe that *you* did."

Kseniya said nothing, not surprised by his claim.

The wizard raised his hand and searing pain ripped across her throat. Blood sprayed about her. Panicked, Kseniya clamped a hand to her neck, desperate to keep her life from flowing away onto his carpets.

For a moment, everything seemed suspended: the guards jumping back in surprise; Jia-li, her mouth open as she cried out; the bodyguard, moving from his place at the back of the room, crossing the dais toward her.

Only she wasn't ready to die, not when escape beckoned. Kseniya caused the wound to seal, stopping the flow of blood. For a moment, she sensed only the paths of her body's energy and the blood pulsing through her veins—what blood remained.

She opened her eyes to see Jia-li leaning over her, red-stained fingers pressed to her cheek. A warm presence at her back told her the bodyguard crouched behind her. Wide-eyed, he leaned over and touched her neck as if searching for the injury.

"I wondered," the wizard said, "what it would take to get you to reveal yourself."

The guards closed on either side of the bodyguard and grasped his arms, pinning them behind him. They dragged him to his feet.

The wizard chuckled. "Well, Jia-li, it is time for you to meet your brother, Yun-qi."

From Kseniya's vantage, she saw Jia-li's eyes go round with surprise. The girl crossed her arms over her chest and said, "If he is my brother, they should let him go."

The wizard pushed himself up from his chair and took two tottering steps toward the edge of the dais. "Stupid girl. He is far more useful to me than you. Why take a child's body when I could have one full grown? Bring him here," he instructed the guards.

Kseniya lay on the carpet, too weak to do more than watch. She couldn't reach the knife strapped to her leg.

"No!" Jia-li cried. "Let him go." Foolishly, neither of the guards heeded her as she strode toward them. Without warning, Jia-li raised her little knife and plunged it into the thigh of the nearer man.

The guard spat out a curse. With one hand, he backhanded the girl. Jia-li shrieked and tumbled over Kseniya's body. The bodyguard jerked his arm loose from the injured man's grasp and slammed the second guard's head against a teak beam. The man fell, slumping over Kseniya's legs. Freed, the bodyguard drew his sword.

Kseniya reached to the face of the guard crumpled unconscious over her legs. Gathering her will, she drained his strength to rebuild her own.

When she opened her eyes, she saw the blur of the bodyguard jumping over her. From outside the sanctuary, two more guards sprinted toward the fray.

Kseniya pushed the guard's body off her legs. Jia-li still lay on the carpet, her hands covering her head. Kseniya rushed to her and dragged her upright. "We have to go. Now!"

She grabbed the girl and ran toward the sanctuary doors, expecting the wizard to use his fire to stop her. Nothing happened. At the threshold, she half-turned. The bodyguard still faced two men.

She couldn't abandon him, she realized, no more than he could Jia-li. She set the girl on her feet. "Stay out of the way, little one."

Yun-qi swung his sword in a wide arc to warn his attackers back. That gave them pause, but only for a second.

Kseniya drew her own blade and ran back to his side. She struck hard, catching one attacker under his upraised arm. Her blade scraped along his ribs, and the man fell.

The bodyguard finished the other one. Kseniya held out a hand toward Jai-li. The girl ran to her side and threw her arms about Kseniya's waist.

Yun-qi set one hand on Jia-li's shoulder and faced their father. "You will not take my life today, nor my sister's. You will not cheat death again."

With a flick of the wizard's hand, red lines appeared across Yun-qi's face. He grimaced in pain, but dashed the blood from his eyes. The wizard raised his hand again. Yun-qi groaned, one hand pressing to his chest. It came away red. Blood soaked through the fabric of his jacket.

Kseniya advanced on the dais but was thrown back by a careless stroke of the wizard's hand. Jia-li tried to help her up, but the ground began to shake.

The dragons, she realized. *He has called his dragons.*

Yun-qi dragged Kseniya to her feet. "We must flee!"

The wizard's skin looked sickly now. He watched them with tired, spiteful eyes. Taking advantage of that momentary weakness, Kseniya grasped Jia-li's sleeve and ran.

When they reached the outer gate of the house, dragons circled above, swooping down to terrorize the guardsmen and servants who ran about the courtyard like ants. Clutching the girl's hand, she hurtled down the steps into the chaos. One dragon dove at them like a kestrel, but they reached the protection of the women's house before it could catch them.

Another dragon set fire to the roof of the guard house. Guards scattered from its doors. A body slammed into Kseniya from behind, propelling her through the gate into the women's house.

"Hurry! Go!" Yun-qi pushed her toward the inner courtyard.

"Where?"

He shoved her, his hand slippery with blood. "Through the side gate. Bao-yu!" he called as Kseniya hurried Jia-li down the hallway. "Grandmother!"

The old woman met them at the gate, a bundle already tied to her back.

"If we flee, he will just have his dragons fetch us back," Kseniya said to Yun-qi.

"It tires him to control them. He will soon lose them. Then he is nothing. We must keep moving."

Kseniya stopped and stared at him. "That was your plan?"

He looked startled, as if no one had ever before questioned his wisdom. Before he could answer, a dragon swooped by the platform on which they stood, and fire blossomed on the roof of the women's house. They would have to cross the unprotected expanse of the courtyard to reach the gate.

"Can you not control them?" Kseniya asked, raising her voice over the sudden roar of the flames.

He wrapped his arms about Bao-yu, shielding the old woman. "I am sworn not to."

Kseniya heard the burning roof groan as one of the creatures settled on it. The bronze edge of a leathery wing protruded over the platform's shelter. Another came close, its baleful red eye winking at them. It couldn't breathe its flame on them, she guessed, for fear of killing the wizard's children—the one thing the wizard needed—but the dragons all knew now where they hid.

She, however, was expendable. Kseniya pushed Jia-li toward her brother. "Stay with him."

She drew her blade, but Yun-qi stopped her with a hard hand on her arm. "No! Don't be foolish. He will only cut your throat again."

"I will not stand here and wait to be burned to death." But she knew he was right. The wizard would enjoy killing her after all these years.

Kseniya glanced down at Jia-li, who held to her brother's

leg, her eyes squeezed shut against the heat. She knelt by the girl and asked, "Can you talk to them?"

Jia-li's eyes opened, startled. "I..."

Then a determined look hardened the girl's features. Jia-li stepped away from her brother to the edge of the platform, her dark eyes wide. She held her hands up and closed her eyes. "He's weak. He's very weak. I am stronger now."

Kseniya put one hand on Jia-li's back and willed the girl what strength she could.

The wind whipped about the four standing on the platform, dragon's wings stirring the air. The smell of sulfur choked her, and Kseniya held one sleeve over her mouth to keep the burn of it from her throat.

The two dragons nearby were joined by another, and then others until a dozen dragons circled in the sky above the women's house. Claws scrabbled on the soot-blackened tiles. The snow melted away, and the water in the spring evaporated under the heat.

Jia-li raised her hands to the sky. Abruptly, the dragons fled the women's house, the hot wind of their passage swirling about the four figures on the platform.

"Quickly." Kseniya drew the girl toward the gate.

"No," Jia-li said. "We don't need to run. They won't follow us." The girl led her off the platform and pointed back in the direction of the wizard's house.

A dozen dragons flew there, the house already in flames. As they watched, a figure in blue robes stumbled down the steps only to be snatched up in the claws of one of the beasts. Like birds, the dragons squabbled over their prize until they tore it to pieces.

Then they rose in the brilliant sky and flew toward the west.

"Where are they going?" Kseniya asked.

"I told them they could go home," Jia-li said, one hand lifted to shade her eyes. "Far away, where they belong."

Water began to trickle from the spring. Yun-qi jumped down off the platform, filled one of the pitchers waiting there, and handed it up to Kseniya. She dropped her sword and took the pitcher, giving it to Bao-yu first.

The old woman drank and then coughed. "He is dead," she whispered.

Kseniya turned back to her. Never had she heard the old woman speak before. "Bao-yu?"

"The spell on me is gone. My son is dead." The old woman sat down on the singed boards of the platform and began to cry.

Kseniya stood in the ruins of the broken central court, the spring breeze tugging at her hair. The wizard's house was gone, burned to its foundations. A few beams remained to mark the location of the guards' house, but the women's house had fared better. Tiles broken off the roof by the dragons' claws littered the ground, charred black.

The warm breeze carried with it the faint smell of sulfur.

Kseniya turned to find its source and saw Yun-qi approaching. He came and set his arms about her, and asked, "Bad memories?"

"I only wish there was something of Anushka I could take back to our father," she said.

"You have her daughter," he pointed out. Jia-li came running in their direction then, her braids flying behind her. They made an odd family, gathered from the ruins of the wizard's cruelties, but they belonged together.

"Look!" Jia-li cried. She grasped the tail of Yun-qi's tunic and grinned up at him. "He came! I called him and he came."

There, rising up in the air, was the native dragon. Scales of white and gold glittered in the morning light. A *true* dragon, master of wind and water, the creature's long, sinuous body twisted in wingless flight. His crest and horns flared about his head.

And out of a cloudless sky, rain began to fall. Water trickled along the stones and tiles of the ruins, rinsing away the stains of soot.

"We had best go now," Yun-qi said, "before he brings enough rain to wash away the buildings."

Kseniya laughed and held out a hand to Jia-li. "Yes, let's go home."

THE END

The Legacy of Dragons

Kseniya stopped in the shade of the pines and rubbed her temples. The dragon's song had begun to fray her nerves. At first it had been a mere bubbling sound, similar to a small stream, but as the weeks passed, the intensity and frequency of the dragon's singing increased. Now it often took on the sound of a waterfall. Cursing the dragon wouldn't be advisable; one didn't treat such a creature lightly. She had to settle for thinking uncharitable thoughts about him.

On the mountain pathway ahead of her, Yun-qi turned back and regarded her with worry on his handsome face. "Do we need to rest?"

Not wanting him to worry, Kseniya set a hand on the hilt of her short sword and hurried down the hill toward him. He was inclined to be overly protective of her these days. "We're close now," she said. "We can rest once we get there."

"If they let us in." Yun-qi gestured toward his travelling garb. They had been walking for several days now, and his tunic and loose trousers were coated with a layer of dust.

Despite that, *her* garb was far more likely to give the guards pause. She hadn't thought to have a proper shift or overtunic made before they left. Instead she wore trousers and a tunic Yun-qi's mother had sewn for her. They were quite similar to Yun-qi's clothing...and in no way acceptable for a Russian woman. "They will," she assured him anyway. "We have something Prince Ilya will want to see."

It might take them a while to get an audience with the

prince of New Kiev. She could only pray he would receive her kindly, but she had no doubt he *would* see her. Being allowed an audience with one of the healers in his household would be a different challenge altogether, but it was her best chance of finding out what was wrong with her.

Jia-Ii came back into view, bouncing along on their sturdy packhorse. "There's a town," she called to them. "In the valley just over the next hill. I saw it."

Kseniya gestured for the girl to come back to them. Jia-li complied, and then scowled when Kseniya tied a headscarf over her light brown hair. "It's stupid," Jia-li complained.

"It is *different*, dearest," Kseniya corrected her. "Here women cover their hair. Your mother did this every day of her life. She would expect you to accept it with good grace."

Jia-li nodded once and adjusted the scarf, resolutely determined not to fail her mother's memory.

They waited in the main hall, while Kseniya wondered how long it would take Prince Ilya to arrive. Had he heard out the man she'd asked to speak with him? She grasped Jia-li's fingers in her sweating hand. "It will be fine, dearest."

Jia-li nodded, her dark eyes wide.

At least the dragon had stopped singing, granting Kseniya a respite. Her head felt like it was her own for the first time since they'd begun this journey. She took a deep breath and looked around to see what had changed.

The hall was even grander than it had been before the dragons' fires destroyed it a decade before. The intricate carvings that marked the columns, the fine wooden planks under her feet, and the rich tapestry that hung at the end of the hall all displayed the wealth of this particular branch of the Vladimirov family. Yet their splendor didn't compare to the household in which Jia-li had been raised, the mountain retreat of the dragon wizard, Jiang-long.

Yun-qi stood back near the door through which they'd come. When Kseniya stole a glance at him, he seemed prepared to wait indefinitely. Fortunately, the boyar's man who kept the door had recognized her; it had saved a great deal of explanation. Yun-qi was clearly a foreigner, and Jia-li looked far more like him than her Russian mother. Both bore the stamp of their father's royal bloodline, even if their plain travelling garb did not reflect their nobility.

The heavy sound of boots approaching warned her a moment before the hall's doors swung wide open. Tall and stern, Prince Ilya stepped over the threshold into the hall, resplendent in a red tunic with fine embroidery about the neck, picked out in gold thread. He paused and stroked his short blond beard as he surveyed the three inhabitants of the hall, the gesture he always used when thinking. Kseniya inclined her head in his direction.

"Leave us," he barked. His guards disappeared back into the hallway, one drawing the doors shut.

Prince Ilya came closer and peered down into Kseniya's face. Ten years had passed since he'd last seen her. Her face was lined now with fine scars, evidence of her travails, but his reaction showed he recognized her anyway. He laid his hands on her shoulders and kissed her cheeks. "My daughter," he said. "We heard the wizard's retreat in the mountains was destroyed by fire in last winter. I feared you dead."

Thank God he recognizes me...and didn't disown me on sight. A tension Kseniya hadn't been willing to acknowledge slipped from her shoulders. "No, Father."

He stepped back, casting a glance down at Jia-li as he did so. "The wizard is dead, then?"

"Yes, Father." The dragon wizard was dead, killed by the very fire-dragons he'd held captive for decades. Jia-li had freed the creatures, and they'd flown away from the mountains in search, Kseniya assumed, of their original homes. The dragon who troubled Kseniya's waking hours—Long—was not one of those. He was, instead, a water dragon whom Jia-li had called up from the south to claim the wizard's newly vacant mountains.

The prince's eyes rose to meet Kseniya's again. "And your sister? Is it true she is dead?"

"Yes, she is." Kseniya kept hold of Jia-li's hand. "What do you know of what happened to us, sir?"

His lips thinned. "Only gossip from traders. We heard Anushka died bearing a child, but when I asked, none ever mentioned your name. I could only assume..."

"Very few ever knew my name, Father. To most I was merely

Anushka's servant."

"Ah." A flush touched his cheeks. Kseniya might be his eldest child, but she was his *bastard*. Although he had taken her into his household, that didn't make her a princess. She had been trained to protect her royal sibling instead and had gone with Anushka to the wizard's mountain as her guard. The fact that no one had known Kseniya was also the prince's daughter had probably saved her life. "How did you come by these scars?" he asked.

The scars crossing her face had faded in the last few months, now that she felt safe using her limited healer's skills to ease them, but her father wouldn't know that. Nor would she tell him that they sketched across most of her body. "The wizard would use me to force Anushka's compliance. He knew she placed value on me, even if he thought me merely a servant."

The prince covered his face with his hand for a moment. Then he dropped his hand. "Can you ever forgive me?"

Kseniya understood the reason behind her exile to that place. No one had suffered more than her father, given the choice between forfeiting his daughter to be the wizard's concubine or allowing the eradication of his people by the wizard's dragons. Anushka had understood. She had gone, not quite willingly, but dutifully. "I have never held you responsible for this, Father," Kseniya told him firmly. "And the man who did it...is dead."

Her father gazed at her, his lips held tight, and his blue eyes flicked down to Jia-li again. While the girl looked a great deal like the wizard who had fathered her, her single braid was a light brown, an unusual color for one of the Han. Not as pale as Anushka's flaxen hair, but remarkable nonetheless. "And is it true about the child?"

"Yes." Kseniya moved her hand to Jia-li's shoulder. "Father, this is Jia-li, Anushka's daughter and your granddaughter."

Jia-li bowed properly, but flinched back when he knelt down to kiss her cheeks. She stepped behind Kseniya's trousers.

"What's wrong, dearest?" Kseniya asked. It wasn't like her to be timid.

Jia-li touched her chin hesitantly.

Ah, it was her father's beard the girl didn't like. Jia-li had seen very few beards before they'd crossed the border. Kseniya turned back to her father, hoping he wouldn't be offended. It wasn't as if he wore his beard halfway down his chest like Father Petrov always had. "Your beard frightens her, sir."

He crossed his arms over his chest and peered haughtily at his granddaughter. "And not my consequence?"

Kseniya knew her father well enough to recognize his gruffness for a joke. He'd never taken himself as seriously as his aunts and sisters urged him to. He was merely one of a dozen Vladimirov princes, the children of the diaspora sent forth from Kiev to claim lands left abandoned when the Mongols were obliterated. In *Old* Kiev, his title meant very little. "Jia-li has royal blood on both sides, Father. Very few people are above her."

Jia-li turned questioning eyes on Kseniya. The girl knew

her mother's tongue, but sometimes missed a word or two. Kseniya patted her back. "Don't worry, dearest. He was jesting."

"Oh." Jia-li squared her shoulders. "I am happy to meet you, Grandfather."

Prince Ilya gently touched the girl's cheek. "And I you, Granddaughter."

Then his eyes lifted to meet Kseniya's again. "There is much you and I need to discuss. Your manservant there can take the girl to the stable to see to the horse you brought."

Kseniya cast a quick glance at Yun-qi, whose face remained expressionless. He'd only been practicing her language for a few months. His eyes laughed, though, which made her think he'd caught the word 'manservant'. "Father," she began," the man travelling with us is my *husband*, Yun-qi. He helped us to escape the wizard."

Her father's jaw clenched. He likely wanted to rail at her for marrying a foreigner, or for marrying without his permission, but he held his tongue. Instead he eyed Yun-qi suspiciously. Prince Ilya spoke the Imperial tongue, but never did so in his own lands. He usually had a boyar pretend to interpret for him. This time he made an exception. "So you have married my daughter," he said to Yun-qi. "And who are you to take the hand of the daughter of a prince?"

Kseniya had expected such a reaction...and she was only a *bastard* daughter. "Father, Yun-qi is a cousin of the Emperor and grandson of the Imperial princess, Bao-yu. His mother Rahime is the daughter of a Tatar clan chieftain, very much a princess herself. And he is Jia-li's half-brother."

Her father had always been quick. He favored Kseniya with a scandalized look. "You married the wizard's *son*?"

Kseniya gazed down at her scarred and idle fingers, clenched in the ochre wool of her borrowed tunic. Her father had instructed his wife Ludmilla to provide suitable clothing for Kseniya, so now she wore a shift and tunic, loosely belted, and a beaded headdress atop her headscarf. It felt like she had stepped into someone else's life, a life she'd long since forgotten how to live.

While the children of Prince Ilya's household played, the women plied their needles in the solar, their worried eyes darting to where Jia-li cradled a cloth doll in her arms. Even dressed now in proper clothing, the girl looked like an exotic flower set among the household's children. All the other girls had fair coloring, some with blonde hair, others with red-gold like Kseniya's own.

One of them, a tiny blonde of six with a voice that was already strident, was Kseniya's half-sister. Princess Ekaterina was the child of Prince Ilya's current wife, a girl a few years younger than Kseniya herself. Like his first two wives, Ludmilla had been chosen for him by his family, a matter of alliance rather than preference. Although she was pretty, Ludmilla had the vacant demeanor of a sheep. Kseniya thought her father could have done better by picking a farmer's daughter at random in the market, although she would never say that aloud.

Not that any of the household's women would listen should she yell it to the heavens. Kseniya had chosen to stay with Jia-li, to make certain the girl wasn't mistreated. But that meant Kseniya must remain in the company of the women of the house throughout the day...and they wouldn't speak to her.

Some of the hostility Kseniya attributed to the fact that she was a bastard and therefore beneath her aunts' notice. Much stemmed from her father's having her trained to the sword like a boy; her aunts had never been comfortable with her, calling her *unnatural*. The fact that she'd married a foreigner—an Unbeliever—only alienated them further. Her week so far had been spent in near silence. Kseniya was bored enough now to enjoy even the dragon's singing.

She glanced up from her scarred fingers in time to spot Princess Ekaterina across the room, about to yank the braid hanging down Jia-li's back. With an absent wave of her hand, Kseniya said, "Don't."

Ekaterina stumbled back as if pushed. She landed screaming on her rump amid a cluster of pottery bowls filled with beads.

Jia-li jerked around to stare at Kseniya, dark eyes wide. She jumped up and ran over even as the household's women swarmed around the wailing princess. She grasped Kseniya's hand. "How did you do that?"

Kseniya frowned. "That wasn't you, dearest?"

Jia-li had inherited her father's powers. Surely she'd been the one who...

"You stupid," Ekaterina shrieked at Jia-li's back. She tore off her beaded headdress and threw it. It landed far short of its target. "Smelly squinty-eyed...stupid!"

Jia-li's eyes went round, but she didn't respond to the inane taunt. She was well-trained to control her reactions, no matter how provoked. With her talents, she could be dangerous.

"Go away," Ekaterina screamed, "you and your ugly, scarry nursemaid, too."

So much for trying to get along with the women of the household. Kseniya rose and lifted her niece in her arms. Out of the corner of her eye she saw that the pottery was indeed broken. She half-hoped the spoiled princess had a piece embedded in her royal buttocks.

She carried Jia-li out of the main hall and back toward the guestroom she and Yun-qi had been given, but only got halfway down the brightly-painted hallway before she set the girl on her own feet. Jia-li had grown heavier of late, and Kseniya carried more than her own weight. She'd tied her belt loosely to camouflage her growing belly, but she wouldn't be able to hide it much longer.

She took the girl's hand to lead her instead. "Why do you say I did it?"

"I felt it," Jia-li insisted. "You used the dragon's touch."

The dragon's touch—the ability to affect things without physically touching them. The wizard had used that gift to cut

Kseniya's skin without even touching her. Jia-li had inherited it, as had Yun-qi, but she...

I should not have it.

Kseniya waited until they reached the guestroom, shut the door, and sat heavily on the wooden bench that ran along the side of the room. A feeling of disquiet had been creeping upon her for some time. That she could hear the constant singing of the dragon she had attributed to her pregnancy. But this was worse. Somehow she was stealing her husband's powers, one by one.

Yun-qi returned after a day walking through the mountains, his handsome face flushed with pleasure. As soon as he stepped through the door, Jia-li jumped up from the floor to throw her arms about him. "I want to go home," she mumbled, pressing her face into his tunic.

The happiness fled his dark eyes. "What happened?" he asked Kseniya over the girl's head.

"Ekaterina was...unkind," Kseniya said with a sigh.

Jia-li stepped away from him and wiped her nose with the back of her hand. "She called me smelly and squinty-eyed, and she said Kseniya was ugly."

Yun-qi sniffed the air. "Clearly wrong in every word."

Jia-li giggled.

They both had their father's dark, hooded eyes—certainly not *squinty*. And while both had inherited a distinctive sulfurous smell to their skin, the legacy of their father's interaction with fire-dragons, Kseniya didn't think that excused Ekaterina's rudeness. "There is another problem," she said.

Jia-li nodded solemnly. "She used the dragon's touch."

Yun-qi didn't even look surprised.

No one complained when, later that evening, they retrieved Jia-li's things from the nursery and made a makeshift pallet for her on the floor of their room. Kseniya felt relieved to have her niece nearer.

"I will miss this bed," Yun-qi said when she blew out the wooden splint. He eased closer, his face resting against the hollow between her shoulder and neck. "It is growing worse, then."

"Yes." She sighed. "Do you still have *any* of your talents?"

He rose onto one elbow. "How should I know?"

In addition to hearing dragons, he could use dragon's touch to move things and also control fire. Nevertheless, Kseniya had never seen him do either of those things. Having watched his father use those skills to torture his mother and later Kseniya, Yun-qi had foresworn using them.

"Did your sister do this when she bore Jia-li?" he asked.

"No, but she wasn't a very strong healer. I always had more strength." She had lasted nine years in the wizard's house, while Anushka only lasted one. Kseniya rolled onto her side to face him. "I'll ask to speak with my father once more. In the morning. I'll pray he's convinced one of my aunts to examine me."

"And if they relent? Shall we leave afterward?"

Kseniya nodded. "I'd like to go home."

"No more nice bed," Yun-qi whispered ruefully.

Her father made time to meet with her in the main hall that morning. His boyars were out hunting, but Father Petrov had accompanied him. Unfortunately one of the young maids had been forced to chaperone Kseniya. The soft-spoken girl was a cousin of hers, but Kseniya had no doubt with whom the girl's loyalties lay. Everything she overheard would be faithfully reported back to their domineering aunts. The priest stayed on the far side of the hall and beckoned for the girl to join him. After shooting a worried glance at Kseniya, the girl complied, giving them a bit of privacy.

Kseniya didn't waste her father's time. "Have you been able to convince them to talk to me?"

"No. They have all refused," Prince Ilya said in an aggrieved voice. "Where one of my sisters goes, the others follow. I have tried getting them alone, but they have set their faces against you, Kseniya."

She had lived her first eighteen years with that treatment, so she couldn't say she was surprised. "Is there some other you know, Father? A woman in the town they don't control?"

His lips pressed together, and she knew he had some idea.

"Please, Father."

He glanced about the main hall as if worried someone

might overhear him. "I do not want to send you off on a hopeless quest. There is a village farther to the east, called Petrivka. Her family name was Lebedev, but it was nearly thirty years ago. I cannot even tell you if she's still there. I've heard nothing of her for years. Ask for Sofiya Lebedeva."

Nearly thirty years ago? For a moment she couldn't breathe. Kseniya lifted her eyes to meet his. "Was she...?

Her father nodded sharply, once.

My mother. He had never before given Kseniya her mother's name. She was shocked he even remembered it. She had always assumed her mother had been nothing to him, a village whore perhaps. But instead she'd been a *healer*, a girl whose name and family and town he recalled even thirty years later. Kseniya laid her fingers against her lips, trying to sort out her emotions.

Her father hadn't wanted her to go off seeking her mother. For her part, Kseniya had feared intruding into a life where she wasn't wanted. Or perhaps discovering a mother of whom she wouldn't be proud. Her adored father had always been enough for her.

Nevertheless, he was sending her to her mother now, and that seemed a weighty portent. She lowered her hand and regarded him steadily. "Do you have a map of where we can find this village?"

He tilted his head back toward the priest. "I will have Father Petrov copy it for you."

She bowed, the beading on her headdress briefly obscuring

her vision. "Then we will be gone by noon, Father."

She stepped back to bow properly before leaving him, but he laid his hand on her arm and drew her close to whisper, "They think you are possessed of a demon. You and Jia-li both."

She looked back at him, aghast. That shed new light on the unwillingness of the women of the household. "Father..."

"I did not say I believed it. Now go with my blessing, daughter." He kissed her cheeks and smiled down at her, and added, "And bear my greetings to Sofiya should you find her."

The habits of travel returned quickly. Jia-li would dash ahead down the road and then come darting back, her energy boundless. Yun-qi seemed pleased to be out of New Kiev as well, his normally sharp humor returning. The clopping of the packhorse's hooves took on a restful and familiar rhythm.

Outside the town's walls, though, Kseniya found the dragon's song ringing in her head again.

"One becomes accustomed to it." Yun-qi smiled, the skin about the corners of his dark eyes crinkling. "When I was in the capital, I would sometimes hear four or five dragons at once."

"Do you hear him now?" Kseniya asked, although she already knew the answer. That had been the first gift he'd lost.

"No," he confirmed. "And I find it odd that either of you can hear him so far north."

"He's come to the northern end of his mountains," Jia-li

said. "That's why we can hear him."

"Is there any chance he's going back home soon?" Kseniya asked, more sharply than she intended.

Yun-qi just laughed. "Dragons do as they wish."

The next morning, Kseniya watched as Yun-qi went about his regular exercises, coaching Jia-li through the measured steps. The girl used the short sword today since Kseniya, her mind distracted by the dragon's insistent song, couldn't concentrate adequately. Yun-qi would stop at times to correct his sister's grip or the angle of the weapon, but Kseniya thought Jia-li did well for her first attempt with a blade.

The girl already showed great promise with a bow. Yun-qi had hesitated to teach her such things, for although he didn't mind having a wife who pursued unwomanly arts, many men would. His mother had reminded him that, as a wizard, Jia-li's life would never be like that of the other village girls; finding a husband for her would be a challenge whether she learned the sword or not. Hearing that wisdom, Yun-qi had agreed, much to Jia-li's delight.

Once they had finished their exercises, Yun-qi helped Kseniya pack up the last of the supplies. "She did well," Kseniya said.

Yun-qi settled the bedrolls across the horse's back. "Well enough. You did better your first time."

"I was much older," Kseniya pointed out.

"More mature. Do you still hear him?"

Kseniya handed him his bag. "Yes, I didn't learn to ignore

him overnight."

Yun-qi rolled his eyes.

Jia-li cupped her hands over the fire and the flames flickered and died. "Long is worried," she said. "He keeps trying to warn me."

Long. Kseniya heard the name only as 'dragon'. The creature seemed to have no other, so Jia-li always referred to him that way. "You can understand him?"

Jia-li shrugged. "He's far away, so I'm not sure."

To Kseniya his song was only burbling nonsense. "So what is he warning you about, dearest?"

"Stone," Jia-li said. "I don't know what that means, but he thinks something's coming. That's why he's come north."

Yun-qi rose, a furrow between his brows. "Yes, something is about to happen."

Kseniya hated it when he said things like that. More often than not lately, he'd been right.

The market town of Petrivka sat among the foothills of the Cholodio mountains, a collection of wooden houses and shops along a few muddy paths, not nearly as fine as New Kiev. The villagers nodded to them in a cautious manner as they crossed paths, but almost all stared at Kseniya rather than Yun-qi and Jia-li, the foreigners. Kseniya lowered her face, hoping she hadn't unwittingly offended.

In front of one of the houses, two elderly men sat on a bench, one chewing a reed. "Sirs," Yun-qi said to them, "we are looking for Sofiya Lebedeva, who lived on a farm north of here. Does she still live nearby?"

The two old men conferred, and one of them surprised Kseniya by supplying directions to a herbalist's shop. They located the shop among a row of buildings joined by wooden walkways, the town's market area. Yun-qi went inside first, pausing to bow to the icon in the corner and admire the selection of herbs hanging from the rafters. Kseniya touched his shoulder and he went farther in, allowing her to enter and bow in turn.

Behind a tall worktable a woman stood binding a bunch of herbs with string. Despite a youthful face, a hint of graying hair showed at the edges of her headscarf.

When Yun-qi repeated his earlier query, the herbalist wiped her hands on a linen towel and tilted her head to look past his shoulder. "Come here, child, and let me look at you. Did you think I wouldn't recognize you?"

Kseniya blinked. "You know who I am?"

The woman came around her worktable and smiled. "You're my daughter. I never dared hope to see you again."

Kseniya's words all froze in her mind. *What do I say?*

Yun-qi gave her a gentle push in the woman's direction. "Go on. I will see to Jia-li."

He bowed and walked out the door, leaving her at the woman's mercy. This close, Kseniya saw features similar to her own, but lined with age—not scars.

"Are you still called Kseniya?" the woman asked after a moment of silence. "Or did your father give you a new name after I took you to him?"

"Yes," Kseniya said, finally finding her voice. "I mean that I'm still called so. How did you recognize me?"

Sofiya Lebedeva touched Kseniya's cheek. "You will probably not believe it, but you look a great deal like I did as a girl."

Kseniya stared at the woman. As a girl, she had spent a thousand evenings wondering what her mother must be like. Now she stood before her like a tongue-tied simpleton.

"What brings you here?" her mother prompted.

Kseniya shook herself to sort her scattered thoughts. "We didn't know if we would find you, madam, or if you can help us, but my father thought you might."

"Ah, Prince Ilya sent you." Sofiya leaned back against the worktable. "How could I possibly help you that he could not?"

Her mother had hazel eyes, Kseniya noted, whereas she'd inherited her father's blue ones. "You are a healer, aren't you?"

"Yes, I am." Sofiya glanced at Kseniya's belly. "Is there something wrong with the child?"

"I don't know," Kseniya admitted, surprised the woman had so quickly divined her concern.

"Then perhaps it would be better to discuss it after dinner. There will be plenty for you and your family." Sofiya gestured to the door through which Yun-qi had disappeared. "Will you introduce me to them?"

The farm house stood a short walk outside the town, and Kseniya could see it had housed a large family. Sofiya had one son and four daughters, she'd said. Only the youngest still lived in that house, though, and that daughter was currently out on the mountainside with the family's flock.

It wasn't a grand house—certainly nothing like her father's house in New Kiev—but it was well cared for, the floors swept clean and the stove maintained. Panes of glass in the windows hinted the Lebedev family had once been wealthy. What would it have been like to grow up here rather than her father's household?

Her mother set her in the place of honor, the corner under the family's icons. After a plain but filling meal, Sofiya came and settled next to her, while Yun-qi and Jia-li checked on the packhorse in the stable below.

"How did you and my father..." How direct could she be without offending?

Sofiya chuckled, evidently grasping where her question meant to go. "You know how attractive a man seems after you have healed him. Your father cut his hand in the stable. I healed it. I was fifteen, and foolish enough that my head was turned by a true flesh-and-blood prince with pretty eyes."

It was hard to imagine her father that young. Coming from a family of healers himself, he would have been aware what effect such a healing would have. Kseniya shook her head. "And he took advantage."

Sofiya nodded. "But I did not mind. He was kind and unhappy about his upcoming marriage. He'd heard the woman was...ill-tempered."

Kseniya thought of Grushka, her father's first wife and Anushka's mother. 'Ill-tempered' described her well. Sofiya Lebedeva was far more likeable. "She was a princess, which was the reason his family made the match."

"So he claimed," Sofiya said. "With a child, I would never have found a husband, so my mother caused the priest to write to him. Prince Ilya offered to raise you when I let him know I carried you. He had more than I to offer you, so...I agreed."

"He asked me to bear his greetings," Kseniya said. "He hasn't forgotten you, it seems."

Sofiya chuckled. "I believe I was his first, so for that reason alone I would be memorable to him."

"Oh." Kseniya gazed down at her scarred hands. "Why did you never come to see me?"

"Child, it's a long way. Only a few months later my father died, leaving me and my mother to run the farm by ourselves. I had neither the time nor the luxury, and I trusted your father's word that he would raise you well."

Kseniya held her tongue. No doubt the woman wanted to hear she'd had a leisurely life within the prince's household. "Did your other children know about me?" she asked instead.

"I never hid you from them, or my husband." Sofiya reached over and lifted the end of Kseniya's red-gold braid, uncovered now they were inside. "They all have dark hair, save the youngest, Ivanka. Hers is almost this color. She looks strikingly like you."

Ah. *That* was why the villagers had stared at her.

"Now, what is troubling you?" Sofiya asked.

Kseniya laid her hand on her belly. "Yun-qi and Jia-li can hear dragons, among other things—talents they inherited from their father. But it seems now that Yun-qi's talents have left him and come into me."

Sofiya rested her chin on one hand. "Left him?"

"I believe so. Yun-qi never uses them because of an oath, so we have no way of knowing if he still possesses them, but I have exhibited hints of those powers. Unfortunately, I lack the skill to control them."

"That, at least, is not surprising," she said. "You are likely borrowing those talents from the child. It has been known to happen with a healer when the father has a gift."

Kseniya let loose a pent breath. At least the woman didn't seem to think that worrisome. "Will it harm the child?"

Sofiya's brow furrowed. "I doubt it, but let me examine you. I should get a feel for your husband as well. Then perhaps I might have an idea as to why he's lost his abilities. That surprises me more."

Yun-qi kept his mouth shut throughout the examination, but his eyes danced.

Sofiya methodically laid a hand to his crown, and then his brow, his throat, chest, belly and groin. "He is perfectly normal," she said. "In fact, he is unusually healthy for a man his age. Forgive me, son, how old are you?"

"Thirty-three, madam," he said. "Am I to call you *Mother*?"

"I think I would like that," Sofiya answered with a smile. "It is not unusual for a man wedded to a healer. To be so healthy, I mean."

Yun-qi raised an eyebrow, and Kseniya flushed.

"Some healing always takes place during the sex act," Sofiya said without pause, "given that the healer is willing. How long have you been wed?"

The tips of Kseniya's ears burned. With her more rigid upbringing in the prince's household, such talk between men and women had been forbidden.

Yun-qi cast a glance in Kseniya's direction. "Less than a year, Mother."

Sofiya gave Yun-qi a warning look. "Legend claims we are descended from rusalki, who steal the lives of unwary travelers. My daughter could drain your body's energy just as easily as heal you. If you value your health, son, you'll keep on her good side."

Yun-qi actually had the nerve to grin at her. "My step-father—who is a very wise man," he said, "says to do as my wife wishes in all things, so she will do as I wish in bed."

Kseniya crossed her arms over her chest. "You have both embarrassed me enough. This is serious."

"I realize that, child," Sofiya said. "But I can't find anything wrong with him."

"Thank you, Mother," Yun-qi said with a half-bow.

She waved him away with a hand and patted the bench, indicating that Kseniya should sit there.

"Perhaps you should go check on your sister," Kseniya suggested. Yun-qi just returned a bland look and sat nearby. "Oh very well," Kseniya snapped. She settled on the bench and glared at him. "So much for doing what I want."

Sofiya laid a hand on the crown of Kseniya's head. "Hush."

Kseniya closed her eyes and let her mind drift as Sofiya's hand moved to her brow, and her throat. The dragon's song filled her head, the gurgle of a running stream now. Kseniya fought to shut it out, but could not.

When Sofiya's hand reached her belly, it stayed there for a long time. "It is definitely the child."

Kseniya opened her eyes and caught her mother's troubled expression. "The healers at my father's house believed I am demon possessed."

Sofiya snorted. "There is something *unusual* about the child, but he is simply made that way. It is more as if the flow of energies in his body is reversed." She turned back to Yun-qi. "Would you permit me to examine your sister? It might help me understand better."

He seemed intrigued. "She has already lain down to sleep. Perhaps in the morning?"

A thundering voice called to Kseniya in the darkness, rasping out a message she didn't quite understand. She sat up, her heart beating in panic.

Shadows obscured Yun-qi's face. "What is it?"

"The dragon spoke to me." It hadn't been the gentle sound of water this time, but the roar of fire.

A cry came from where Jia-li slept on the other side of the room. Kseniya struggled to her feet. More agile, Yun-qi slipped past her and dropped to his knees next to the girl's pallet. He shook Jia-li's shoulders, and the girl's dark eyes opened.

Kseniya peered over Yun-qi's shoulder at her. "What is it, dearest?"

Jia-li hugged her arms around herself. "The dragon is coming. It told me so."

"I don't understand." Kseniya's blood pounded in her ears. She'd heard the same words. "Why would he...?"

"No, not *Long*," Jia-li said. "One of the others, like my father had captive. One that breathes fire."

"Why would it come here?"

"It wants the baby."

"It wants what?" Kseniya asked.

"The baby. My father promised it a baby," Jia-li whispered. "It is coming to take one."

Sofiya firmly put off discussing their departure, claiming she needed to examine the girl first. Jia-li sat patiently while Sofiya did so, appearing mystified by the whole process.

"She is quite healthy," Sofiya told Kseniya after she sent the girl out of the room. "However, her body's energies do flow differently."

"Flow differently? But Yun-qi's do not?" Kseniya caught herself chewing her lower lip.

Sofiya sighed. "Can you tell me more of their father, this wizard?"

Kseniya thought back on the stories Yun-qi's grandmother had told her. "He was an apprentice to the court sorcerer but he dreamed of controlling dragons. Because of that, he was banished and fled to the west, to the places where the dragons who breathe fire dwell."

"And he brought them here," Sofiya said.

Kseniya glanced at Yun-qi. He nodded, so she continued. "He used the dragons to crush the horsemen of the Steppes. In return, he asked for Yun-qi's grandmother as his prize. For some reason, he could only possess the body of a child he'd fathered. She bore him a child, and when that boy was fifteen, he possessed the boy's body. Yun-qi was *that* wizard's first child, and Jia-li the second."

Sofiya frowned. "He sought to make a new body for himself?"

"Yes," Kseniya said. "He demanded Anushka as his concubine because he learned she had a healer's powers. He hoped to gain that gift as well through the child."

"How fortunate for you, girl, he didn't realize you come from a stronger line of healers than the princess," Sofiya said without a hint of smugness. She turned to Yun-qi. "What made your mother special?"

"In her family line," Yun-qi said hesitantly, "the men are sometimes seers. That is what made him choose her."

"And are you a seer, son?"

"I am not certain," he said after a moment.

Kseniya stared at him. "You have *never*..."

He shook his head. "Recently, I've had cause to question. I seem to know how some things will fall out."

"Luck, perhaps?" Sofiya asked.

"It could be. If I do have a seer's gift, I have no training to use it. And I cannot explain why I've never felt this before." He gave Kseniya a helpless shrug.

Sofiya eyed him shrewdly. "Tell me, son, of something that will happen today."

He closed his eyes. After a moment, he opened them and said, "One of your daughters will come down from the mountainside. With sheep."

Sofiya cast a questioning glance at Kseniya, who in turn regarded Yun-qi as if he'd turned into a radish. "Why didn't you tell me?"

"I wasn't certain," he said, throwing up his hands. "I still am not. It's like grasping at leaves in the wind."

Sofiya drummed her fingers on the work table. Then she crossed over to where a large, lidded basket rested on the floor and brought it back. She dug a handful of fresh leaves out of the basket. "It helps me think," she said in response to Kseniya's confused look.

She gathered a handful of leaves, arranged the stems and tied them off with string. A moment later, Yun-qi joined her, sorting the herbs for her. His own mother was an herbalist and had trained him in that art. Kseniya held her tongue while they worked through much of the basket's contents in annoyingly companionable silence.

"Jia-li is too young for us to know if she has the healer's gift," Sofiya finally said. "Do your brothers have the seer's talent?"

"No," Yun-qi said.

Sofiya rose and slid the herb-laden stick onto the rafters. "I suspect that you, son, were born with energies like your sister's. Your inherited powers must require that reversal of energies to flourish, but your association with your wife has caused them to realign. And once corrected, your seer's gift began to emerge."

Kseniya shook her head. "I've known Yun-qi for less than a year, but I've been in Jia-li's presence since the day she was born."

Her mother smiled. "But your contact with him has been of a more *intimate* nature, has it not?"

Yun-qi raised his eyebrows and opened his mouth, but before he could speak a knock sounded, forestalling whatever clever words he had in mind.

A young woman waited at the door. The red braid peeking from beneath her headscarf hinted that Yun-qi had been correct.

The panicked bleating of sheep in the yard outside confirmed it.

Sofiya turned back to Yun-qi. "It does seem you have the seer's talent now, son. Kseniya, I would like you to meet your youngest sister, Ivanka."

"Mother, there is something terrible on the mountain," the girl interrupted, her eyes wide.

"The dragon," Yun-qi said under his breath.

Ivanka shot him a frightened glance. She would have been a child when last the fire-dragons flew over these lands, but likely recalled those times all too well. "Did *you* bring it here?"

It was not the sort of introduction Kseniya would have chosen. "It followed *me*, I think,"

Kseniya eyed the short sword lying on their pallet. No use against a dragon, so she left it there with her bag. But Yun-qi armed himself as if on guard duty in the Emperor's palace, donning his long sword and the shorter one, as well as his knife. His movements bore an air of finality that sent a chill down her spine. "What does a dragon want with a baby?"

"I suspect the same thing my father did, to possess the child."

Why hadn't she realized that? "How did it even know I'm pregnant?"

Yun-qi glanced at her. "Dragons know what dragons know."

She hated it when he answered like that. "But you've told me a story where a man kills a dragon," she reminded him.

"And you've told me a story with a house on *chicken* legs. Foolish children's tales are not going to get us out of this." He turned to her, a grave look on his face. "I am not a fool, Kseniya. You and I both know what the dragon wants. I won't allow it to claim my child; that has happened once too often in my family. Nor will I let it take Jia-li."

"We are agreed, then," Kseniya said.

"Then you know what the beast must have."

Her stomach clenched when she understood him. "No," she protested. "You are not to offer yourself in the child's place."

He came and laid one hand against her cheek. "There is no other way. What else do we have to barter with? If we refuse the creature, imagine what retribution it will exact on the countryside here. Your people would pay, Kseniya, and this is not their doing. It is *my* family's legacy."

Kseniya wrapped her hands in his tunic. The back of her throat ached with the effort of stilling her tears. "Give me time to think of something."

He laid his hands over hers. "There is no time. The dragon is here now."

She pressed her lips together, trying to form some other protest than a simple *no*. Yun-qi would hate it if she begged. "Please listen to what it has to say before you make any promises."

"I will," he said. "But we know how this must be."

When he walked up the hillside, she lagged a few steps behind. If she only had time, surely she could *think* her way out of this, find a way where they would all escape intact. But Yun-qi knew dragons better, even if he could no longer hear them, and she was going to have to follow his lead.

They could smell the creature long before they saw it. The scent of sulfur hung in the air. When they topped the rise, Kseniya spotted the dragon down in a shallow valley below, its leathery body nestled around an outcropping of stone. The nearby grass had withered, baked brown by the creature's mere presence.

It turned its head so one burning eye faced them. "I have come for my prize."

The dragon's voice whispered in Kseniya's mind like dried twigs rattling in the winter. She glanced over at Yun-qi, but he didn't react to those words—he'd heard nothing. "What right do you have to ask this of us?" Kseniya called down.

The dragon's head turned. It appeared to look directly at her, not Yun-qi. "Jiang-long bargained with me that I should have a child of his in return for the twelve I gave over to him. You carry a child of his line, which I now claim as forfeit."

Jiang-long was the title Yun-qi's father had given himself—*Dragon Lord*.

"But *we* made no bargain with you, dragon," Kseniya said.

"The child is bound by his ancestor's words," it replied.

"What is it saying?" Yun-qi whispered.

"What we expected." Yun-qi opened his mouth to speak to the beast, but Kseniya laid two fingers over his lips. "Dragon, the child is not yet born. We cannot give him to you."

The dragon came in their direction. It moved in an ungainly

fashion, like a bat forced to crawl, but far more quickly than Kseniya would have thought possible. They stood their ground at the top of the rise as the sulfurous wind of its approach blew about them.

Almost three times her height, it reached out with a clawed wingtip. Yun-qi moved between them, but the dragon jerked that claw in his direction, sending Yun-qi sprawling without even touching him.

"Stop," Kseniya cried.

The dragon made a rattling sound that resembled laughter. Burning heat accompanied the sound. Kseniya threw an arm over her face to shield it.

"Is this your champion?" the dragon asked. "I will roast him if he interferes again."

Yun-qi had risen to one knee, so Kseniya repeated that claim to him. He went still.

The dragon startled her by touching her belly with one claw. "It is not hatched? It matters not," the dragon said. "I will take the child now."

Did it mean to rip the babe from her belly? "You must not," she protested. "The child will die if taken from me too early."

The dragon angled its leathery head with one eye looking down on her. "Hmmmph. Then send me the other one—the *female*."

Jia-li had only been convinced to stay behind because Kseniya could speak to the dragon herself. Kseniya was grateful they'd taken that precaution. "It knows of Jia-li," she told Yun-qi, "and has asked for *her* in the baby's place."

Yun-qi rose and came to stand at Kseniya's side. "Take me instead. I am the wizard's son."

Kseniya held her breath, praying silently that it would not accept.

The dragon's head dropped closer to them, the single eye peering intently at Yun-qi. "This man is not of the blood. He is *useless* to me."

Yun-qi's hand grasped Kseniya's shirt as if to throw her to one side, but when she repeated the dragon's words, his fingers loosened. "What?"

She was simply relieved the dragon didn't want him. "Why is he useless to you?" she asked the creature.

The dragon's eye drew closer. "His flesh cannot house one of my kind. That was Jiang-long's wizardry, to create between us a creature able to bear a dragon's spirit. This one cannot."

Because I changed him. Kseniya's mind spun. The creature failed to recognize Yun-qi as one of the wizard's children. Whatever made one acceptable to the fire-dragon must be that same quality she had *healed* out of him. And if she could heal Jia-li somehow...

She raised her face to the beast again. "Dragon, can you give me time to decide? If I must choose between them, I need time."

The fire-dragon drew back, allowing a cool breeze to stroke past Kseniya's face. It felt like a breath of hope.

"What will you give me in exchange?" it asked.

"I will bring you a sheep in the morning," she promised, hoping her mother would sell them one.

"Why would I want a sheep? I would take one if I did."

Kseniya turned to Yun-qi. "Is there anything I have the dragon would want? In trade for time, I mean."

"What are you thinking?" he asked.

"What might a dragon want?" she asked him quickly.

Yun-qi drew his long sword and handed it to her, saying, "They like steel."

She took the blade carefully and held it up for the beast to see. "Give me a day for this, so I may make my decision."

The dragon eyed the blade in what Kseniya could only consider a lustful manner. "Done."

With its clawed wingtip, it took the blade from her. Kseniya had to jump back to avoid being cut by its clumsy handling.

The beast turned away from them, clambering back down to its hollow by the rocks. "In the morning," it rasped in Kseniya's head. "When the sun rises, I will have the girl—or I will take the babe, hatched or not."

It turned its leathery back on them and curled about the sword like a miser with his gold.

Kseniya grabbed Yun-qi's hand. "Quickly—I don't know how long it will take."

"What have we traded for?" he asked, not having heard half the conversation.

"Only for time. It has given me until tomorrow morning to decide." She hurried back toward the farm, anxious to speak with her mother. If anyone would know how to heal that difference out of Jia-li—and do it quickly—it would be Sofiya. She explained to Yun-qi as best she could, the extra weight of the babe making her breath shorter than she liked.

He caught her arm. "And if you succeed in changing Jia-li, the dragon will take our child instead. You won't survive that."

She'd thought of that. "Perhaps the babe can be changed as well. It is desperate, Yun-qi, but I can think of no other way. It is worth a try, isn't it?"

His jaw clenched, but he nodded once. "I fear the dragon's actions if it decides it's been cheated."

That worried her as well...but they had no assurance the dragon would leave them peaceably alone should they capitulate anyway.

Sofiya considered Kseniya's request gravely. "We can *try*. But your husband's change has likely been gradual, over the whole of your marriage. To change the girl in one night...I don't know if that can be done. It is like trying to make a river flow backwards."

"But you believe we can," Kseniya said, hoping she'd understood correctly. "What of the babe?"

Sofiya laid a gentle hand on Kseniya's belly. "I will send Ivanka to fetch all of your sisters. Between the six of us, perhaps we can work a miracle."

Kseniya threw her arms about her. "Thank you, Mother."

Sofiya pulled back after a moment, a fond smile on her face. She hurried off toward the town while Kseniya and Yun-qi went to hunt Jia-li.

They found the girl sitting motionless against the southern side of the house, her eyes closed. When Kseniya explained what they intended to try, Jia-li rose and crossed her arms over her chest. "No," she said. "You can't do that to me."

Kseniya tried to be patient. "Dearest, if this can be done, the dragon will have no use for you. You will be safe."

Jia-li lifted her chin defiantly. "That dragon won't touch me."

Kseniya grabbed the girl's arm to drag her niece back into the farmhouse, but Yun-qi's hand stopped her. "Sister, the dragon rejected me. When it realizes it cannot take the babe, it *will* come for you."

Jia-li pulled herself up to her full height. "I heard all it had to say."

Kseniya had forgotten that even at a distance Jia-li would hear the dragon's words. "Then you understand why we must try this. You would no longer be troubled by..."

"No!" Jia-li jerked back, her eyes wild.

Yun-qi's brows drew together. "Jia-li, if the fire-dragon takes you, it will possess your body."

Jia-li held her ground. "It won't touch any of us. Long is coming to be our champion."

Yun-qi knelt in front of his sister, his eyes level with hers. "You called him here?"

The girl nodded.

Yun-qi sat back on his heels. "And *what* did you promise him in return?"

Jia-li's chin quivered. "It is my bargain. Not yours."

Kseniya's newly-met sisters had come at their mother's call. They had taken Jia-li's refusal well, though, and now slept on pallets on the floor of the main room. Kseniya eyed the sleeping women, trying to recall the name that went with each face. They all favored their mother, which made the task a difficult one, although only Ivanka had her mother's red hair. Each of Kseniya's half-sisters had seemed pleased to meet her, despite the trouble she'd brought down on the family. They didn't look at her oddly for carrying a sword, nor did they comment on her choice of husband. They were far kinder than the family among which she'd been raised, noble or not.

Kseniya didn't believe she would sleep that night, so later she made her way outside. Yun-qi wrapped one arm about her where they leaned against the western wall of the house. A faint glow in the hills above reminded them of the burning presence of the creature waiting there.

"What could Jia-li have offered him?" Kseniya mused. The girl refused to tell, a surprising lapse in her usually biddable nature.

"What could a dragon possibly need?" Yun-qi asked in turn.

"The other took your sword readily enough, and it wants a child."

"It wished to consume the sword," Yun-qi said. "And now we know why it wants a child; it seeks a human body to possess."

"It wanted to eat your sword?" Her husband knew far more about dragons than she ever would, but that made no sense.

Yun-qi shifted against her. "These dragons, the ones our father controlled, they are not like true dragons, not like Long. Fire-dragons belong beneath the earth, or in places where the ground erupts with molten rock. They consume stone and metal."

That explained why her offer of a sheep hadn't been well received. "What *does* Long eat?"

"Not little girls," Yun-qi said musingly. "It is said that true dragons need only air and water to thrive. I've no idea what he might ask in trade."

She leaned her head against his shoulder. "I only hope he made a fairer bargain than your father's."

She woke hours later, her head pillowed on Yun-qi's leg. The sky was still dark. "How long until sunrise?"

"Not long. I would have woken you soon in any case."

He helped her up, and they made their way into the house. Jia-li sat on her own pallet on the other side of the room. "I'm sorry I yelled," she said sheepishly, and then added, "When he came back to his mountain, I promised Long I would speak with him sometimes, so he wouldn't be lonely so far in the north. There aren't any other dragons this far from the capital. That's why I can't let you change me. It would break my promise to him."

At least that had been a fairly benign promise, Kseniya thought. "But now you've made him another one."

Jia-li nodded. She rose and nervously straightened her tunic as if going to meet the lord of the province. "He'll be here soon. Do I look well?"

Kseniya frowned. "You look fine, dearest."

The graying of the sky heralded the first signs of daybreak, the glow over the western hills now rivaled by the one in the east.

"Where are you?" a voice rasped in Kseniya's mind. "It is time."

"We are coming," she called out, hoping the fire-dragon could hear her the same way she heard it.

Jia-li remained behind at the shop under Sofiya's watchful eye, but Yun-qi walked with Kseniya up the hillside, his hand to her back. She'd considered asking him to stay behind, thinking one of them should survive this, but she knew better. He would only refuse.

When they reached the crest of the hill, the outcropping of rocks to which the beast clung looked diminished. Had it been eating the rocks?

The dragon's head snapped about on its neck. "What have you decided? The boy inside you, or the girl?"

"I am here," a voice trumpeted before Kseniya could answer. The cool sound flowed about her, far different than the voice of the creature below.

"We have chosen neither," Kseniya called down. "We have a champion now."

With a great blast of hot air, the fire-dragon rose awkwardly into the air, its wings laboring to bring it into flight. Ashes of dead vegetation stirred about them. Kseniya held her sleeve over her mouth to stifle the acrid taste. "What do we do now?" she asked Yun-qi.

"I have no idea," he answered.

The dragon rose into the sky above them, red-stained by the sun's rising rays. Once in flight it was graceful, flame trailing from its leathery wings.

"Perhaps we should run," Kseniya suggested.

Yun-qi scanned the skies, one hand raised to shield his eyes from the early sun. "And look like cowards?"

"Coward or burned to death, which sounds better?"

Yun-qi grabbed her hand and led her quickly down the mountainside. One of the things she loved about him—he had sense enough to recognize impossible odds. She coughed into her sleeve, the air dry with the dragon's fury.

A shadow passed over them. Yun-qi caught her against him and pointed. Long flew overhead, couched in the winds. Scales of white and gold glimmered in the stray beams of light that fought their way through the gathering storm. His crest flared about his head, and he roared, a fearsome sound.

The other dragon threw itself at Long, bellowing out flames. As huge as the creature had seemed on the ground, Long was twice its size. He twisted out of the path of the flames, and the clouds steamed away wherever the fire trailed.

The fire-dragon turned about, swift like a bat. It caught the end of Long's tail and blood flowed—golden drops falling in the sunlight. Long's massive claws caught one of the fire-dragon's wings, arresting its flight. The two grappled with each other. For a heartbeat they hung suspended in the sky, but then the entwined beasts began to fall. Misaimed flames belched outward as they plummeted through the air.

Yun-qi knocked Kseniya to the ground and threw himself atop her. Fire blazed all about them. The smoke from burning grass filled Kseniya's lungs.

Panicked, she willed the fire back. To her surprise, the flames answered her demand, and the air about them cooled.

Still tangled together, the two dragons slammed into the mountainside. Water exploded outwards, drowning all the remaining fires. It rushed over Kseniya and Yun-qi where they lay.

Nothing moved once the water had passed.

For a moment Kseniya lay there, trying to catch her breath. Her hip ached from where she'd hit the ground, but she thought no harm had come to the baby. Yun-qi hadn't fared as well. Blisters already showed on his side where his tunic and shirt had burned away before she'd managed to beat back the flames with her stolen talent. "Lie still," she ordered.

"Where is Long?" he gasped, pointing to where the dragons had fallen.

Kseniya turned to look. The fire-dragon had struck the ground spine first, and lay in a pool of water. Dark blood seeped from its torn wings and a great rent in its side. No flame licked about it now, evidently extinguished in the same moment as all the other fires.

Of the water dragon, Kseniya saw no sign at all.

She closed her eyes and listened with her mind, but could hear nothing from either creature. "He's gone. I don't know what that means."

Yun-qi grimaced. "Help me up."

"No. Let me heal this first." She laid her hands against his burned side, drawing the worst of the heat from his skin. He hissed out a tight breath as if he'd been holding it. She forced the heat through her own skin, allowing the cool wind to dampen it. "I need to do more."

"Not now," Yun-qi said. "Help me up."

Leaning on each other, Kseniya and Yun-qi surveyed the hillside. The carcass Kseniya had seen only a moment before was gone, and in its place lay a pile of broken bronze-colored stone, foreign to these hills. "What happened?"

"It's dead," Yun-qi said. "Truly dead. The spirit that animated the stone is gone."

"And Long? Where did he go?"

Yun-qi gazed up at the rapidly-thinning clouds. The sun shone through in spots, sparkling on the pools standing all about them. Water glittered among the dried out grasses. The wind ruffled Yun-qi's damp hair. "He is still here, all about us."

Kseniya glanced at his face. "What do you mean?"

He gave her a tired smile. "He'll be back soon to claim his prize, I expect."

While Yun-qi rested, Sofiya gathered Kseniya's hands into her own. "You forced away the flames?"

Kseniya nodded. Control over fire, the last of her husband's gifts, was now *her* burden. "Yun-qi thinks he can teach me to control it. I would hate to burn down this house, Mother."

Sofiya shook her head, smiling. "You wouldn't do so, girl. Might it not be better for you to remain here through the rest of your pregnancy? To be near healers who can help if something should go awry?"

Kseniya didn't know what to say. It was hard to believe her mother still wanted them there after all the trouble they'd brought. It would give her a chance to learn something of the healer's art though, training her aunts had refused to give her. And she could learn more of Sofiya Lebedeva, too.

"And to give us a chance to know you," Sofiya added.

"I would like that," Kseniya said, feeling the back of her throat tighten. She was perilously close to tears. "If we are not too much of a burden."

"Never." Her mother touched her cheek. "Never."

A day passed and still they saw no sign of Long.

"You said he was fine," Kseniya reminded Yun-qi the next morning as they walked up the mountain path. Jia-li had come with them this time. "Why hasn't he come back?"

"Not *back*," Yun-qi said. "He's right here. He simply needs to...pull himself back into one creature."

Kseniya turned disbelieving eyes on her husband. "What?"

"He is here," Jia-li agreed. She held her hands wide. "I can feel him."

Mist began to steam from the ground all about them at the sound of the girl's voice. Clouds formed in the sky above, and the wind lifted in a fresh breeze. Kseniya looked up and saw the shadowy form of Long above them, growing more substantial with every breath. Starting with a whisper, the liquid sound of his singing rose in Kseniya's ears. "Oh, no," she moaned.

Long came down from the skies, his serpentine form settling on heavily-clawed feet on the charred mountainside. His gilded crest and horns flared out about his head, glowing in the scattered light. "I am here."

"We thank you for your aid, Lord Long," Yun-qi said with a bow.

"A bargain was made," Long said, inclining his head.

Jia-li paled, apparently nervous now that the moment of her making had come.

"What is needed in payment?" Kseniya asked, setting her hands on her niece's shoulders. She had a good idea now, even if Jia-li had refused to tell them.

"The girl is to be my bride," the dragon said.

Yun-qi turned a disbelieving look on his young sister. Kseniya covered her face with one hand and groaned. Yes, that was precisely what she'd feared.

"It was all I could think of," Jia-li whispered.

Yun-qi turned back to the dragon. "Surely you can see she is too young to be married, Lord Long."

Long's great head tilted as if evaluating Jia-li. "She *is* small."

Jia-li raised her head and stood straighter.

Yun-qi set one hand on the girl's shoulder. "Lord Long, surely in your wisdom you know that the girl made a bargain not comprehending the complexities of it. I cannot ask that you release her, but I would suggest you give her time to grow up before you take her to your household. So she can be trained in the *duties* of a wife, as she has not been before."

The dragon tapped a massive claw on the stone remains of the fire-dragon.

"Lord Long," Kseniya asked, "what use does a dragon have for a human bride?"

"Be more polite," Yun-qi told her under his breath.

A bubbling sound rumbled through Kseniya's mind, one remarkably like laughter. "I do not know," Long said, "but that is the bargain I was offered. I chose to take it."

Jia-li cast an anxious look in Kseniya's direction.

"I will give you three years," the dragon pronounced.

"She is only nine years old," Kseniya protested. "Surely you can wait longer."

Long leapt into the sky and circled among the clouds. "We will discuss it again then."

He began to sing more loudly as he faded from their sight, his voice a waterfall in Kseniya's head. She rubbed her temples.

Yun-qi laughed at her pained expression. "Only a few more months." He set a hand under her elbow to help her over a break in the path. "And now I no longer need worry about finding my sister a suitable husband."

Kseniya managed to hold her tongue, but only with great effort. The die was already cast. So hand in hand they headed back down the path toward the farmhouse, while Jia-li ran ahead, her steps a dance in time with the dragon's song.

THE END

Early Winter, Near Jenli Village

When Li-huan's family first arrived at the house near Jenli Village, the ghost rattled bowls on their shelves and howled through the house as a rush of wind, stirring up the mats and musty old bed-curtains. The priest told Li-huan's father that the house's previous owner, a wealthy merchant, had died with no one to remember him and so sought their attention. The family dedicated a small shrine to the merchant in the corner of the inner hall and, so appeased, he left them unmolested...until Lili came.

Li-huan gazed at his bride where she lay sleeping. They had not yet attached the winter curtains to keep the heat in around the platform of the bed, so the early light streamed in through the screens, illuminating her smooth skin. Her glossy braid lay over one shoulder, and the long tunic she wore to bed managed to show no more than her slender hands and the arch of her neck.

Li-huan reached across the space between them and ran the back of his hand along her braid. Her eyes fluttered but she remained still, tensed as if afraid to move. "It's only me," he told her.

A pent breath sighed past her lips and the tension in her flowed away. She turned halfway to face him.

He stroked her winter-pale cheek. "May I kiss you?"

She nodded, yet her wide eyes showed her mistrust. When he pulled away, her lips trembled.

He sighed and said, "Lili, you know I wouldn't hurt you."

"I know," she whispered through her tears. Her fingers clenched again in the blankets. "Just do what you must."

He had tried to be patient. In the two weeks since their wedding he had only lain with her once, and the tears afterward made him feel like a monster.

Hoping for another kiss, no more, he leaned toward her again. That was when something struck him on the back of the head.

Cursing under his breath, Li-huan searched behind him until his hand found the object—the leather-bound journal in which he wrote his poetry. It had been on the table across the room the night before. He had no doubt who slung it at him, though. The ghost had taken to defending Lili every time she started to cry.

"You are unfair," Li-huan protested to the air. "I would not hurt her."

"Don't yell at him," she said, coming to the ghost's defense.

For a second, Li-huan thought uncharitable thoughts about the ghost and his wife both. Determined not to say anything that would frighten her further, he got up from the bed, dressed and went out into the courtyard.

The chilly air helped. A light snow had fallen only a week before, promising a colder winter than those of his childhood in the capital. Powdery drifts collected about the edges of the courtyard and covered the pots of over-wintering plants in his mother's carefully-tended herb garden.

The vast house itself was new to their family. The emperor had gifted the dead man's entire estate to them, but duty took Li-huan's eldest brother to visit the family of his wife. His second brother had gone to oversee the work on the other house belonging to the estate, which left Li-huan and his parents, along with old Bao-yu, to manage the workers at Jenli Village.

There was much to be done to make the house what it had once been, made evident by the bricks and tiles the workmen had left piled in the first courtyard. Li-huan gazed up at the second floor of the main hall in the center of the house. With its missing windows and roof tiles, he reckoned the family might spend the entire winter as cold as he was at that moment. Shaking his head, he rubbed his arms and then crossed to enter the inner hall.

His mother and old Bao-yu were already at work, and the scent of steamed buns reminded his stomach of his hunger. His mother glanced up and smiled at him. "Where is Lili?"

Li-huan scowled. "She will come when she is ready."

"Ah." His mother came over to join him at the table. One of the Cordara people, she was of the minority in Jenli Village. Her brown hair bore streaks of gray now and her face was lined, a testament to the struggles in her past, but she clung to the belief that things worked out for the best in the end. "No better?"

"No, Mother." He shook his head. "She still does not want to be touched."

"You must be patient," she said. "She will warm to you."

He sighed and wondered how many years she expected that

would take. His parents possessed great wisdom and tolerance, but he knew he could not claim either virtue yet. "I know, Mother. It is only unfair."

His mother's lips pressed together, and he felt guilty for having complained. It had seemed a good idea, taking a bride from among the local families. After all, Li-huan was twenty, and a wife could help greatly in the fledgling household. The girl came from a respected family and, for her part, Lili had seemed pleased at the prospect of the marriage despite Li-huan's mixed blood. His mother found the girl well-mannered and lovely enough to please her son, and so had approved the match. They'd had no way of knowing that Lili would react so to him.

"I have no other counsel for you, son," his mother said in a regretful tone.

He smiled for her sake. "Do not worry. It will work out, Mother."

Lili came in through the courtyard door, then, a placid expression on her beautiful face. It would be as if nothing had passed between them, he knew. Another day of pleasantries and meaningless words from her. Li-huan understood little more of his wife's mind than he had when he first laid eyes on her at the wedding.

Li-huan glanced out from the empty space where one of the upstairs windows had been and looked over the courtyard. A stonemason worked below, splitting bricks to be fitted around the window once they replaced it. His father oversaw that effort, so Li-huan dug through the refuse left behind by years of squatters in order to see what might be saved from the room. Most everything in the house had been ruined, only a few pieces of furniture and the oven salvageable. Still, the wood would fire the oven and broken glass could be ground down for use in the herb garden.

He heard a voice somewhere in the hallway and walked back to see who dared the chilly upper floor. He caught sight of Lili as she came up the last of the steps and walked into one of the other rooms. He had no idea why she might have come, so he went to the doorway where she'd disappeared.

Lili stood before one of the empty window frames, the wind off the courtyard blowing back a stray strand of hair. "I don't see you, Uncle," she said, her voice sounding like a lost child's. "Where have you gone?"

Li-huan stepped over the threshold and his boot crunched on a broken shard of pottery. Lili whipped around, her braid flying with the motion. For a second she merely stared at him. Her expression was one Li-huan had not seen before, a look of terrible loneliness.

"Lili, are you well?"

Her face fell, and then the placid smile returned. "I came to see if you need help."

His mother's suggestion, he guessed. Lili had not so far shown any preference for his company. "I could use some help cleaning the other room. If it is not too cold for you."

"I don't mind," she answered. So she swept the room while he placed the wood scraps into a bucket.

"To whom were you speaking?" he asked after a time. "In the other room, I mean?"

For the briefest second, she stopped sweeping. "I don't know what you mean."

That was her usual response whenever he asked about some odd behavior. Annoyed, Li-huan picked up the bucket of wood and carted it downstairs.

After a quiet dinner, Lili went early to their bedchamber, pleading tiredness. Li-huan stayed up, though, sitting before a brazier with his father and mother. Zhuang was a quiet man and rarely spoke unless he had something profound to offer, but Li-huan had taken after his mother, and enjoyed their conversations in the evening.

When he told them of the morning's odd incident, his mother frowned. "Uncle? I haven't heard of an uncle. I'll ask around in the village tomorrow and see what I can find out." She picked up a handful of herbs and began bundling them together to be dried. "I have found others to be rather closed-mouthed about the family so far."

One of the difficulties of being new to the village—their family missed out on much of the gossip. "I wondered if she might be talking to the ghost," Li-huan said then.

His father scowled, but didn't comment. His mother put

down the bundle she'd been working on. "He was quiet enough until she came here," she said with a sigh. "But the merchant died years ago, I'm told. And was he not of the Chou clan? He cannot be her uncle, or at least not one she would know."

Li-huan shrugged and said, "She called him so, I think—the ghost. I can't see him, but I believe she does."

When Li-huan went back to his bedchamber, Lili had already fallen asleep, her lovely face still. Her hands were folded over her breast and her braid lay neatly over her shoulder. She looked as far away to Li-huan as if she were in the capital and he here in his cold bedchamber.

He lay down on the far side of the bed and watched her sleep until he slept himself.

In the early morning, Lili woke grasping the sheets with white-knuckled fingers. Li-huan kept his silence, not wanting to startle her. When he neither moved nor spoke, she relaxed. Then she slipped from under the covers and stepped away from the bed. Li-huan watched her with one eye half-open, wondering what she sought.

"Uncle?" she asked. "Are you here?"

A faint glow started above her, like the drift of dust motes on a sunny day. Li-huan opened both eyes to be certain he wasn't imagining it.

She gazed at the spot. "I know I'm safe when you're here, Uncle. Don't leave me."

But the shimmering in the air shifted, moving toward the bedchamber door and then flowing out past it. Lili followed, her bare feet hardly making a sound on the reed mats. She eased the door open and slipped out.

Li-huan jumped up and went after her. The house was still dark, so he kept his eyes on the light fabric of her tunic. She made her way back to inner hall, then to the stairs and up to the icy second floor. When Li-huan came out of the stairwell, she stood in the same room where he'd found her the previous day, staring out the window.

The faint sparkling light he'd seen in their bedchamber fluttered in the darkness outside, but faded as the first sliver of the sun peeked over the horizon. Li-huan suspected that whatever he'd seen was still there. Then Lili stretched out one hand toward it, confirming that she saw it even if he could not.

"Uncle, please don't leave," she begged, leaning out through the empty window-frame.

"Lili!" Li-huan jumped forward and drew her back.

She stiffened in his grip and then blinked. "What are you doing here?"

"I thought you were going to fall out that window." He turned her loose and asked, "Are you well?"

Her eyes shifted about the room. Li-huan couldn't tell if she was simply confused, or preparing to lie to him again. "I don't know why I came up here," she finally said.

He put a hand on her cheek to make certain she was looking at him. "You were speaking to your uncle. I didn't know you had one. I did not meet him at the wedding."

A sadness touched Lili's eyes. "No, my uncle is...gone away."

Li-huan stroked her cheek. "You miss him."

Her eyes looked past him, seeing into some place he could not. "He was..."

Li-huan suspected she stood on the edge of some revelation, and so dared not push her.

"He protected me," she whispered.

The village was a safe one, where all the neighbors knew one another. Surely the uncle hadn't much to protect her from. "Where did he go?"

"It's my fault." Her eyes began to tear. Not the sobs Li-huan dreaded, only two pale tracks glistening in the light of the rising sun. "It's my fault."

Li-huan wiped the tears from her eyes. "What is, Lili?"

"It's my fault," she said.

And wherever her mind had gone, Li-huan suspected he could not follow. "Why don't you come downstairs with me, and we'll have some tea."

He placed an arm around her shoulders, and led her away from open window, back down into the warmth of the house.

Once she'd gotten warm though, Lili returned to her normal detachment, which made Li-huan want to shake her. When he asked her what her earlier words meant, she merely said, "I don't know what you're talking about."

Before he started sorting on the second floor again, Li-huan asked one of the workmen to come upstairs and help him cover the open window frames. Not skilled with a hammer, Li-huan managed to blacken his thumb in the process, but felt better knowing his wife wouldn't fall out the window should she wander up there in the middle of the night again.

Lili made a fuss over his injured hand when he came down to eat and fetched him a bowl of snow. He felt silly sitting at the table with his thumb stuck in the bowl, but it was the first time she'd ever done such a thing for him. Her concern gave Li-huan hope that his wife might warm to him after all.

"There *is* an uncle," his mother told him after her excursion into the village. "He used to visit regularly, but he left suddenly a couple of months ago and hasn't returned. Apparently, there was some argument with her father."

"And she blames herself for it." He told his mother of the incident in the early hours.

"I wonder what he protected her from," she said softly, a furrow between her brows.

"I do, too," Li-huan said, "but she will not tell me."

That night when he took himself off to his bedchamber, Lili already lay underneath the covers. Li-huan laid down next to her. "We will be married a month soon, Lili, and I know very little about you."

"It is only two weeks," she said.

"Will you tell me about your family?" he asked, seeking a safe topic. "What of your mother? What was she like?"

"She died when I was young," she whispered, "when my sister was born."

"What is your sister like?" he persisted, recalling a girl of eight or nine with serious dark eyes who strongly resembled Lili. "I saw her at the wedding, but never spoke with her."

"Father doesn't like her to talk to people," she said.

Li-huan noted that her knuckles had gone white on the blankets. He'd strayed into that delicate territory which made her deny things, so he tried something else. "What sort of flowers do you like?"

He'd startled her—that much he could tell.

"Lilies," she answered hesitantly. "Mother and I used to dig them up from the mountainside and plant them in the courtyard."

She must have been a little girl, he reckoned. "Mother will use most of the beds to grow herbs but there is enough space for you to plant some lilies here as well."

And she smiled at him. "Truly?"

"Of course, Lili." He touched her cheek. "This is your home now. Whatever you want, you can ask."

That idea seemed to startle her. "Husband, I...I do not know what I would ask."

He nearly laughed at her bemused expression. "You do not need to choose everything tonight, Lili. I think it will be a few months before we can hunt lilies on the mountainside."

She smiled again. "You are very kind. And what do you wish for, husband?"

Li-huan bit his lip to keep from blurting out an honest

answer that might start her to crying. "I think I would like," he finally said, "for you to call me by my name."

" Li-huan," she said softly.

And he should be content with that progress for one night, he told himself. "May I kiss you?" he asked anyway.

She nodded shyly, and Li-huan set his lips to hers. He intended to be gentle, no matter what hunger he felt. That kiss led to another and then a third, and she didn't try to escape him. He murmured her name against her lips.

But he felt a trembling in her limbs then, so he drew away.

"I am sorry," she whispered, her jaw clenched. "I am sorry."

"Shhh." Hc stroked her cheek and eased away from her, settling back to the far side of the bed. "I will wait."

She didn't cry, though, which he considered a good sign. Nor did the ghost throw anything at him. After a time, her shivering passed, and she slept.

Li-huan had already dressed when she woke. She rose and did the same, and they walked together to the main house to eat. When he took her hand, she didn't pull away.

"Are you almost done sorting in those rooms?" his mother asked. "Or do you need Lili's help?"

"As much as I would enjoy her company," he said, "I am mostly done." The workers would be able to replace the windows this morning, he guessed, a good thing since the air felt of snow again. "And it is cold up there."

"Would you like to come to the market with me then, today, daughter?" his mother asked.

Lili smiled faintly. "I would like that."

His mother bestowed a warm smile on her. "We're low on flour and rice both, so I can use your help."

The workmen came early, in hopes of finishing their work on the windows before the snow arrived, so Li-huan and his father went out into the courtyard with them.

Near noon, his mother came out to them with steaming bowls of rice and fish. "You should go speak to your wife," she told Li-huan quietly. "She saw her sister at the market. She would not tell me what passed between them, but she's very upset. I told her to go lie down. She's in your bedchamber."

Li-huan handed back the bowl and headed directly to their room. When he pulled back the bed-curtain, though, Lili wasn't there. He ran up the inner hall and climbed the stairs, thinking the ghost must have led her back to that same room he'd found her in twice before. By his request, the masons had put in that window first.

She wasn't looking out the new window. Instead, he found her huddled on the floor sobbing. The bucket of broken glass he'd left behind lay tipped onto the floor, and red marred the pale blue of her sleeves—blood.

She didn't seem to recognize him when he spoke to her, so Li-huan lifted her in his arms and carried her down the stairs. When he reached the ground floor, he called for his mother.

Lili sat dazed and tears streamed down her pale cheeks. There were cuts on her forearms, the fabric of her dress torn. "It's my fault," she whispered.

"Shhh, do not worry," Li-huan told her. His mother came in then and shook her head remorsefully when she saw her daughter-in-law's injuries. "The ghost must have thrown the glass at her," he said.

His mother's expression turned to a frown. "Go get me some clean linen."

A trained herbalist, his mother always kept a ready store of bandages, which saved him the work of shredding one of his shirts. He located the basket and brought it back.

His mother sat cleaning her daughter-in-law's wounds. She had cut away the ruined sleeves, exposing Lili's bare arms. Li-huan didn't think he'd seen his wife's arms naked before, and now he knew why. Dozens of old scars marred her forearms.

"She did this to herself?" he whispered.

"And has been doing so for some time, it seems. I have seen the like before," his mother said, hardly louder. She wrapped Lili's injured arms carefully. "I am going to make her an infusion of valerian to help her sleep. Perhaps a cup of wine as well. Stay here with her."

Li-huan knelt before his wife, who no longer even cried. "Why, Lili?"

"It's all my fault," she whispered.

He wasn't certain if she'd responded to his question, or simply repeated that self-damning mantra. Her eyes remained focused on some place within. The ghost whipped up a wind and threw the basket of bandages to the floor. Li-huan let them go. "What did you do, Lili?"

His mother returned with a bowl of wine. "Will you drink this, daughter?"

Lili took the cup and sipped dutifully, but never answered Li-huan's question.

After a time, his mother brought her a larger bowl and, once Lili drank that, Li-huan walked with her back to their bedchamber. "Just a nap," he told her as he tucked the blanket carefully around her bandaged arms.

He sat next to his wife until he was certain she slept, and then went back to speak with his mother. He found her still at the table, folding the bandages the ghost had scattered.

"I should have realized it earlier," she said. "I have seen the like before, in a girl taken against her will. She blamed herself and would cut her skin as...a way to punish herself. As if she'd had any choice in the matter."

Li-huan sat down. "You mean...You think Lili was raped?"

His mother raised one eyebrow. "You would know better than I. Was she a virgin?"

Li-huan's jaw clenched. He hadn't intended to speak of it, not wanting to denounce his lovely bride. He hadn't been a virgin himself. "I do not think so," he finally answered.

"Then I must suspect the other. Lili doesn't strike me as the sort to take a lover."

Nor did he. "What can I do?"

His mother touched his cheek. Her hand carried the potent scent of valerian with it. "Be even more patient, son."

Given his new understanding, Li-huan thought that would be much easier.

Li-huan sat near Lili later that afternoon and waited for her to wake. He could not bring himself to hold it against her. Many years before he'd been born, his mother had been an unwilling concubine. Women were often forced to a man's will, he knew.

He had to wonder then if the man had escaped unpunished.

Someone in the village must know of the incident, but they would not have told his family. Newcomers never heard all the secrets.

"My arms hurt," Lili said in a plaintive voice, the little girl voice he'd hear upstairs when she'd sought her uncle there.

Li-huan leaned closer. "Do you not remember? You cut them." She didn't answer, so after a moment he tried a more direct question. "My mother thinks a man forced you, Lili, and that you blame yourself. Is that why you did it?"

She spoke then, words loosened by either the wine or the herbs. "Father said it was my fault Mother died, because I did not help enough with the work when she carried my sister. That I must be a wife in her place."

Li-huan froze as the chill in the air flowed into his soul. He felt ill, the enormity of the crime against her suddenly clear in his mind. "Your father?"

"It is always my fault," she mumbled. "My fault that Mother died, my fault that Uncle died."

Li-huan wanted nothing more than to leave the bedchamber, aghast at her admission, but he could not afford to miss her rare words. Her mother had died in childbirth; surely that could not be blamed on her, so he asked about the other. "What happened to your uncle, Lili?"

Her eyes began to run again. "Uncle wanted to take me and Mei away with him to live with his family, but Father grew angry. I planted lilies in the courtyard where Father buried him. I am never to speak of it. I must say Uncle went home."

Li-huan could not decide what more to ask.

"I tried harder," she whispered, "but it was never enough, and now Mei must do everything herself, and she is too young."

Her voice trailed off, and Li-huan realized she'd drifted back into her uneasy sleep. He stroked her cheek, wondering what other dark secrets hid behind those delicate arching brows.

The ghost had taken up residence in his bedchamber. Sparkling motes of dust floated above the bed. Li-huan sighed and shook his head. "Do not entice her into anything," he told the ghost sternly. "She needs to rest."

Nothing answered his request. Li-huan doubted the ghost had any respect for him anyway.

His parents did not appear too surprised when he told them

of Lili's words, which told Li-huan that he knew very little of the world. He could not imagine such a thing happening, but evidently they could.

"Surely someone knew," Li-huan protested.

"Or suspected," his mother agreed. "But they did not choose to interfere in another family's business."

His father rose, his dark eyes hard. "I will go speak to the village headman."

"Zhuang," his mother said, "you must bring the younger sister here."

His father nodded shortly

"I will go with you," Li-huan said.

"You will stay with your wife," his father said. Li-huan wanted to argue, but his father held up one hand. "Do not waste my time with talk, son."

His mother put one hand on his arm. "Go stay with Lili. Your father can handle this discreetly. Two call attention, where one can slip into the village unnoticed."

Li-huan was relieved to find his wife still asleep when he returned to the room. He wrote in his journal, intending to resolve his frustration, but the ink refused to flow into the words he wished. Humiliation and helplessness ended up on the page instead, meant for her plight and not his own.

His father came back long after darkness had fallen, a grim expression on his face. Zhuang gestured for his son to join him outside the bedchamber.

Something had gone amiss, Li-huan could see that. "What

happened?"

"We were too late," his father said. "Whatever passed between Lili and her sister at the market must have forewarned the man. He took his own life sometime this afternoon, rather than have his guilt exposed."

Li-huan felt a moment of perverse pleasure. "Good."

His father held his arms tightly over his chest. "Hush, son."

"What of little Mei?" Li-huan asked then, recalling his mother's request.

His father shook his head and looked past Li-huan's shoulder, and Li-huan knew that Lili stood there. He turned in time to catch her as she collapsed to the floor.

Li-huan had never felt so helpless in his life. Lili cried even in her sleep, sobs that must surely rob her of any true rest. When she woke, the ghost would wake with her. Wind rose in their bedchamber, tearing at the screens. Li-huan removed everything breakable from the room, more from fear that the ghost might hurt his wife than himself.

The village's headman arranged the burials, but Lili did not join the procession. Li-huan did not have the heart to force her to it, no matter what others might say of disrespect.

After several days, Lili's distress eased. She settled back into the detachment that Li-huan recognized from the very first days of their marriage, but unsmiling this time. She rose and dressed, did as his mother bid her, but no more.

Lili drifted through her days, haunted by her past and pursued by the ghost. It called her from the bed at night, leading her up to the upper rooms in the house. Li-huan took to sleeping outside the door to stop her wanderings.

One morning, he found her in that upstairs room, staring out the now-sealed window. The workers had finished them all and that floor kept its heat better. *At least she won't freeze*, he thought. "Lili, you should go back down."

He saw no recognition in her eyes when she turned to look at him. "Where has Uncle gone?" she asked. "He spoke to me just a moment ago."

"Lili? That isn't your uncle. It's the ghost. He's lying to you." When he drew her back down the stairs, she didn't resist. But the wind yowled at him angrily and the screens rattled. And later that afternoon, he found her there again.

"I think you should take her away," his mother said one afternoon. "Perhaps to your number two brother's house. The ghost won't follow there."

Li-huan glanced over at his wife. Two weeks had passed since the funerals, and Lili only grew worse. She had cause for her woes, he knew, but the ghost did her no favors with his constant importuning. Even as Li-huan watched, Lili's face lifted as if she heard a voice calling her name.

His next elder brother house lay at the far end of the estate, up in the mountains. While Li-huan didn't wish to leave his parents and Bao-yu alone, he agreed it would best for Lili. The smell of snow hung in the air, so he suspected it would take a full day's journey. "We will leave in the morning," he decided.

His mother nodded. "Then perhaps she will have a chance to heal. And we will see if we can find a way to tame our other problem in your absence."

Li-huan went out to the yard to help his father direct the workmen. Their ladders filled the courtyard. They had only to replace the missing tiles from the rooftop of the inner hall. A light snow began to fall as the workmen used a pulley to hoist tiles up onto the highest portion of the roof. Li-huan eyed the slippery tiles and hoped they could finish their work before the snow became problematic.

When his mother came running out into the courtyard, dread filled him. She held one hand to her head, and her steps wavered. Li-huan ran to her, one step behind his father.

"Lili is gone," his mother cried. "Something hit me over the head, and she is gone."

One of the workmen touched Li-huan's shoulder and pointed up toward the main house. Li-huan saw a flutter of white and saw that someone had climbed one of the ladders to the rooftop. And then enough of the sleeve became visible that he knew who.

Li-huan ran for the ladder. He reached the roof and climbed onto the wet tiles. Barefooted, Lili took a step along the ridge and then another. One hand reached forward, and Li-huan knew the ghost had called her.

The wind whipped about him on the rooftop, and Li-huan struggled to keep his balance. "Lili," he yelled. "Come down. It is not your uncle."

She didn't turn to look at him. Still gazing out into the air above the courtyard, she extended one hand. Li-huan edged closer but then paused, still half the rooftop's length away. In the pale swirl of the snow, he saw the outline of a man's shape stretching one hand out to her.

She went one step closer and, for the barest instant, Li-huan saw that ghostly hand grasp hers.

That the ghost felt lonely, Li-huan thought, did not give him the right to coax Lili into the afterlife with him. They later learned from the village's headman that the wealthy merchant had cast himself down onto the courtyard flags from a second floor window. Li-huan did not need to ask which one.

The house had two ghosts now, and Li-huan only hoped they could comfort each other. He lit incense for them and placed it in the holder behind the bowl of rice on the shrine. Properly honored, neither the merchant nor Lili returned to haunt them. But when spring came, Li-huan found lilies on the side of the mountain to plant in the courtyard for her sake anyway.

THE END

The Dragon's Pearl

Kseniya Ilyevna had been expecting the young man who stood at her entrance gate for weeks, but she'd expected him to be a dragon.

The irises of his eyes gave away his identity, golden in a face where one expected to see brown. Otherwise he looked much like any other youth of Jenli Village, with black hair bound back by a white ribbon. His garments were unadorned, but the white of his tunic shone in a way Kseniya never achieved with her own laundering. *Magical*, she decided. "Lord Long, it that you?"

The golden eyes narrowed. "Are you Jia-li's aunt?"

He *had* met her before, but three years had passed since. Even so, she hadn't aged noticeably and her red-gold hair made her distinctive among these people. To receive directions to the Zheng family home, one could ask anyone in the village for the 'northern' woman living among them. "Yes, my lord. Have I changed so much?

He gave her a long, thoughtful appraisal before answering, as if he didn't know the polite answer would be to deny it. "I do not know," he finally said. "To these eyes, everything seems different."

Kseniya resisted the urge to chuckle at his answer. She opened the gate as she considered his words. "Please, come inside."

He followed her on silent feet around the spirit wall and through the first courtyard. His golden eyes surveyed the halls with their fine lattice screens and tile roofs. "Is this house the proper size?"

Kseniya opened the door to the inner hall. "I don't understand what you mean, my lord. The proper size for *what*?"

He stood with his hands folded respectfully—or as if he feared touching anything. "The proper size for a human man with a wife."

The last time she had seen him, he'd been a dragon as large as four houses. He'd killed another dragon that day in exchange for the promise that her niece Jia-li would become his bride. Now Kseniya thought she detected a hint of nervousness in those golden eyes.

She gestured toward a low table set near the window. "Please come and sit down with me, my lord. I will bring tea. My husband will be back shortly, I think. Perhaps he can answer your questions better than I."

He settled at the table and waited patiently while she gathered the pot and bowls. Her pregnancy, advanced as it was, made her slow but finally she sat on a cushion across from him and poured his tea. "Grandmother and Mother are at market. My husband, his father and Jia-li have gone hunting deer."

The sun fell across Long's face through the lattices, high-lighting those odd eyes. "That is how many people live here?"

"Well, my husband's second brother, Li-huan, also lives here, although he is often gone with the flocks. We have a son, Quon, who is nearly three, and will have a second son in a matter of weeks." She laid a hand on her swollen belly.

His dark brows drew together. "He is *inside* you?"

Kseniya put down her cup of tea and gazed at him for a moment. How best to ask this politely? "Lord Long, how much do you know about humans?"

The dragon kept his eyes averted, his expression troubled. "Very close to nothing, mistress. I know you must eat and drink. I know most live in houses. I know some pray to me for rain, and other days not for rain."

As a dragon, he was master of wind and weather, as close to a god as any creature could be. She expected many farmers prayed for his favor, but surely their homes must look tiny and distant to him when he flew in the clouds. He must know as little of people as she knew of ants. "Have you ever been human before, my lord?"

"I have never needed to be so, mistress. But if I am to take a human bride, must I not be?"

Kseniya caught her lower lip between her teeth. It seemed a logical supposition. Of course, despite his prediction that Long would show up *soon*, her husband Yun-qi had never once foreseen that it would be in this form. It would have been more helpful if his erratic seer's talent had shown them *that*. "I assume so," she finally answered.

She was saved from further confusing conversation by Yun-qi's appearance at the side entry of the inner hall. He entered and set his bow in the corner. Then he turned toward her and stilled when he saw their guest.

Kseniya used the column as a crutch to help her up, the other hand under her belly. "We have a visitor, as you promised."

Yun-qi's dark eyes stayed on Long. He came closer and bowed. "My lord Long, you are welcome in our home."

Long had risen behind her—likely far more gracefully. He bowed and returned to that humble pose that once again made Kseniya wonder if he might be nervous. "Are you Yun-qi, the wizard's son?" the dragon asked.

"Yes, my lord." Yun-qi's lips twisted in a suppressed smile. "I must look much larger to you now."

Long seemed relieved to be understood. "Yes, you do. Everything is different to these eyes."

Yun-qi just smiled. "I apologize, my lord, for being away when you arrived, but hunting must be done."

Yun-qi's foster father came in with Jia-li behind him. Both paused when they spotted the visitor.

Twelve years old now, Jia-li still barely reached Yun-qi's shoulder. She wore loose trousers with a sheepskin tunic over them. To keep her light-brown hair from her eyes, she'd pulled it up into a top-knot that streamed down her back like a horse's tail. Her bow rested across her shoulders and blood stained one cheek. Kseniya surmised the girl had made her first kill.

A furrow appeared between Long's brows again when he saw his intended bride. He cast a quizzical look in Yun-qi's direction.

"My foster father, Zhuang, and Jia-li," Yun-qi supplied.

Quietly—*but not quietly enough*—the dragon asked him,

"Have I misunderstood? Is Jia-li a boy?"

The girl's eyes went wide. She spun about and fled back out through the side door.

Shaking her head, Kseniya went after her. She found Jia-li in the shed, huddled down against the straw they kept for the ponies. The girl had thrown her beloved bow onto the floor and now sat with the heels of her hands pressed against her eyes.

"Dearest, hiding in the shed will not improve things," Kseniya told her. "Come inside and get cleaned up."

"Why didn't anyone tell me he was coming?" Jia-li asked.

"Ah, so you realize who that was? Your brother *did* tell you he was coming soon."

"Not today," Jia-li added with a dramatic sniff. "I wouldn't have gone hunting if I'd known. I would have worn a proper tunic."

Kseniya almost laughed at the image of a demure Jia-li perched on a cushion to wait for Long's appearance. "Dearest, do you want him to think of you as that sort of girl?"

Jia-li crossed her arms over her chest and scowled. "At least he would have known I am a girl."

"I take it his eyes are different now. He does not recognize people he may have seen before in his other form. Given that, it was an understandable question. And I suspect he doesn't know much of humans, despite the fact that he's managed to look and sound like one of us. He seemed surprised that I keep my baby inside me, so don't feel singled out. Clearly, he knows *nothing* about women."

"*You* don't have to marry him," Jia-li sulked.

Kseniya considering reminding the girl the arrangement was all her own doing; Jia-li had made her bargain with the dragon without her family's knowledge. She could also point out that the dragon didn't seem overwhelmingly pleased by the prospect. Kseniya decided not to do either. "Your brother and I will speak with him. Perhaps we can talk him into putting it off as you are too young to marry."

Jia-li opened her mouth to protest *that*, but wisely shut it.

"Come inside," Kseniya said. "He has already seen how you are dressed. There's no point in hiding. Better he knows now that you prefer to have some freedom."

The girl had far more leeway to do what she wanted than most girls. Part of that came from Yun-qi's standing in Jenli Village, and Kseniya's. Yun-qi claimed that he allowed Kseniya her way in most things because she came from a foreign people, and others never gainsaid him because Kseniya was the village's healer. Given her example, surely most of the villagers expected Jia-li to exhibit a few unconventional behaviors.

The girl rose from the straw, a pensive look on her face. "Do you think he might change his mind?"

"About marrying you? I do not believe his kind go back on their word. Do you intend to cheat him out of it?" Jia-li shook her head, and Kseniya picked stray bits of straw out of the girl's hair. "Now, hold your head up. I will carry some water back to your room so you can bathe...or cause your brother to do so. And then we will try again."

After a second, more proper introduction, Jia-li retired to her room. She emerged a short time later in her best tunic, the blue one with bright embroidery across the shoulders. She'd braided her hair back neatly and scrubbed the red stain from her cheek. Kseniya doubted the dragon would mistake her for a boy again.

Long rose and bowed. "I apologize for my earlier words, Lady Jia-li. They were ill-considered."

Jia-li sat on a chair by the work table, her narrow shoulders squared, and said, "It was an understandable mistake, my lord."

The dragon appeared more comfortable now that Yun-qi had returned. As usual, Yun-qi's foster-father had little to say, but observed the conversation with respectfully averted eyes.

"And Jia-li has proven to be an excellent archer." Yun-qi finished his story of the hunt with a smile for his young sister. "Although I must explain that she cheats, my lord."

The girl's lips pressed together, vexation replacing her earlier flustered look. "That is like the blind man complaining of the marksmanship of the sharp-eyed man, brother."

Yun-qi turned back to Long. "She can control the flight of the arrow with her mind, my lord. She never misses."

"If I have the talent, should I not use it?" Jia-li asked with her nose held high. Although her healing talent barely sufficed to heal a cut, the dragon's touch—that power inherited from her father—was a great deal more potent. She could use her mind to move things, control fire, and hear dragons.

"A reasonable question," Kseniya pointed out. "So long as she does no harm with them, I see no reason not to use her talents. The takin will provide our meat for some time."

Long's brow furrowed again. "Takin?"

"Goat-antelope," Yun-qi explained. "We left it with Mrs. Wei to be butchered. If you would be our guest for a few days, you might share some with us."

Kseniya hid a smile behind her sleeve. It was an excellent plan. To host Long at their home would give Jia-li a chance to be accustomed to her intended, and give them time to convince him to wait before asking for his bride.

A small smile appeared slowly on Long's face, almost as if he'd not practiced such before. "I had hoped you would be willing to allow me to stay for a time, Master Yun-qi, but I do not know what your customs are."

Kseniya found that unsurprising. "We are an odd household, my lord, melded together out of three peoples. Any irregularity in conduct can always be explained away as foreignness."

"Ah, I am fortunate then," the dragon said, as if grasping her evasion for what it was. "I know little of how humans live...and it is a long way back to my mountain."

"I'll let the women discuss the arrangements," Yun-qi said. "You are very welcome here."

Jia-li was clearly trying hard not to look terrified, her dark eyes the size of coins.

Kseniya had always admired her husband's ability to remain unflustered. Yun-qi managed to set the dragon at ease, offering him a tour of the village. Long cast a sidelong glance at Jia-li and accepted, leaving after a few minutes in Yun-qi's company.

"What is he thinking?" Jia-li burst out as soon as her brother had gone. "Why did Yun-qi ask him to stay?"

The sound of voices at the main door warned her that the other womenfolk of the household had returned. Old Bao-yu, Jia-li's grandmother, smiled widely when she saw Jia-li finely dressed—something that didn't happen as often as the elderly woman would like. Rahime, Yun-qi's mother, carried a tired-looking toddler on her hip. Kseniya went to retrieve her exhausted son.

"He has come, Grandmother, and Yun-qi has invited him to stay here." Jia-li grasped the old woman's sleeves, her voice taking on a frantic note. "With us!"

Rahime's dark eyes twinkled in her scar-lined face. She turned to Kseniya. "May I assume her dragon has arrived? How can he possibly stay here?"

"He is in human form," Kseniya informed her in a dry voice. She shifted Quon on her hip, and the boy yawned. "Yun-qi wants him to stay for a time, so we'll need to find a place for him to sleep."

Rahime rolled her eyes. She laid the bag of vegetables she'd purchased on the workroom table. "We can put him in Li-huan's room for now," she said, naming her youngest son who had gone north with the flocks. "Perhaps we should consider adding a new bay to the house."

Long's golden eyes watched Yun-qi's movements as they ate a simple dinner of soup and fish. He imitated them carefully. He nodded respectfully when Rahime explained the sleeping arrangements, evidently not too prideful to borrow another man's bed.

Kseniya lay next to her husband in the stillness of the night, her mind yet occupied with the day's events. "Jia-li was quite flustered."

Yun-qi chuckled. "Yes, I have no doubt she was. But we have a rare opportunity here. We have the chance to influence her husband, to make certain he is..." He paused, evidently trying to get the words situated properly. "I would not be pleased if he were to treat her poorly."

Kseniya recounted what she'd said to Jia-li in the stable. "Did you get any idea if he wanted to take her away *now*?"

"No, I didn't think so. I believe he's come just to learn how to live as a man." He shifted against her and placed a careful hand on her belly. "How old should we tell him, should he ask?"

Although they'd had three years to think about it, the dragon's impending visit had always seemed a distant thing. "Well, I would like her to be fifteen at the very least. Three more years?"

"Hmm," he said.

"Honestly, I would prefer seventeen or eighteen. Perhaps a bit older."

"Perhaps thirty? He won't be put off forever." Yun-qi's voice sounded troubled. "I did not expect him to be human."

"Yes. As a seer, you seem to have missed a few vital aspects of his coming visit," she said in a playful tone. A source of more confusion than clarity, Yun-qi's foresight only fed him bits of information, and rarely useful ones at that.

He chuckled and then sobered. "It tells me he's actually serious about this. About the marriage."

Three years before, when she first learned of his bargain with Jia-li, Kseniya asked what the dragon could want with a human bride. *I have no idea,* Long had answered.

She didn't think that had changed.

In the second courtyard the men went through their morning exercises. Jia-li joined them as usual, something that wouldn't be permitted in a more traditional household. To her surprise, Kseniya saw that their guest also participated.

It must be the first time for him. He watched Yun-qi and

Zhuang closely, but his movements had a grace that made the martial nature of the exercises seem more of a dance. The dragon still wore his overly-white tunic and trousers. Not a hint of dust clung to his garments.

Long accompanied Yun-qi that day as he made his visits at the tenant farms, leaving Kseniya at the house with the other women. Jia-li chafed at the confinement and spent the day unhappily sewing a new shirt for Quon under Bao-yu's critical eye. Jia-li hated sewing.

"You could have gone as well," Kseniya reminded her.

Jia-li just scowled. "He likes Yun-qi better than me."

Kseniya smiled at the hint of jealousy in her voice. "You would prefer for him to court you?"

"That isn't what I meant," Jia-li snapped and crumpled the shirt in her lap.

"Stop that, girl," Bao-yu said in an exasperated voice. She snatched away the shirt and smoothed it with her wrinkled fingers. "You made the choice to marry him. I had no choice at all in my husband, so do not think to complain."

Jia-li's shoulders slumped.

Kseniya took pity on her, and said, "Your brother and I have agreed that we would ask him to wait at least three more years, dearest, before you marry."

"That's a *long* time," Jia-li whispered.

Kseniya didn't agree, but there was no point trying to convince a girl of twelve. "You will survive it. And this will give him time to learn what humans do. Or do you think that once you wed him you will spend the days floating in the clouds?"

Jia-li opened her mouth, but said nothing.

"You are a human girl," Kseniya reminded her, "and I think there will still be laundry and cooking and, yes, hunting to do, dragon or not."

Jia-li's brow drew together in an expression of dismay. "Do you not think he has servants?"

"Given how little he knows about humans, I very much doubt it. Why should he need any?"

"Oh," the girl said.

Bao-yu pushed the shirt back into the girl's hands. "Silly to marry off two babes who know nothing of life, if you ask me."

Kseniya bit her lips. For all they knew, the dragon might be thousands of years old. "They have time to learn to work together, Grandmother. We shall just have to count on Jia-li's experience...and his patience."

Jia-li spent the next several days alternating between wanting to spend every moment in Long's company and avoiding him completely. Yun-qi in particular found it amusing, but wisely refrained from saying so in his sister's presence.

For his part, Long remained unfailingly courteous. He proved to be a reticent human, far more reserved than any of Yun-qi's family save the taciturn Zhuang. The dragon watched and listened far more than he spoke.

One night after dinner, Long asked how Yun-qi's father came into his powers.

"I do not think he was truly human any longer," Yun-qi said, "merely a human body that housed the spirit of a fire-dragon. I think the talents Jia-li inherited, being like a fire-dragon's, must come from that melding of flesh and spirit." Yun-qi had inherited the same gifts, but they had faded away following his marriage to a healer. He did not regret that, having seen as a child the way his father used his powers.

"A wizard came to the mountain in the spring," Long said, "and the villagers in the valley told me he sought your father's books."

"They were all burned," Yun-qi said, a furrow appearing between his brows. "When we returned to his house, we found nothing but ashes."

"I do not know if he found them, but he believed I knew where they were." Long shook his head. "He offered me his daughter in exchange for them."

Jia-li's dark eyes went wide. "What?"

"I told him I had a bride already," the dragon said, apparently unoffended by her outburst. "I do not know what he expected me to do with another one."

"What did you do?" Jia-li asked.

"I do not often find humans on my mountain, so I had let him stay," he said, "but after *that* I thought he should leave."

Jia-li had once said that Long was lonely up on his distant mountain. With no other dragons nearby, that must be so.

Afraid that Jia-li would ask more impulsive questions, Kseniya changed the subject. "My lord, you have seen much of my husband's duties. I wondered if you might wish to learn what the women of the household did."

Long turned to her. "That would be helpful, mistress."

The marketplace bustled on the last day of the week, when people came in from nearby farms to sell their wares. As close to harvest as it was, they had a goodly selection of fruit and grains. Long seemed fascinated with the variety of produce and quizzed Kseniya about many of the ones he hadn't seen before.

"Did you have all these where you are from?" he asked. "In the north?"

"No, it's much colder there," Kseniya said. "They're not able to grow many things this valley produces."

"And the market is every day like this?"

"No, only twice a week."

He nodded sagely, and asked, "A week is ten days, yes?"

It had taken her a long time to become accustomed to the idea of ten days in a week. Here the Church didn't reign over time. "Yes, my lord."

But Long had wandered away, his eye evidently caught by a seller's brightly colored fabrics.

Kseniya stopped to look at kumquats displayed on a blanket by one of the farmers who lived south of the village. The fruit looked ripe enough. She glanced up at the farmwoman to begin haggling, but instead her eyes caught those of a boy sitting on the dirt next to the blanket.

An adolescent, he had an odd appearance, almost as if he were unfinished. His ears were misshapen blobs and his nose strangely flat. His eyes seemed malformed as well, but avidly followed some movement across the pathway. Kseniya turned to determined what had captured his attention, only to see Long squatting down to cautiously touch the fabrics laid out on another seller's blanket.

The baby kicked hard, and a prickling ran down Kseniya's spine. Even though the boy looked harmless, something in those eyes seemed very familiar. They burned, making her suspect that what was behind them wasn't human at all.

Kseniya laid one hand over her moving belly and crossed quickly to where Long crouched. "I believe we should go back to the house now."

He rose obediently, his expression regretful. "They are such lovely colors."

Kseniya cast a glance backward and saw that the boy still watched them. "Please, my lord. We should go."

He gave in and followed her as she edged her way through the crowded market. When they reached the house on the edge of the village, Kseniya was relieved to find Yun-qi in the courtyard, carving a new bow. She abandoned Long for a moment.

"Could there be someone else like your father?" she asked

her husband without preamble.

Yun-qi put down the bow and turned to meet her eyes. "Not that I know of, but I cannot say no, either."

"At the market, there was a boy with Mrs. Hu. He looked wrong, somehow. He had eyes like your father's," she said. "And he watched Long."

"Eyes like my father's?" Yun-qi brushed the wood-filings from his trousers. "I'll go and have a look at him."

But he returned not much later without success. "Mrs. Hu told me they found him standing by the side of the road a few days ago and took him in. They thought he could help work the harvest if he wasn't too simple. She told me he got up and ran away just after you left the market and they haven't seen him since."

"That alone should be something of a warning." Kseniya placed one hand over her stomach as the baby began kicking again.

"You left so quickly that Mrs. Hu was concerned your time had come unexpectedly," Yun-qi said, sparing a glance for her rippling stomach. "Has it?"

"No, the baby is only kicking a great deal." She sighed, wishing she could take the whole afternoon back. "So what can we do?"

"Do? Nothing."

She regarded him over the abandoned bow and asked, "Will something happen?"

Yun-qi closed his eyes and for a moment, said nothing.

Then, "Fire."

Bells and gongs in the village rang out not long after moonrise, and Kseniya knew already what passed. Yun-qi rose swiftly and helped her up from their bed. "I will go," he said.

"Be careful." She had no better advice for him, so she drew a tunic on over her old shift and went to the inner hall. She got there in time to see Yun-qi slipping out the side door, his sister begging to go with him. "No, Jia-li, stay here," Kseniya ordered.

Jia-li turned back. "If there's a fire, I can control it."

"And if there is a fire-dragon there, I don't want it to see you." Three years before a fire-dragon had wished to possess Jia-li's body, just as one had taken over her father's in the distant past. She was different, the energies in her body running in a reverse order. *That* was the quality the dragons sought in a host for their spirits.

Jia-li's mouth gaped open, but Kseniya held up a hand to stop her protest. "I saw a stranger in the village this morning. He had eyes like your father's. And now this happens." Kseniya shook her head. "I cannot believe it's a coincidence."

"Like my father?" Jia-li repeated in a frightened voice. "It can't be. He's dead."

Catching a movement in the corner of her eye, Kseniya saw Long standing on the threshold of the inner hall. Fully dressed in his usual pristine garb, he looked very alert.

"It must have followed me," Long said. He shook his head

wearily. "I am tired of these creatures, and had hoped that at least in *this* form I would have some peace from them."

"Lord Long? Do you know of what I'm speaking? It was the boy at the market."

"And he has started a fire to draw me out, I expect. I didn't see him, but I heard you speak with your husband about him when we arrived here."

Yun-qi had been out in the courtyard, but far from the inner hall doors. "You heard us? Lord Long, are you certain?"

"I have very good ears," he said.

"Good ears indeed, Lord Long." She frowned. "You have seen one like the boy before?"

Long frowned. "I do not know how he managed to take human form. Those creatures cannot do so on their own, they are not truly *alive* to begin with. A wizard must have created the body for him."

The mysterious wizard who had visited Long's mountain must have, indeed, located the books of Yun-qi's father, even if Long didn't know of it. "Not truly alive?" she asked.

"They are stone, brought to a semblance of life by the spirit of fire that inhabits them."

"How do you know that?" Kseniya asked before she thought better of it.

He folded his hands together. "It is a thing...that concerns dragons, mistress."

Jia-li came closer. "Is this stranger a fire-dragon? Like the one you fought three years ago?"

"Yes," he said. "One of the twelve. Five have come after me already. As long as they do so one at a time, they do not concern me overmuch."

The fire-dragon he'd fought for Jia-li's sake had twelve hatchlings that she'd given to the dragon wizard in a bargain. Jia-li had freed them after her father's death, but apparently that didn't carry any weight with them. Kseniya sighed. "Are they seeking revenge?"

"Yes," he said. "It seems to be intrinsic to their kind."

They'd brought this on him. Judging Jia-li's stricken expression, Kseniya decided the girl had drawn the same conclusion. "My lord, I must apologize. I regret that we ever drew you into this."

"It was my decision to accept Jia-li's offer." Long stood with his hands pressed together and his eyes downcast, looking meek and not particularly dangerous. "I can call rain, if that will help, although not as much as in my other form."

"I believe that would be helpful, my lord," she said.

So he called the rain, although *how* he did so, she couldn't tell. He didn't move, just stood in the middle of the room with his eyes closed. She'd expected something more dramatic. At first Kseniya heard a faint pattering on the tiles of the roof, then a steady drumming.

The dragon opened his golden eyes. "It is more tiring in this form. I believe I should rest, mistress."

Kseniya watched him turn and walk back down the hallway. He wavered and, for a moment, leaned with one hand against a beam before continuing on and disappearing from her sight. From behind her, she heard Jia-li's faint voice protest, "I didn't know."

The miller's storehouse had caught fire, a pile of wheat exploding into flame. "Not unheard of," Yun-qi said in a weary voice, "but suspicious. If not for the rain, there might not be flour this winter."

She brought him a cup of tea to ease his throat. "Long called the rain."

"Ah," he said, and drained the cup. "I did wonder. I warned the other men to be wary of strangers who might set a fire out of maliciousness."

"Did you mention the boy?"

He nodded. "I did."

She felt pleased that he trusted her judgment. She related all that the dragon had said to her as she fetched him more tea. "Jia-li is quite upset and blames herself."

Yun-qi sighed. "She has always taken more responsibility than is due her. This boy—you think he was watching Long?"

"Long agrees. He believes it's one of the hatchlings, having taken human form. Or rather that a wizard must have helped it to take such a form."

Yun-qi sat down on the bed platform and ruffled a hand through his sooty hair. "It seems another wizard *has* found my father's secrets. Why would a wizard do such a thing for a fire-dragon?"

"I'm certain the wizard hoped to gain something."

He gave her a dry look. "Yes, I expect so, but what?"

"If he already found your father's writings, what else could he want? Would that not be enough to satisfy him?"

"Wizards are never satisfied with what they have." Yun-qi stripped off his soiled tunic.

Kseniya folded it to put with the other laundry in the morning. "Would a fire-dragon be stronger in human form?"

Yun-qi shook his head. "It would not have been a match for Long before, as some of them have already discovered. Now it must be even weaker."

That only posed more questions. "Then it came here to die, which serves no purpose."

The next day, a fire caught in the Yuan's store of straw and burned down one wall of their house before the rain quenched it. Later than evening, the clay oven outside Mrs. Wei's home cracked, spilling coals onto the shed floor. Having gone with the other men to extinguish the flames, Yun-qi returned that evening tired, wet and sooty.

"I believe I would do better to seek him out," Long said. "He came for me. That is their way. I do not believe being in human form would change it."

"Why would a wizard give a fire-dragon a human body?" Kseniya asked him, still not having found her answer.

"I do not understand how humans think," Long said with a rueful shake of his head.

Kseniya could not argue with that. "How do you suggest we proceed, Lord Long?"

Long's features took on a grave expression. "I shall draw him out. I can still defeat him, especially since he has taken human form as well."

"Can you not take back your other form?" Yun-qi asked.

"Not without returning to my mountain."

"Ah," Yun-qi said, "your pearl is there?" A dragon's magic, it was said, was kept in the form of a pearl which the dragon, if he had any sense, would never reveal to a human.

A faint smile touched the corners of the dragon's lips, but he didn't laugh. "In truth, Master Yun-qi, my other form is simply much larger. I left most of it there. I would only make a very small dragon now, should I try to change."

Yun-qi considered that answer gravely, an odd expression crossing his features. "I see."

"I don't wish any more harm on this village," Long said, "but I believe I must rest for a time before going to find him." He rose and made his way toward his borrowed room.

Kseniya looked across at her husband. "What *were* you thinking?"

"I have a terrible image of a rotting dragon body left behind in some mountain cave," he said softly. "I only hope that wasn't foresight. How could he have left part of his body there?"

Jia-li puffed out a breath. "It's water, brother, in a pool or a lake. Remember, a *water* dragon?" she said in a tone that clearly condemned Yun-qi as dense. "I'm going to go rest, too."

Yun-qi watched his sister go with raised eyebrows. Kseniya wanted to laugh but elected not to in favor of familial harmony.

"If either of you is hurt," Kseniya said patiently as she pulled on a pair of loose trousers, "I should be there. You could be burned."

"I want neither you nor the baby there," Yun-qi said, casting a pointed glance at her belly. "We don't need your sword."

Fortunately, she knew she would win the argument. She drew on a plain tunic, tied the tapes, and belted it loosely. "I will stay back, I promise. It would be easier if you gave in and let me go with you, rather than having me follow you at a distance in the dark. Besides, I can identify him for you."

Although it had been years since he'd left the Emperor's personal guard, armed and dressed in a dark jacket and trousers, Yun-qi looked very much like one of them at the moment. He watched her with narrowed eyes while she continued to dress. "Very well, but if I ask you to run, do so."

Kseniya reckoned running was impossible, but she could waddle away quickly. "I will."

His sighed. "I am sorry. My father's evils keep coming back to try us..."

"No matter how good we are," she finished with a wry smile. "We have Long on our side, though, which is a blessing."

"I doubt he thinks so."

She touched his cheek, concerned by this morose track his thoughts seemed to be following. "We will weather this, and there will be one less dragon to hunt him."

They found Long already waiting for them in the inner hall, Jia-li with him. Kseniya didn't catch the girl's words, but Jia-li grasped the edge of his sleeve, conveying urgency. She was close enough to hear his answer, though.

"He will continue this until I find him or he finds me," Long said. "I prefer he not come to this house."

"Could I not try to control the fire-dragon?" Jia-li asked her intended hesitantly.

Long shook his head. "I do not believe that would be wise. A spirit such as this possessed your ancestor. I suspect that yours would be a preferable body to the one it wears now." He frowned slightly. "And such an outcome would place *me* in a most difficult position."

Would his promise to wed Jia-li would still bind him if her body were possessed? Or would he simply dislike killing her should that happen? Kseniya decided not to ask. "You will stay here," she told the girl.

Jia-li looked as if she wished to protest, but Long took her hand, the very first time Kseniya had seen him touch any of them. "I ask it of you as well," he said in a grave voice.

For a brief instant, Kseniya saw a glimmering light about

his form. Was he using his magic to persuade Jia-li to his will? But her let go of her hand and Jia-li stepped back, still looking rebellious. Yun-qi repeated Kseniya's order, and Jia-li flung herself gracelessly onto a cushion to sulk.

They set out from the house in Long's company under a glowing moon. His white tunic blazed under the pale light, a beacon to whomever might seek him. Kseniya stayed back as promised, so she didn't hear what passed between her husband and Long. They conferred, deciding their path along the way.

Kseniya clutched her jacket about herself. The noises of the dogs and pigs, normal in the village, were all absent. They knew there was evil afoot in the streets of Jenli. A piebald hound rose silently near the gate of the Huang family home, then crouched with its hindquarters raised as if it bowed to Long. It made no sound, though.

Long stopped, turned his head to the left and pointed. The two men went in that direction, and she followed. After a time, Long's path led them back to the silent marketplace. Some stalls were regularly left behind, lined up against the back wall of the miller's storehouse. Long walked past them slowly.

Kseniya stopped at the storehouse doorway and settled back against the cool stones. The men walked along the aisle, Yun-qi pulling back the hemp hangings of the stalls with his sword as they went. They had neared the end of the aisle when, in a flurry of fabric, the boy erupted from the next-to-last stall.

"That's him," she called. Yun-qi raised his sword to strike, but the boy backed away, his ill-shaped hands wide. For a moment none of them moved.

"Do not try to escape," Yun-qi warned him.

The boy's head didn't turn toward Yun-qi, as if he neither heard nor comprehended. His gaze stayed fixed on Long's white form. Fire blossomed about his hands, confirming Kseniya's suspicions.

The boy raked one hand through the air. Yun-qi fell backwards like a rag doll tossed by a spoiled child. His sword flew out of his grip and clanged down against the storehouse steps.

Without thinking, Kseniya ran to where he fell and knelt next to him. He blinked up at her in an addled fashion, but showed no immediate signs of injury. The dragon's phantom touch could cut skin, Kseniya knew from painful experience. Yun-qi wasn't bleeding, fortunately.

Long stood unmoving with his hands pressed together. "Do not concern yourself with them," he said. "You came here for me."

Rain began to fall over the marketplace, a heavy rain that doused the boy's flaming hands. He stood there in the falling water and gazed blankly at his fingers.

"Where is my sword?" Yun-qi asked Kseniya over the din of the downpour.

"On the steps." Kseniya half-rose and helped him up, both of them ungainly now. He clutched one arm to his side and groaned when she touched it. Ribs, she decided, cracked or broken, and beyond her power to heal.

The boy's eyes returned to his quarry. He screeched unintelligibly in a voice that shook the walls.

Kseniya slapped her hands over her ears. Yun-qi's eyes squeezed shut in pain. They were still some distance from the steps where they could get out of the hard rain, when she glanced back and saw the boy running at Long.

Long stepped out of the boy's way, a fluid motion like one of their morning exercises perfected. Shrieking, the boy spun about and attacked again.

Kseniya stopped in the street and watched, astonished to see Long rise into the air like a feather. For a moment, the dragon stayed suspended there, out of the boy's reach. The boy gazed up at him and howled in fury.

Then the boy spun about and turned his attention on Kseniya. He started running toward her. Yun-qi was in front of her before the boy got close. He clutched his short sword in his off hand, the other arm still held against his side. One-handed, he swung downward. The blade sliced through the boy's outstretched wrist like mud.

The boy backed away, screeching. He didn't bleed, though. The severed hand lay on the gravel of the street, the flesh unraveling until a pile of dark rocks lay there.

"The water makes him weak," Long called down to them.

Hearing that, Yun-qi glanced back toward the steps, apparently searching for his long sword. He pointed it out to Kseniya where it lay against the stone wall. She started that way, only to turn back when the drenching rain abruptly stopped.

Clutching his heart, Long fell from his perch in the sky, perhaps twice the height of a man. He landed on his side on the gravel with an audible grunt and didn't move.

Seeing an advantage, the boy ran toward him. His hands blazed with flame again. Yun-qi started after him.

"Get down!" Jia-li's voice pierced the darkness. She stood on the steps of the storehouse, Yun-qi's long sword in her hand.

Seeing Yun-qi drop to the pavement, Kseniya ran for the wall. Out of the corner of her eye, she saw Jia-li throw the sword like a spear. Not balanced for that, it should have fallen...but it flew true, like one of her arrows. The sword slammed into the boy's back, piercing his chest as easily as the earlier cut had severed his hand.

The boy stumbled and fell to the ground, only a few feet from where Long lay motionless. As Kseniya rose and went closer, his body crumpled into a pile of stone, Yun-qi's sword caught amidst it. Flame licked about the stone only for an instant, then was gone.

Jia-li ran past her and dropped to her knees at Long's side.

Keeping one eye on the pile of stones, Kseniya went to help Yun-qi. "What happened to him?"

"She killed a dragon," he said in an awed tone.

On his good side, Kseniya slipped one arm around his waist to steady him. "I meant what happened to Long? I don't care what happened to that thing."

Yun-qi leaned on her as they made their way over to where Long lay in the street. Jia-li held one hand against his pale cheek.

The girl's healing talent was weak, Kseniya knew, but it should at least tell her if her dragon was alive. "What is it, dearest?"

"I don't know," Jia-li said in a frightened voice. "It's like he's far away."

Getting everyone back to the house proved to be a nightmare of its own. Long didn't wake and, unable to carry him, Yun-qi finally agreed with Kseniya that they should wake the miller and beg his aid. So the miller, Jia-li and Kseniya lifted Long's limp form into a borrowed cart under Yun-qi's frustrated regard. They also retrieved the sword, encased in a sheath of melted stone.

Fortunately, back at the house Zhuang and Rahime waited for them, and helped to carry in their guest. Rahime clucked over her son's injury, but left him to Kseniya's healing mercies. Instead she turned her stern eye on Jia-li. "Go to your room. Change clothes. Go to bed. Now."

"But..." Jia-li started. Rahime glared at her. Jia-li folded her arms over her chest. "He is my intended. I only want to be certain he's well."

Rahime raised an eyebrow, usually enough to intimidate any of her sons. "Are you implying I will not see to our guest's comfort? You are in enough trouble for stealing out of the house at night."

Jia-li snapped her mouth shut and bolted down the hall.

Zhuang carefully lifted the dragon and bore him back to

the room he'd been using, with Rahime a few steps behind. Kseniya regarded her husband, who stood staring ruefully at his ruined sword. They were both drenched and liberally covered with mud. With a sigh, she touched his shoulder and then led him back to their room, where she would heal what injuries she could.

The dragon didn't wake that day. Jia-li paced about the inner hall like a caged tiger, her eyes bloodshot either from lack of rest or tears. She had already begged their forgiveness for sneaking out behind the others and given her promise not to do it again. Kseniya had some doubt *that* would last.

Zhuang had dressed the dragon in a shirt of Li-huan's. Compared to the dragon's usual garb, it seemed a very dull shade of white. Long looked more human, then. Kseniya did note, however, that he didn't seem to be in need of a shave. Trained as a healer as Jia-li was not, she laid her hands to the top of his head, his forehead, and his throat. When she reached his chest, she knew she need go no further. "He isn't injured from the fall. His head and his bones are intact. He is very weak, though. I don't know why."

"That's what I thought," Jia-li said softly from the doorway. "He felt weak but not hurt."

Kseniya scowled. When had Jia-li's healing powers improved enough to allow her to feel the flow of another's life force? She recalled then Jia-li's control over a sword that should not have reached its target. Had the dragon done something to her?

A few minutes later, Jia-li sat on a stool in the kitchen. Kseniya laid one hand on the crown of her head. She forced the life energy in her body along the pathways of power within Jia-li's body, and found them all far stronger than they'd been the last time she'd examined the girl.

The dragon slept on, and the next day the family tried to resume their normal routines. Yun-qi convinced Jia-li to accompany him to the smith's shop to try to rescue his sword from its stone prison.

So Kseniya was alone, grinding bark into powder when the dragon appeared at the end of the hallway. He stood with his hands folded together, like he had the first day he'd come. "I must leave now, Mistress Kseniya."

She put down the pestle. "My lord, are you well enough to leave?"

He came closer, his paleness evident in the light filtering through the lattices. "I do not believe I have a choice. I must return to my mountain."

"What has happened, my lord?"

"It was a distraction, that fire-dragon in the market. He was sent here to keep me occupied, so I would ignore what happened on my mountain. My body has been destroyed."

She feared something like that. "The wizard?"

"I think so," Long said. "He must have found my hidden place in the mountains. The lake which held my essence was drained. I must return to gather my form, or there will be no rains there this fall."

Kseniya wiped her hands. "*Gather* it, my lord?"

"I do not have a better word for it, mistress."

"Will you be safe returning there? If this wizard has drained your lake..."

His faint smile touched his lips. "The wizard does not concern me. He did not find what I suspect he truly wanted, and as such, is barely a threat."

"What *did* he want?" she asked.

"My pearl," Long said. "I have given it to Jia-li for safekeeping."

His pearl contained a great part of his magic, if she understood correctly. "Does she know, my lord?"

"No." For a brief instant he seemed almost sheepish, an odd thing for a dragon. "I passed it into her when I held her hand. Nothing more, mistress. I have not hurt her in any way, and it will protect her should the remaining fire-dragons come after her here."

Now she understood why Jia-li's powers seemed stronger. She had a dragon's hidden magic within her somehow. "Do you have enough magic left to do what you must?"

"It was only a portion of my magic, mistress." He smiled

gently and came toward the door. Kseniya could see that he no longer wore the borrowed shirt. He had on his own glowing tunic instead. "I think it best I go before she returns. The pearl will bind her to me, and I believe she is too young for marriage just now. How old did you say? Sixteen or seventeen?"

Kseniya tried to recall when she'd said as much to him. With his good hearing, Long must have overheard Yun-qi speaking with her that first night in their bedchamber. "That is what I said."

"Was Master Yun-qi joking when he said thirty? I couldn't tell."

She suppressed a grin. "Yes, my lord. He was joking."

"Then I hope to return in the next harvest season, mistress, if I may." He bowed to her a final time. "Please keep her safe for me."

Kseniya followed him into the courtyard and watched as he rose in the sky, his white raiment blending with the clouds until she couldn't see him any longer. Jia-li would be unhappy to have missed his departure, but Kseniya felt sure they would see him again soon

THE END

The Eretik

On a distant hill a bonfire burned. Ivanka watched the glow of the flames, not much more than a bright blotch in the dark sky, and wondered what fools danced there. A year ago she had jumped over that fire. She had believed a man's lie, and that had come near to ruining her life.

Li-huan leaned up on one elbow and gazed down at her. In the light of the waxing moon, his eyes seemed dark and mysterious. "Why are there fires?"

"Midsummer's Eve," she told him. A foreigner, he spoke her language passably, but she wasn't certain whether he would recognize those words. "They will burn the straw man."

He took a hank of her unbound hair and used it to tickle her nose. "Straw Man?"

Ivanka batted his hand away. "Do they not do that where you are from? What do you do?"

Li-huan was from the Han Empire, and Ivanka had no idea what customs their people had to honor the solstice. Or whether they even marked the longest day at all. Being so close to the border between their peoples, the town of Petrivka often saw foreign traders passing through. But they surely did not make close bedfellows, not when their ways were so different. For Li-huan, Ivanka was willing to make an exception.

He was the younger brother of her half-sister's foreign husband. They had come north to Petrivka to visit Ivanka's mother, and Li-huan had come along to help herd the sheep they'd brought as a gift. While his elder brother looked very much a descendant of the Imperial Throne, with dark, hooded eyes and raven-black hair, Li-huan did not. He had curly brown hair, eyes that laughed, and a distinctive hook to his nose made her suspect him to be part Turk. And Li-huan smiled far more often than his elder brother did.

In a few weeks time he would be gone again, but she would remember him with great fondness. She would miss him.

"No, no man of straw," he said after a moment. He leaned closer, laying a hand against her cheek to draw her eyes to his. "Tomorrow is midsummer, yes? In the morning I will ask..."

She never learned what he intended to ask.

Within the fold, one of the dogs barked. Ivanka sat up, and Li-huan came to his feet smoothly. He crouched down to dig among his garments, rising again a moment later with his short sword. Both dogs began to growl in earnest then, so Ivanka grabbed her shift and dragged it on over her head. Her breath coming short, she scrambled back into her hut, drew her knife from her belt, and ran to where Li-huan stood peering into the darkness. Her blood pounded in her ears.

Birds erupted from the trees in a rush of wings.

"Man," Li-huan said softly, pointing with his chin. He'd managed to pull on his trousers one-handed but gave her his sword to hold while he tied the strings. A moment later his fingers pried the hilt from hers, and he asked, "See him?"

Ivanka shook her head. In the moonlight, the trees were simply blackness filled with more blackness. Who could be out here, up on the mountain?

"Whore!" A voice rung out from that direction, one eerily familiar to her. For a terrified moment, Ivanka thought her husband had returned from the dead. Then she caught a glimpse of the man moving toward them, heavier and taller than her husband had been. It was Bogdan, his younger brother. Her stomach tightened—this could not be chance.

Li-huan stepped between her and that distant threat.

Sheep began bleating within the fold, agitated by the dogs.

"Go away, Bogdan," she yelled, "or I'll set my dogs on you." It was a toothless threat. Anyone familiar with the dogs would guess that. They would stay with the flock. The shape in the darkness paused, though, as if reckoning the odds.

"Couldn't wait for a grown man, could you?" he called back. "You take up with a beardless boy, instead. Have you bewitched him as well, *koldunya*?"

Bogdan didn't mean that title respectfully. In the time before the Church had come, *koldunya* had been a term of honor, a name for the wise-women and healers of the mountain villages. But some had turned their talents to ill use, and the name had come to mean *witch* in many people's minds. Bogdan and his sister had done their best to make the people of Petrivka see Ivanka that way. "I never did anything to you, Bogdan," she protested.

He laughed harshly. No more than a dozen feet away now, Ivanka could see that his pale hair was disarranged. His ornately embroidered tunic looked rumpled, as if he'd slept in it. She caught the scent of soured wine and sweat carrying past him on the faint warm breeze. Li-huan edged toward him.

"What do you want?" she asked, hoping to keep his eyes off Li-huan. Bogdan had no idea her 'beardless boy' was the true threat, not her or her dogs.

"I could have saved you," Bogdan said, pointing a shaking finger in her direction, "remember that when he comes after you."

He comes after you? Ivanka had no idea what—or who—*that* meant. "I don't need your help with anything, Bogdan."

He took another step toward her, but Li-huan blocked his path and said, "Go back now."

Bogdan pulled his knife from its sheath and stabbed at Li-huan. Ivanka cried out, but Li-huan raised his arm, deflecting the blade easily. His short sword flashed in the moonlight and Bogdan yelped. He jumped backward out of Li-huan's reach, his hands going to his belly where a dark stain spread across the light fabric.

"A warning," Li-huan said. "Go now."

Ivanka held in a gasp, her hand to her mouth. Bogdan had struck first, but he would lie about that when he got back down to the town. Li-huan would be blamed, and it was her fault.

Bogdan surveyed Li-huan with an insolent sneer, then laughed in Ivanka's direction again. "Consorting with an unbeliever? What will the Father say? He already thinks you and your mother are witches."

He sketched a mocking bow and then turned and strode

toward the trees.

Her stomach knotted. That wasn't simply musing on Bogdan's part. He would send the priest after her, claiming witchery and debauchery. This time people might be more inclined to believe his family's claims.

The main room of the farmhouse was dark when Ivanka slammed open the door, but her mother and sister both rushed in to see what caused the noise, lamps in hand.

Ivanka held one hand to her side, winded from her run down the mountainside path. "He saw us," she gasped out.

Her mother clutched a blue-dyed woolen wrap about her shoulders, but the nightdress beneath told Ivanka that she'd already lain down to sleep. She set her lamp on the worktable that stood in front of the loom that filled most of the main room. "It's late, Vanka. What are you talking about?"

"Bogdan saw us together." She laid a hand over her mouth, wishing she could unsay it.

Her half-sister Kseniya eyed her narrowly. Ivanka was mildly terrified of this eldest sister of hers, not only because the woman had been raised in a prince's household, but because she had a man's ways. Kseniya's royal father had ordered her trained to the sword rather than a woman's skills. The priest in Petrivka had denied communion to such an unnatural creature; that was one of the few things Kseniya and Ivanka had in common.

"What did you mean by *together*?" Kseniya gave her a stern look, but then her blue eyes slid to the doorway of the farmhouse. "Ah, no need. I think I can figure that out."

Ivanka followed the direction of her sister's gaze. Framed in the lamp-light, Li-huan stood in the doorway barefooted, still wearing only his loose trousers. Running after her, he must have left his tunic by the sheepfold. Ivanka grimaced, wishing she'd used her brain instead of bolting for the protection of her mother's house. She ignored her sister's acerbic tone. "Bogdan will tell the priest, Mother."

"What were you thinking?" Her mother closed her eyes tightly, as if that might chase away this new catastrophe Ivanka had brought down on them. "And why was Bogdan up on the mountain?"

"I don't know, Mother. I expect he sought the sort of thing he usually wants from women." She always carried a knife on her belt, but had more reason to keep it close because of Bogdan. A year before, his brother Grigori had taken Ivanka to the Vasiliyev house near the stream. And while Grigori had *called* her his wife, he'd never treated her so. Knowing that, Bogdan had decided he could freely pursue her. That had been as unacceptable to Ivanka as everything else in the Vasiliyev household.

She wrapped her arms about herself. She thought she'd escaped them. For the last six months since she'd left Grigori's household, she'd lived in near exile up on the mountain with the flock, denied both the church and the bathhouse because of the rumor of witchery. Only her mother ever came up to talk to her. It had been peace bought at the price of isolation, but now Bogdan Vasiliyev had come up to her mountainside and shattered her fragile tranquility. Would they never leave her alone?

Ivanka took a deep breath and stood straighter, her aching side having forgiven her. She would simply have to think of some way out of this.

With her red hair unbound and uncovered, she suspected she *looked* like a witch—a whore, as Bogdan had called her. She'd left her headscarf at the hut, as well as her over-tunic and belt. She gathered her hair back with her hands and tried to regain some dignity.

Her wits gathered, she gave her mother a clearer answer. "Bogdan saw us together up on the mountain," she said. "I don't know why he came, but he and Oksana will tell everyone in the town by noon." Oksana—Grigori and Bodgan's beautiful sister—was at the heart of all of Ivanka's problems. The woman would surely love having grounds to persecute Ivanka further.

Li-huan came to stand next to her, apparently as unconcerned by being caught half-dressed as if he were in the bathhouse. A sheen of sweat glistened on his bare chest. "I do not understand what is wrong," he said to her quietly. "Who is Bogdan?"

"My husband's brother," Ivanka said. Li-huan raised a dark eyebrow and gazed at her. His brows were drawn together as if to say that her explanation fell short. She tried again. "He and Oksana—she is his sister—told everyone it is my fault my husband died. They said I used my gift to weaken him."

Li-huan's eyes narrowed. "You had a husband? But...?"

Ivanka covered her face with her hands. She hadn't seen any reason to tell him about Grigori. Li-huan knew she'd never lain with a man before him, though, so the claim of a husband must make no sense. She wasn't sure whether his voice carried hurt or anger, but she'd never meant to deceive him. She hadn't meant for him to be drawn into her problem, to give him cause to despise her.

Kseniya took pity on her, then, embarking on an explanation in Li-huan's tongue.

Ivanka wilted onto the bench on the side of the wall. Her mother came and sat next to her. She wrapped one arm around Ivanka's shoulders and said, "We will work something out. If nothing else, Kseniya and her husband can take you with them for a time when they return home over the border. Or you could go to one of your other sisters."

Ivanka doubted that any of her sisters wanted her on their hands. Until now, the people of Petrivka had always trusted their family to use their talents wisely. They had seen them as *healers*. The rumors started by the Vasiliyev family had damaged that trust. "I'm sorry, Mother," Ivanka whispered. "But if Oksana can get the townsfolk to turn against me, they will turn against you as well."

Her mother shook her head. "I will be fine. Your problems

with Bogdan and Oksana are not your fault. And this..." Her mother glanced up at Li-huan where he spoke urgently with Kseniya. "...this, I cannot fault you for."

Ivanka turned her eyes on her eldest sister. Ivanka had never even met her until a few years ago. Kseniya looked the most like her of all her sisters, though, her hair a few shades lighter but with the same face and tall, slender form. Despite that, they were only half-sisters. Kseniya was their mother's *bastard*, fathered by a prince who'd stayed at the farmhouse for one night on his way to some city even farther east.

Kseniya's stern expression told Ivanka that she and Li-huan argued over something. Li-huan crossed his arms over his chest, favoring Kseniya with a frustrated expression. His forearm was covered with blood, Ivanka saw then. Bogdan's poorly wielded knife had struck home after all. Ivanka felt wretched again.

Kseniya frowned down at her. "He doesn't think this is a problem. He says you should claim you are already married."

What? Ivanka's breath caught in her throat.

Kseniya went on. "I've explained that the priest will not permit the two of you to marry, but Li-huan figures that if we claim it is already done under their rites, the priest can't force you to set it aside. And then if Bogdan Vasiliyev tries to make trouble, it won't carry."

When had marriage entered the conversation? Had Kseniya told him that he *must* marry her after bedding her? Ivanka tried to catch Li-huan's eyes, but he had turned back to Kseniya to say something else.

"Is it legal under their law?" her mother asked, wearily tucking a strand of escaped gray hair behind one ear.

"Yes," Kseniya answered with a wry smile. "Their people don't view a marriage relationship as consanguineous. The priest here will fine you for allowing it because Li-huan's not a Christian, but we will pay that for you, Mother. And there will be a penance, I'm sure."

Her mother nodded. "I will suffer the penance, gladly, if she's safe away from here..."

Ivanka sat unmoving as they spoke past her, uncertain what she should do. Everything had spun out of her control. Li-huan smiled down at her then. He seemed unruffled by the situation, as if being forced to marry her was of no consequence. "Is that what you want?" she asked him. "You need not..."

The door opened again and Kseniya's husband Yun-qi came back in from the night. Ivanka hadn't even heard him go out, he moved so quietly.

"I have been all around the house," he said, "and I found nothing following them." When no one responded, Yun-qi raised his eyebrows and gazed at his wife.

"Your brother has decided to marry my sister," Kseniya announced.

Yun-qi's dark eyes flicked toward Li-huan. Then he took in Ivanka's rumpled state. "Ah. That makes sense."

It seemed the strangest thing in the world to have Li-huan join her in her bed under her mother's roof.

He had spent the last two weeks seeking out her pallet up on the mountainside, near the sheep fold, but Ivanka had never thought any would discover them. When he left at the end of their visit, she would go back to being Grigori's shunned widow, with a reputation questionable enough to warn away any possible husband. At least she had planned it so.

"I did not intend this," she told Li-huan when he lay down beside her. She had shared the narrow bed with her next oldest sister as a girl, but it wasn't built for two adults.

He eased closer and wrapped his arms around her. "I know."

Ivanka pressed her face to his chest. She liked the way he smelled, no justification for her tumbling into his arms. She had managed to avoid *other* men who thought a lonely young widow an easy conquest. Surrounded by the smell of the fresh straw of the mattress, Li-huan smelled even better—healthy and alive. Unlike Grigori who had, once she figured out the perfume he wore, reminded her of over-worn shoes.

"Midsummer is a good day for a marriage, is it not?" Li-huan asked.

How many midsummer mornings as a girl had she walked barefooted in the fresh dew, hoping to hurry the arrival of a husband? But Grigori had taken her to his home on midsummer morning a year before, and it had *not* been a fortunate alliance. Ivanka shook her head to chase away those memories.

"Yes," she finally managed in a tight voice. She choked back the tears a moment longer, but then they flooded forth.

"Do not worry," Li-huan whispered, his hand stroking her back.

After a time, Ivanka drew away. She recalled the cut on his arm and pulled back enough to tug his arm from around her. "Let me heal this."

She'd never tried to heal him before, but he seemed to understand her need to concentrate. He had likely seen Kseniya use her talent—all the women of the Lebedev family, bastard or not, were healers. Ivanka laid one hand over the center of his chest and the other on that wrist. The cut was shallow and had already stopped bleeding.

Ivanka gathered her strength. She forced her will into the power centers of her hands and through his body, drawing away the lingering pain and inciting the skin to knit.

It was far easier than before. She didn't know whether it was only that she was no longer a maid, or that it was *him*. Her mother had once told her a healer's strength always responded best to the man she'd lain with first, her powers forming a bond to him. If true, Ivanka was grateful that Grigori hadn't wanted her.

Exhausted from worry more than the healing, she curled into Li-huan's warm arms and slept.

The house had glass in its small windows—a sign that the

Lebedev family once had wealth—and Li-huan shaved in the eastern light that streamed through. Already properly dressed in her primmest shift and tunic, Ivanka sat on the bed and watched him, fascinated. She had never seen a man do so before. Every man she knew wore a beard. Even Yun-qi did when he came with Kseniya to visit, although Kseniya had confessed to Ivanka that her husband disliked it.

"Should I not?" Li-huan asked her, one dark eyebrow quirking upward. "Do you think I am a boy?"

Ah, he'd understood Bogdan's insult. Li-huan was, in truth, a couple of years older than her, nearly twenty-four. Despite his smooth cheeks, she'd never mistaken him for a boy. Ivanka shook her head. "I do not."

"Good." He gave her his hand to help her up.

A twinge of nausea surged through her as she rose but she suppressed it, determined not to allow her worries over the coming day to defeat her. She tied on her headscarf and followed him downstairs to the main room.

Her mother kissed Li-huan's cheeks as if he were her son, and then bade Ivanka to sit on the bench. When Ivanka settled there, her mother directed Li-huan to sit next to her. Then she untied Ivanka's headscarf and began unraveling her single braid.

"At least I can do this for you." Her mother combed out Ivanka's hair, and then parted it to braid it into *two* plaits, like a proper wife.

Ivanka fought the urge to cry again. She hadn't had anyone to comb out her hair when she'd gone to Grigori's house. It was custom for the groom's mother to divide the bride's hair and bind it up, the visible change between being a girl and a wife. Ivanka had pinned her hair up, but having done so herself, she'd never felt as if she were truly married. The lack of any ceremony had made it seem mere playacting. The simple blessing her mother granted her now made her feel, for the first time, a *wife*. It made her feel forgiven despite all the troubles she'd caused.

Li-huan must have seen the unshed tears in her eyes. He took her hand in his, a reassurance that she needed at the moment. Her mother took the two plaits, pinned them close at the nape of her neck, and then set Ivanka's headscarf back in place. She leaned down and kissed the top of Ivanka's head. "I have no crowns to give you, children, but you will always have my love."

No, there could be no wedding in the Church, Ivanka knew. Not when she was not allowed to enter its doors due to her reputation for witchery. Not when she chose to marry an unbeliever. But to Ivanka, her mother's forgiveness mattered far more. She reached up with shaking fingers to settle her headscarf.

Li-huan thanked her mother and rose to go speak with his brother by the door.

Her mother settled next to her on the bench, and touched her cheek. "He is a kind young man. No matter what the priest may say of his family, I know you will never lack for anything. You will be safe, and I believe he cares for you. It is a good start."

Ivanka sniffed and wiped her cheek with the back of her

hand. "I am sorry I have caused you so many trials, Mother."

"Of my daughters," her mother said, "you are the most like me. Your mistakes are the same ones I made, Vanka."

Her mother's mistake had left her with child, although Prince Ilya had agreed to take the infant Kseniya and raise her himself. And her mother had certainly never been accused of witchcraft. Ivanka caught her lower lip between her teeth and then said, "Mother, I can't tell if I'm...I felt sick this morning."

Her mother turned on the bench to lay one hand on Ivanka's forehead and one on her belly, reading the flow of energies throughout her body. After a moment, she sat back. "You are with child, although it is very early. Does he know?"

Ivanka laughed shortly. "Surely he knows it's...*possible*."

Her mother's lips thinned, a sign of vexation. "You should tell him anyway. Some men are children about such matters, believing this or that could never happen to them, only to other men."

Ivanka didn't think Li-huan was one of those men. "Is that what your prince thought?"

"I don't believe he thought about the possibility of a child at all," her mother said, and rose to finish setting breakfast on the table.

Ivanka wrung her hands together. If Bogdan had not come up the mountain, would Li-huan have offered to marry her? Or would he have left at the end of the month's visit and never seen her again? She didn't know enough of him to answer those questions, and had no idea how to bring up the topic.

Breakfast proceeded in a normal manner, but Ivanka ate half-heartedly, waiting for catastrophe to strike. Her mother may have forgiven her, but she didn't think Bogdan had forgotten his threats. When a rapid banging came at the door, none of them was truly surprised. At her mother's nod, Yun-qi rose and went to open it.

Predictably, the priest jumped back a step when he saw Yun-qi holding the door. But then he bowed to the icon in the corner in a perfunctory fashion and crossed to where the women waited at the table. Mud clung to the hem of his robe, an oddity in such a fastidious man. He stroked a shaking hand down his gray beard.

"Madam, I need to speak with you urgently," he said to Ivanka, bypassing her mother completely—a further hint as to his agitation. "About last night."

Ivanka raised her chin and met his eyes. "I don't know what Bogdan has told you," she said, "but he lies."

"Bogdan?" The priest shook his head. "I haven't spoken with him."

Ivanka grimaced inwardly. It was worse then, if Oksana had been the one to tell him. Everyone believed beautiful Oksana, no matter how spurious her claims. "I was up by the sheepfold as usual last night," Ivanka said, hoping to head off his accusations. "With my husband."

The priest's mouth fell open. Then he gathered himself to ask, "He was there? How is this possible?"

Ivanka glanced over at Li-huan, who simply regarded her with that raised eyebrow. She didn't know if he'd understood. She managed a casual shrug. "Yes, he was there, Father. He has come there every night for the last two weeks."

"But the grave," the priest protested. "It was only opened last night."

Her mother's hand descended on Ivanka's arm before she could say anything more. "Father, do you mean that Grigori's grave has been disturbed?"

"Such desecration." The priest wrung his hands together, looking more lost than Ivanka felt. "I found it this morning, along with the boy's body."

"The boy?" Ivanka repeated faintly, her stomach turning again. She pressed a hand to her belly to still its distress.

"Little Alexei." The priest laid a hand over his face. "His hair not even cut yet."

Oksana's son would only be five years old, Ivanka knew. "Alexei is dead?"

Her mother came around the table and set one hand lightly on the priest's arm to calm him. Despite their frequently adversarial positions, the two had known each other many years, and both had the people of Petrivka's health and safety in mind. "I think it best if we see, Father. We'll come back to the church with you."

The priest shook his head—apparently not denial, but

distress. "It is too gruesome."

"Come, Father," she repeated firmly. "We must deal with this."

Once Yun-qi had secured a blanket in which to wrap the boy's body, they followed the priest down the wooden walkway toward the town. The farmhouse stood only a short walk outside Petrivka, so it was not a long journey. Ivanka fell to the back of the procession, Li-huan lagging with her. She dreaded going into town—the whispers and the averted eyes.

Li-huan walked beside her. "Who is Alexei?"

"Oksana's son," she told him. On Grigori's instructions, Ivanka had spent the better part of six months catering to the boy's every whim. He'd been a spoiled and quarrelsome child, inclined to whine and insist on his way, and Grigori had always allowed him to have it. Even so, Ivanka couldn't wish the boy dead. Perhaps spirited far, far away, but not dead. She whispered as much to Li-huan, who listened with a furrowed brow.

The town was mostly empty at this hour, the previous night's revelries having taken their toll. They walked along the wood slats between the buildings toward the church. Although that building was made of wood like the rest of the town, the bright paintings that adorned the outer walls made clear the richness of the people's regard. Far behind it, near the wall of trees that skirted the town, a series of ancient standing stones marked the entry to the church's graveyard. A raven perched atop one, regarding Ivanka with his bright eye as she neared.

She lifted her skirts to keep them from the mud and tucked the excess fabric into her belt, ignoring the creature.

Her mother had complained more than once about this place. Ivanka suspected every healer, every *koldunya,* had since the arrival of the Church and its priests more than two centuries before. Bodies buried in the ground were an invitation for troublesome spirits.

Ivanka looked for the marker of Grigori's grave back near the trees, the carved stone a show of the Vasiliyev family's wealth. Then she caught sight of the tattered and bloody thing that lay among tumbled earth at the side of the grave. Long pale hair streamed across the face, hiding it, but brown stains of dried blood covered the boy's ruined nightshirt.

Poor child, Ivanka thought, turning her eyes away. It hadn't been an easy death.

His jaw clenched, Li-huan stayed at her side. Her mother walked on toward the grave with Kseniya and Yun-qi following behind. She stopped near the headstone, leaned forward and gazed down into the earth. The she faced the priest. "Did we not warn you what would come of burying the dead rather than burning them?"

"We cannot burn them," the priest said, laying one heavily ringed hand to his breast. "In the final judgment..."

Her mother interrupted the priest's budding sermon. "Midsummer's Eve is when the earth gives forth its secrets, they say." She crouched down and surveyed the grave. "Surely you can see that the earth was pushed up from within, not dug with a shovel. Grigori clawed his way out of his grave, Father."

"Blasphemy," the priest whispered and shot a suspicious look at Ivanka. "She said he was with her."

For a few breaths, Ivanka wanted to flee, her heart pounding again as it had last night. Then she felt Li-huan's hand under her elbow, reassuring her that he'd not abandoned her. She spoke clearly—and loud—so the priest could not mistake her meaning this time. "My husband was with me. My *new* husband."

The man's gaze flitted between her and Li-huan. He drew himself up and frowned. "You cannot marry him. It would be incest."

Ivanka hoped Li-huan didn't know that word. Since Yun-qi was married to Kseniya already, the Church *did* consider Ivanka and Li-huan brother and sister by marriage, and thereby too closely related to marry. But Kseniya said his people saw the matter differently, so Ivanka crossed her arms over her chest, prepared to fight. "Not by his people's reckoning, Father."

The priest's mouth flapped like a fish's. "Did Bogdan approve this?"

Fury shot through her, her hands curling into fists. "I am not a part of the Vasiliyev family. I returned to my mother's household more than six months ago. I do not need Bogdan's approval."

Her mother stepped between them. "Can we stay to our purpose here?" She sighed and added, "I gave my blessing, Father. He is from a good family that will treat my daughter well." She gestured toward the body. "Now, given that the blood has dried on the cloth, I would guess this happened several hours ago. I have to say I believe the boy was eaten."

Ivanka clapped her hand over her mouth, nausea sweeping through her. Cold sweat trickled down her spine.

Yun-qi took the blanket from under his arm and laid it out on the damp earth. Li-huan left Ivanka's side then and helped his brother move that small, broken body. While Yun-qi crouched down to make a thorough inspection, Li-huan stepped back. Ivanka could see him frowning—a rarity.

Kseniya stood behind her husband. "Mostly the soft parts," she mused. "It could have been wolves."

Yun-qi shook his head. With one hand he indicated something on the body. "These bites did not come from the teeth of a wolf. They look human."

Ivanka closed her eyes, feeling a rare moment of sympathy for Oksana. Although the woman had never doted on her son the way Grigori had, Alexei was still her flesh and blood. "Have you told Oksana yet, Father?"

The priest shook his head vehemently. "I went to the house, but neither Oksana nor Bogdan was there."

Of course the priest would go *there* first. The Vasiliyevs were newcomers, but as the richest family in the small town, they paid a good deal into the Church's coffers. The priest valued their word, even to the point of ignoring the truth.

"The boy's body *must* be burned, Father," her mother said. "And if Oksana and Bogdan are missing, perhaps we should be hunting for them, because I suspect the creature that came out of that grave is."

"What are you suggesting, madam?" he asked in a voice so low that Ivanka almost didn't hear.

Her mother stood with one hand under her chin. "An eretik, Father. A demon has raised Grigori's body. For what purpose I do not know, but he will live by eating others' flesh."

The priest held his hands wide to indicate his graveyard. "But this is hallowed ground."

"And Grigori did not belong in it," her mother snapped.

Yun-qi said something to Kseniya, who shook her head. Then he and Li-huan lifted the small blanket-wrapped body. The priest sputtered, but followed as the two brothers carried the blanket-wrapped bundle along the walkways to the fine Vasiliyev house down by the stream. The near door to the stables hung open, a warning to Ivanka that all was not well. Oksana had always been careful about keeping doors closed.

A scent of fresh blood warned Ivanka before she followed the others into the stable. The gray mare Oksana favored lay in her stall, her innards torn out. Bloody handprints smeared the walls and the sight of it was simply more than Ivanka could bear. She turned and retched into the other stall.

A cool hand slipped under her headscarf and pressed against the back of her neck. The brothers had laid down their burden against one of the walls, and Li-huan knelt at her side. He stayed while she wiped her lips on her sleeve and then helped her to her feet. He waited until the others had passed into the house and said, "I do not think you are one to..."

He paused, clearly unable to find the word he wanted.

"To vomit," she said.

"Ah, to vomit when you see blood." A worry line showed between his dark brows.

"I am usually not." Neither her mother nor Kseniya had turned a hair at the grisly sight. Ivanka straightened her headscarf with trembling fingers. She should tell him now that she was with child. But her courage failed, and she shook her head instead. "It is only too much."

Li-huan rubbed her back with one hand. "Do not worry."

He was fond of saying that. She suspected that for the most part, he *didn't* worry—one of the things that made him so easy to get along with. She gestured toward the empty stall. "One of the horses is missing. There was a gelding."

He nodded and drew her toward the door to the house. The others had already gone inside, but Ivanka paused before the threshold, one hand to her knife. She hated this house.

Li-huan turned back and gazed at her. "We need not go in."

That decided her. She was not such a coward that she could not face a house. She stepped over the threshold and inside. The hallway was chilled, as if the door had stood open for hours. Occasional touches of blood along the brightly-painted walls showed that the person who'd killed the mare had come inside.

They followed the trail of gore to one of the bedrooms. The bedclothes were rumpled and blood marked the sheets. A fine, blue woolen blanket lay discarded on the floor. A musky scent clung in the air, along with that of fresh dirt and blood.

After a cursory glance, Kseniya and Yun-qi had gone to inspect the rest of the house, but Ivanka's mother remained inside the room. "Well, the creature came here," she said. "Whose bed is this, Ivanka?"

"Oksana's," she answered, her sympathy for the woman flowing away. She understood now. Oksana had called forth the demon in Grigori's flesh herself. Little Alexei had mere been a bartering chip.

Her mother surveyed the room, the finely carved bed and thick down-filled mattress. She leaned closer to inspect a handprint on the headboard. "Ah, this would be the place where Grigori died, then?"

"Yes, mother." Ivanka folded her arms across her chest, chilled.

The priest's eyes went wide. He stroked his beard nervously. "Oksana must be in terrible danger."

"She likely is," her mother said, "but I suspect it's danger she brought upon herself."

"How can you say that, Madam?" His tone sounded affronted. "She has done no wrong..."

Ivanka met her mother's eyes and then said, "If Grigori has come out of his grave, it is because Oksana wanted him back. I tried to tell you, Father, but you refused to hear me."

He frowned at her. "Of course she wanted her brother back...."

Ivanka's hands balled into fists again, her temper snapping.

"They were *lovers*, Father. I know. I saw them together. Why do you think they had to leave Novgorod and come to this town? They ran from the censure of others. I cannot prove it, but I am certain that Alexei was Grigori's son." The priest stared at her with his mouth agape, but Ivanka could no longer hold her angry words in. "Why do you think he died in Oksana's bed and not his own? Did you never think to question that, Father?"

His hands waved uncertainly. "But..."

Ivanka looked away, all her ire suddenly lifting like the mist. He would believe what he wanted to believe. Everyone did. "I had good reason to return to my mother's household, Father."

"But you were his wife..."

She shook her head. The priest would keep making excuses for Grigori's behavior. "He brought me to this house, Father, but he never treated me as a wife in any way. I was a slave, nothing better."

"Surely Grigori..." he began again.

Ivanka left the room, walked through the house, and out the front door, desperate for fresh air. The morning breeze was crisp and mild. A touch of dew still clung to the grasses. People were moving about in the town now, going about their morning chores with slower steps than normal. None were staring at her yet.

She *had* been a slave. Never allowed out of the house, always bowing to Oksana's orders save that one she couldn't accomplish. She hadn't been able to heal Grigori as Oksana wished, and in the end his heart had given out—only days after

Ivanka escaped. That unfortunate timing made it simple for Oksana to cozen others into believing Ivanka guilty of using her talent for ill, a witch.

Ivanka heard the door close again, and a moment later Li-huan stood next to her. She glanced up at his face, wondering if he would tell her not to worry.

"I do not think you should go anywhere alone," he warned instead.

She hadn’t expected that. She stared down at her felt shoes, collecting her thoughts, hoping she could give him an explanation that he could understand. "Last Midsummer's Eve, I met him at one of the fires. He told me I was beautiful and that he was taken with me. That he wanted me for his wife." Ivanka wiped her face with her sleeve. "He was rich and handsome. I was pleased when he asked me to be his wife."

Li-huan said nothing.

"It was all a lie. He had a weak heart, but I didn't know that. Oksana picked me only because I'm a healer. She’d heard that the husband of a healer is usually very healthy. She thought I could heal Grigori's heart, so she told him to offer for me. But I couldn't." If Grigori had been her lover she might have been able to make a difference, being so attuned to his body. But that hadn't happened. "He didn't want me. He wanted her. And she...she wanted him to live."

"The boy," Li-huan said after she'd run out of words. "He was the son of your husband and his sister? She killed their child to bring him back from death?"

Ivanka chewed her lip. "I am sure of that. She loved him, to the point of madness."

Oksana had been extremely possessive of her two brothers, although Bogdan had always been the lesser. She had kept them on short reins, playing one against the other, punishing them and rewarding them turn with her body. Poor little Alexei had merely been an afterthought to her. Ivanka laid a hand against her flat belly. She would never treat a child of her own the same way. At least Grigori had loved the boy. She doubted Grigori would have killed his son to bring anyone back from the dead, even Oksana.

Li-huan touched her elbow, drawing her thoughts back to him. "Your mother said we must find Oksana...and Bogdan." He gazed up at the mountainside where they'd seen Bogdan the night before. "And the sheep are still in the fold."

"Damnation," Ivanka said under her breath. "I will go tell my mother."

Li-huan went with her back into the house. Her mother still argued politely with the priest, who turned an angry eye on Ivanka when she entered, as if he blamed her for all this trouble.

"If the creature is what I think it is," her mother was saying, "it will hunt down the members of its family first, so Ivanka is at risk."

Ivanka shook her head. "I am not a part of that family any longer, Mother."

Her mother's brows rose. "And you think a demon cares what you say?"

Back at the farmhouse, Ivanka gazed at the hard rolls her mother had put out and felt queasy. She didn't think she'd be able to eat for a while. "Mother, the sheep are my responsibility. I need to go."

"I will go," Li-huan said quietly.

Ivanka wasn't certain if he meant to go in her stead, or go with her. "I can take care of them."

"If it is an eretik," her mother said, "it will hunt its own family. You are not safe anywhere."

Yun-qi shook his head. "I think it is seeking to..."

When he cast a helpless glance at his wife, apparently lacking the proper word, Kseniya sighed. "Yun-qi thinks it's a mogwai, an evil demon. If so, it will want to...procreate. The state of Oksana's bedroom suggests there might be truth in that."

Ivanka felt her cheeks burning. Trust Kseniya to say such a shocking thing aloud.

Their mother just shook her head. "It doesn't matter what we call it. It's a demon, and surely has nothing good in mind."

Having seen what the demon had done already, Ivanka couldn't argue.

"You should not go alone," Kseniya told her. "I will go with you and Li-huan. Yun-qi can stay here with Mother."

Ivanka opened her mouth to protest, but set it aside as unreasonable. A former member of the Emperor's personal guard, Yun-qi could easily defend her mother should anyone come to the house, and Ivanka supposed that Kseniya and Li-huan together would be sufficient to defend her. She didn't dare believe her own little knife would be any good against a demon.

After a moment, Yun-qi nodded his approval of Kseniya's plan. Ivanka suspected he didn't like the idea, but he handed his short sword to his wife, and she slid the scabbard through her belt. She gestured for Ivanka to precede her out the door.

A raven flew past, headed up toward the sheepfold—a worrisome omen. In the daylight, the mountainside looked peaceful, but an odd scent tainted the warm breeze. Ivanka started up the well-worn trail anyway, Li-huan a step ahead of her. Kseniya followed at some distance, her sharp eyes on the trees.

Ivanka hitched up her skirts and tucked them into her belt, baring her ankles. It wasn't as if Li-huan had never seen her legs before. "I am sorry you are tangled in this," she told him.

Li-huan stopped in the pathway, the wind tugging at his curly hair. "I am not."

Ivanka chewed her lower lip. "I am a poor choice for you."

His brows drew together. He waved one hand at Kseniya, as if asking her to wait. Then his eyes flicked back to Ivanka. "Poor choice?"

Ivanka felt tears sting her eyes again. Did he not understand those words? Or did he want to hear her say the words? "I have no dowry, and I left my first husband. And now he wants to kill me, I think. Or get me with child, as Kseniya said."

"Was he your husband?" Li-huan asked. "He did not lie with you."

"He did not want me." It was not required that her husband lie with her, at least not in the Church's reckoning. He had *called* her his wife, which was all that mattered. So even though Grigori hadn't touched her, she would never escape the association. Ivanka sniffed and wiped away a tear. "I cannot speak your language either."

"I do not need your dowry. I do not understand about this man, but he is stupid if he did not." Li-huan stepped closer and touched his forehead to hers. "We will not let him kill you. And if he wishes to get you with child, he cannot, can he?"

Ivanka went taut as a bowstring. Li-huan *knew*, even if she hadn't yet found the courage to tell him. "No," she whispered. "It is too late."

His lips curved upward in a smile, and he laid one careful hand against her belly. "Bao-bei."

It took a moment for her to understand. That was his people's word for a baby. "Say it again."

He repeated the word and waited while she tried to say it correctly. It fell from her lips awkwardly, but after three tries, he nodded. "You see, you will learn. Do not worry."

And with that he took her hand in his and continued up the path. Her feet felt lighter for his words, as if his optimism had become contagious. But when they reached a spot where the ground leveled, she heard birds squabbling. By the edge of the woods dozens of ravens feasted on something lying in tall grass.

"Wait here," Kseniya ordered, passing them by. She drew her sword and then stooped to pick up a handful of dirt. She pitched it at the birds. The ravens rose screeching into the air and settled a few feet away. Kseniya peered into the trees and called back, "What color hair does Bogdan have?"

"Yellow," Ivanka shouted.

"We don't we need to worry about finding him any longer." Kseniya slid the sword back into its scabbard and started back to where they waited on the path. "Not too long ago. I'd guess after dawn."

The ravens returned to their meal, and Ivanka turned away, all her happiness fading. Kseniya drew her aside, evidently not wanting Li-huan to hear their words. "Bogdan had a bag and a horse tied up back in the trees. I think he waited here to take you with him."

Ivanka shook her head vehemently. "I would never have agreed."

"I suspect he meant to take you unwilling." Kseniya surveyed the mountainside. "How long can the sheep stay in the fold?"

Ivanka shaded her eyes to search for the sun. It was nearly noonday. "They should have already grazed this morning."

Lips pursed, Kseniya looked like she intended to refuse and herd them back to the house.

"Please," Ivanka begged, grasping her sister's arm. "They are my responsibility."

Kseniya glanced at Li-huan where he waited several feet away. "If there is any trouble, get behind me. Li-huan is at best a half-hearted swordsman," she said, "and you have only a knife. " When Ivanka opened her mouth to protest, Kseniya held up one hand. "I do not know if he has the instinct to kill, Ivanka. That may make the difference here."

Ivanka felt a chill down her spine. "And you do?"

Kseniya touched the hilt of the weapon. "Yes. I have killed both with my sword and my talent."

Ivanka gaped at her sister, shocked. That was forbidden, one of the things that gave a healer a bad name. Some said it was the first step toward becoming one of the rusalki. "With your gift? That's wrong. "

"I didn't mean to kill the man," Kseniya said softly. "I needed his strength. I was gravely injured and fighting for my life. I left him alive, but the house burned down around him. His death became my doing. I would do it again to protect my family, so stay close to me."

Now more afraid of her sister than before, Ivanka turned and started marching up the hill. Li-huan followed, looking miffed to have been left out of that discussion. Ivanka walked as fast as she could, sprinting at times while her wind lasted, but it was far more difficult to run up the path than down. They reached the meadow where the fold waited, and she found the dogs lying patiently by the gate. Li-huan climbed inside the stone fold and, as soon as she opened the gate, began herding the sheep out. They straggled out past Ivanka in search of fodder.

Kseniya watched from the edge of the meadow, her eyes on the trees. "How long do we need to stay here?"

Ivanka didn't know what one did in a prince's household, but Kseniya clearly had no familiarity with sheep. "Some time," she said. "They need to calm down."

Kseniya's lips pressed together. "As quickly as possible then."

Ivanka set the dogs to herding the sheep toward the stream on the far side of the meadow. The dogs moved the flock there quickly to drink and then brought them away. They had nearly gotten the sheep calmed and grazing when the calls of birds alerted them to some disturbance in the valley. A raven flew through the meadow, and then another. Ivanka felt a prickling down her spine and spun around to look for her sister, her breath going short.

Kseniya ran back to the pathway to look downhill. "People coming," she shouted. "Too many. Get out of sight."

Despite the summer warmth, Ivanka felt cold wash over her. Had Oksana succeeded in turning the townsfolk against her? Ivanka took a shuddering breath and bolted.

She ran between the trees heading for the meadow on the other side. None of the townsfolk knew the woods up here as well as she did. She'd heard Li-huan behind her, but when she broke though the line of trees into the next meadow, she had lost him. She walked a few steps down the grassy slope, scanning the trees. Her hands had gone slick with sweat. " Li-huan?"

Perched in one of the trees, a raven cawed. The birds often

followed hunters, eager for the scraps of death they left behind. Ivanka peered up and saw several of its fellows among the loose branches of the pines.

Dry laughter like the rustle of fire in old leaves sounded behind her. Her breath stilled in her lungs. Unable to stop herself, Ivanka turned slowly about. A whimper of fear eased out of her throat at what she saw.

Grigori Vasiliyev stood at the edge of the trees—or what had once been Grigori. He looked handsome as he always had, his blond hair neatly brushed back from his fine-cut features. But brown stains marred the red of his embroidered tunic, as if he'd been too eager to feast on his brother's flesh to care. Oksana stood at his side. With her wheat-colored hair falling loose over her shoulders and her pale blue shift unbelted, none would now mistake her for anything other than a witch.

Ivanka wanted to live. Her feet recalled that suddenly, and she fled. She scrambled toward the trees. She had nearly reached them when a hand on her back caused her to stumble. She fell into the brush, crying out when she hit the ground face first. Her heart pounded in her throat.

A hard weight settled on her back. Hot breath brushed her neck. It was the demon.

Ivanka tried to pitch him off, to no avail. His knee just ground harder into her spine. He pulled her free arm behind her with a fever-warm hand and twisted, enough to make her elbow tear. Ivanka sobbed with the sudden pain. She did not want to die here, not like this.

"Ah, I've found my little widow." It wasn't Grigori's voice, but some dryer version.

"You are not my husband," she gasped out, face in the soil. "You have no claim on me."

"You think I need a claim on you to enjoy you?" A dry laugh followed that. "Why would I? For now, Oksana wants you to suffer."

His weight suddenly left her back. He hauled her to her feet, wrenching her twisted elbow. Ivanka cried out again with the pain but managed to get her feet under her. He wrapped one hand around the back of her neck and forced her to look up at his face. He grinned, displaying blood-stained teeth, and then spun her about to face Oksana.

Ivanka wasn't sure which of them scared her more. The demon would kill her, but Oksana was vengeful. Oksana would *torture* her.

"How could I let you get away?" Oksana lifted her skirt daintily to approach them. Her voice sounded honey-sweet as always, but Ivanka knew the poison behind her soft words and beautiful face. "You let my Grigori die, and now you try to steal Bogdan away too?"

She had *never* tried to gain Bogdan's attention. *Never*. Ivanka prayed there was some reason left in Oksana's mind. "Oksana, this isn't Grigori. It's a demon. Don't you know that?"

In response, the creature shifted his grip on her neck, pressing her head back into his shoulder and forcing her to stand on her toes to keep from choking. Ivanka whimpered, scrabbling at his fingers with her own. This demon could do whatever he wanted to her. He was too strong.

Leaning closer, Oksana laid a hand on the creature's blood-stained chest, over his heart. "Feel how strong his heart beats now," she said. "He's better. He'll live forever."

Ivanka shrunk back, horrified by Oksana's madness. And as she did so, the tip of a sword emerged from the creature's chest, thrust from behind, only inches from Ivanka's own shoulder.

Oksana screamed and fell away, clutching her hand.

Abruptly set loose, Ivanka fell against the trunk of a tree. She collapsed to the ground, crying out when her injured arm sent a burning flare of pain through her body.

Above her, the creature spun about, his movement tearing the sword from Li-huan's hands.

He struck at Li-huan, catching his shoulder and sending Li-huan stumbling back. Li-huan's head hit the trunk of a tree with a thud that Ivanka heard even from several feet away. The demon reached one arm around his back at an unnatural angle and drew Li-huan's sword free from his body.

Ivanka opened her mouth to scream, but had no wind for it.

Grigori advanced on the stunned Li-huan then, sword raised.

Ivanka struggled to her knees and threw herself on the creature's leg, using her weight to slow him. He kicked her hard in the side and she fell back again, unable to catch her breath for the pain. Then Grigori stooped down, lifted Li-huan by his neck, and held him against the tree where he'd fallen.

Desperate, Ivanka fumbled for the knife at her belt. Her lungs finally responded with a huge gasp. She crept on her hands and knees and, even as Grigori prepared to thrust the sword into Li-huan's chest, she jumped up and used her good hand to drive the knife into his back.

Grigori just grunted. Half turning, he cast a mocking glance at her...and thrust the tip of the sword between Li-huan's ribs.

Li-huan's eyes opened, unfocussed, as the sword slid slowly deeper through his body until stopped by the tree's bark. For a moment longer, Grigori held him there. Then he let go, and Li-huan crumpled to the ground, a soft moan the only sound he made.

Ivanka screamed. She tried to reach Li-huan, but with one hand Grigori grabbed her tunic. He lifted her off the ground and dragged her close. She could feel the heat of his skin—far warmer than any man's should be. His breath smelled of freshly butchered meat.

"I was promised I could have you, little wife," he said.

"Never!" she cried, setting her hand on his chest to push him away.

Under her hand, fresh blood stained his tunic from the cut Li-huan's sword had made. *That* was a physical injury she could understand. Whatever else, the body that housed the demon was human. Hope grew in her. While a demon's will was strong—strong enough to force a dead body to its commands—it could not truly defeat a living will decided against it.

Ivanka encircled his throat with her fingers and focused. She closed her eyes, tracing his strength through his body's centers of power. Then she drew it through her hand and into her own body. Unnatural heat flared through her as the life-force animating his corpse added to her own. Her injured elbow knitted itself together, the pain flowing away.

Still she pulled strength from him. His blood stilled in its courses. Grigori gasped, lungs immobilized.

She could sense the demon fighting her will, struggling to revive the flow of blood. With no sacrifice given, the demon wouldn't be able to reanimate this body. Not once Ivanka killed it. She could let go now, and it would likely not have the strength to survive.

Or she could draw more.

Taking that body's life force into her own would be terribly dangerous. Yet if there were any chance of saving Li-huan, she must steal every bit of power the demon had.

She opened her eyes. Grigori's face was ashen, his mouth open in pain. Past him, Li-huan lay among the pine needles, gasping, the sword piercing his chest. He still breathed, at least.

There would be a price. Nothing could ever be bought without a price.

She would pay it to have Li-huan whole again. Ivanka clenched her jaw, squeezed her eyes shut, and drew more of the demon's strength from Grigori's flesh. Sweat broke out all over her body.

When she opened her eyes, she couldn't sense his long-dead heart beating any longer. Grigori's skin had taken on a gray tint. His blue eyes watched her balefully, though.

I need a place to go, a dry voice in Ivanka's mind claimed.

Oksana lay in the grasses a few yards away, sobbing. She held one hand clutched to her bloodied chest.

"I am no heretic," Ivanka said. "You have no right to me and mine. *She* brought you here. Take her." She stepped back, and the hand that had been clutching her tunic fell away.

Grigori slid to the ground. Around his corpse the grass trembled, the movement reminding her of the digging of a shrew. Ivanka jumped back to avoid the slowly-moving disturbance in the soil as something tunneled out in the direction of the weeping Oksana.

Ignoring the other woman, Ivanka ran to where Li-huan lay on his side. Breath still rattled in his chest, the sword through his body keeping the bleeding in check. "Do not move," she warned.

She turned him fully onto his back and grabbed the hilt of his sword. With one arm on his chest, she wrenched it out as swiftly as she could and flung it away. Blood flowed then. She ripped his tunic and laid one hand to his chest. Listening to the body's complaints, she could tell the sword had sliced into his lung and heart. One rib was cracked. And although his skull was unbroken, blood gathered inside.

With her stolen strength, she caused the bleeding to cease and began urging the tissues to knit. The excess blood flowed away from his brain and eased out of the sack that held his heart. Li-huan took a deeper breath and then another. *He would live.*

Released from fear, Ivanka leaned with her shoulder against the tree. She felt dazed, too worn to move. For a long time, she sat there, staring at Li-huan as the fever heat bled away from her body. Needles fell from the pine tree she touched, browned and burnt, cluttering her skirt, falling atop her hair.

Oksana no longer moaned. The faint bleating of sheep could be heard over the breeze in the trees. Grigori's body lay unmoving a few feet away. Ivanka watched it with a distrustful eye.

"How did you do that?" Li-huan's voice whispered above the sound of the wind.

Ivanka smiled down at him wearily. "I'm a healer."

The dogs barked in the meadow. Ivanka heard voices, but they didn't sound angry. She hoped not, for she couldn't stay awake much longer.

"No," Li-huan said. "That."

She followed his gaze. Several feet away, his sword blade was driven halfway through the trunk of an aspen tree. "I threw it," she said, and laughed, tears coming to her eyes.

Li-huan laughed as well, but then began to cough up blood. She helped him turn onto his other side so he wouldn't choke. She curled up against him, too exhausted to move.

One of the dogs came, whining and wiggling, and licked her cheek. Then Kseniya stood over them, sword in her hand like an avenging angel. She checked first to be certain Grigori was dead, and then leaned over and picked something off the ground. "Vanka?"

Ivanka opened her eyes halfway to regard her sister.

Kseniya knelt down to tug at Ivanka's arm. "Are you all right? Are these yours?" She clutched something in her hand that looked oddly like pale sausages. "Ivanka!"

Ivanka tried to focus. Then she realized what Kseniya held and felt ill. Now she understood what had happened to Oksana. When Li-huan had driven his sword through the demon's chest, he must have severed Oksana's grasping fingers. Ivanka opened both hands so that Kseniya could see that her own were intact. "They're Oksana's."

Kseniya glanced about. "She was here?"

Ivanka pointed out toward the grasses...but Oksana was gone.

The townsfolk had come up the mountain not to hunt down Ivanka, but Grigori instead, Ivanka's mother told her. The priest, for the very first time heeding her warnings, had gone from home to home to warn his flock of their peril. In turn they had decided to root out the demon before it had a chance to kill anyone beyond the Vasiliyev family.

Several of the men carried Ivanka and Li-huan down from the fold to the house, while one of the young boys stayed to care for the flock. On her mother's instructions, an aspen stake was driven through both Grigori's and Bogdan's hearts to keep the bodies from rising again. They would burn them face down later that afternoon.

Ivanka listened dully to the tale as her mother examined her. "You're well enough, other than being dried out," her mother said. "Keep drinking."

Ivanka lifted the wooden cup in her hand and cool water slid down her throat. Li-huan slept in her bed at the moment, fortunate to have the attention of three healers who very much wanted him to live. They could give him strength, but they could neither replace the blood he'd lost nor heal the injured rib. Some things only time healed. Ivanka sighed.

Her mother sat down on the bench next to her. She laid one hand against Ivanka's belly, her lips pressed into a thin line.

"I've lost the child, haven't I?" Ivanka whispered.

"Taking that much power into yourself," her mother said gently, "it was inevitable."

Ivanka stared at the floor, too tired to cry anymore.

"Did he know?" her mother asked.

Ivanka bit her lip. "Yes."

"I will let you decide how to tell him this, then."

Ivanka took another sip of water and nodded. Could he forgive this, as well? She had known that the child would surely be lost. She had *known*, and had chosen to steal the demon's power anyway to save Li-huan from death. Did that make her what Oksana was? She had used her talent to kill. She had reacted with horror when Kseniya had confessed to stealing a man's strength. Yet faced with the decision herself, she had done the same. And she would do it over again, if it meant Li-huan would live. She wasn't sure what to think of herself now. "Have they found Oksana yet?"

Her mother shook her head.

"I did what she did," Ivanka admitted. "I sacrificed the child for his life. I've sinned..."

"Hush," her mother insisted. "Grigori has been dead for months. Li-huan never was. Yes, you saved his life at a price, but Oksana willingly broke the veil between life and death. I suspect God will judge her act far more harshly than yours."

Ivanka chewed her lip. She hoped Li-huan would feel the same.

It seemed easiest to have the fire near where Bogdan's horse lay slaughtered. Many more of the townsfolk had come to gawk over Grigori's body, and perforce stayed to help carry wood and move the bodies. The priest and his wife even came, giving tacit sanction to the act. Ivanka suspected the man didn't want Grigori back in that grave far behind the church, for fear that Grigori would come out of it again next Midsummer's Eve.

Li-huan sat next to her on the ground, watching the spectacle of the townsfolk building the pyre. It hadn't been done since the priest had arrived, so the men of the town did the best they could, guided by old men who shouted up conflicting instructions. Several women from the town actually greeted Ivanka, when they had not done so for months. It surprised her how quickly opinion could turn on her and simply reverse again, as if the previous six months of shunning could simply be forgotten. Even so, it warmed her to be treated as a person again.

Yun-qi brought Alexei's blanket-wrapped body from the house in town and laid it on the pile of wood between those of Grigori and Bogdan. By the time the priest declared that everything had been done properly, it was near sundown.

He carried a torch over to where Ivanka and Li-huan sat. "You must start the fire."

She craned her head to gaze up at him. "I am not of the Vasiliyev family, Father."

She thought he would protest, but he gave in and took the torch away. He set fire to the branches himself, moving around the pyre to light it in different spots. Flames blazed up as if set among dry tinder. Many of the townsfolk settled about as the sun set, most watching the first pyre they'd ever seen. Little surprise then that the gathering began to take on a festival air, almost borrowed from the previous night's revelries. Sparks from the pyre floated up into the air like glowing night-flies.

"I have lost the child," she whispered to Li-huan in the darkness.

The light from the fire turned his skin golden, hiding its paleness. "The demon?"

"I knew it would happen, if I were to kill the creature." Her throat felt tight. "If you no longer want me, I will stay here."

His brows drew together. "Do you want to stay?"

She wasn't sure if he'd not understood her, or if he asked

something else. "Do *you* want me to stay?"

His fingers reached down to grasp her hand. "No."

"I know you did not intend to take a wife." It hurt even to admit that.

He smiled. "Yes, from the start. I waited for Midsummer to ask. It is lucky."

She gazed at his face, trying to gauge the truth. Had he intended to marry her before Bogdan threatened her? Before he knew of the child, even? She had so little to recommend her as a bride that she found it hard to believe. "Truly?"

He seemed perplexed. "You are Kseniya's sister. Did you think I would lie with you and leave you?"

Ivanka lowered her eyes, hoping he couldn't see the flush that warmed her cheeks. She had thought *exactly* that. She had never reckoned he might marry a shepherdess. His family was wealthy, related to their emperor somehow. Surely he needn't seek out an alliance with a poor family in Petrivka. "Why?"

His other hand reached up, his fingers stroking her cheek. "You are beautiful," he said softly, "and I am taken with you."

She blinked back tears. It was the same claim Grigori had made a year before, only that hadn't been true. This time it was, she felt sure of it. Smiling, Li-huan set his arm about her shoulders and drew her closer. Ivanka laid her head against his shoulder, amazed by her good fortune. It seemed he had forgiven her mistakes, too.

They sat longer in the falling darkness as the pyre burned. Ivanka finally rose and helped Li-huan to his feet. He wobbled, but didn't seem too embarrassed to slip an arm about her shoulders so that she could help him walk. He glanced down at her face and winked.

Ivanka smiled at him and shook her head, doubting he would obey her mother's orders to rest. "Do not think of it, not as weak as you are."

His expression turned innocent, as if he had no idea what she meant.

A cry rang out through the crowd. People began rushing away from the fire, some haring off down the pathway to the town. Ivanka watched, mesmerized, as Oksana stumbled out of the woods just where Bogdan's horse had been slaughtered, her pale face lit by the fire's glow.

Oksana's hair still streamed loose, but now it looked as if she had crawled through the underbrush. Twigs and pine needles tangled in the heavy strands. She clutched her maimed hand to her chest. A stain spread down the front of her pale blue shift. In the dim light of the fire the fabric looked white, the color of death.

She approached the people nearest her, the miller and his family. The miller wisely fled, and others followed his lead.

"Murderess," one woman shouted at Oksana.

"Witch," another called over her shoulder as she hurried her children away.

Soon only a handful remained beyond the priest and Ivanka's own family. Ivanka watched unmoving, unsure what to do. Now that the priest knew Oksana to be a witch, *she* would be the one isolated from her fellows. Ivanka knew how that felt.

Oksana stretched out her hand toward the priest. "Father, help me," she begged.

The priest turned his back on her. "There is no help for you here."

Before the pyre, Oksana sank to her knees as if she couldn't bear her own weight any longer. She began to sob.

Kseniya came to stand at Ivanka's shoulder. "Saves us hunting her," she said softly. "I expect the priest will want her taken to Novgorod for a trial, or at least to Prince Ilya's household in New Kiev."

Ivanka wasn't surprised by the hard glint in her sister's eyes. "Trial?"

"For witchcraft, of course," Kseniya said. "And for the murder of her son. The Church will deny that Grigori came out of the earth, so who can they blame but her?"

Oksana keened Grigori's name. Ivanka had no cause to love the woman, but she knew what it was to be that alone. At least she could ease Oksana's wounds before she was taken away. She went to her and laid one hand on the woman's shoulder.

Oksana's head snapped up, a fire in them that Ivanka recognized. The other woman leapt to her feet, and her hands encircled Ivanka's neck. One whole, one maimed, they still had the strength to choke off her breath. Ivanka kicked at her, blackness filling her vision.

Then she was released. Ivanka stumbled and nearly slumped to the ground, but Li-huan gathered her against him.

His breath sounded harsh in her ear...or perhaps that was her own. She pressed her face into his shoulder for a moment, and then turned back to see what had happened.

Kseniya stood over Oksana's slumped form, her sword buried in the woman's side. She tugged it free and stepped back, warily watching the body as it twitched. Then Oksana's corpse went still.

"Look to the ground," Ivanka cried out.

In the flickering light of the pyre, she saw the disturbance of the earth as the demon fled the body. The tunneling came in her direction, as if *seeking* her. Li-huan shoved her out of the way, drew his short sword, and plunged it into the dirt right where her feet had been. A terrible squealing sound came up from the earth, and steam rose. The priest's wife screamed and ran away.

Li-huan used his sword to flick the thing from under the earth. It was a black-furred creature like none Ivanka had ever seen before, with tiny eyes and heavy-clawed feet. Its snout erupted with strange appendages, almost like a flower of red worms. Li-huan lifted the hideous thing with his blade and flung it onto the pyre. A billow of dark and oily smoke rose from the spot where the creature landed. Ivanka covered her mouth to keep the foul stench from her lungs.

A loud pop sounded as one of the logs in the hurriedly-built pyre gave way, spilling down burning embers, wood and flame. After hours not much would be left of the bodies, but Ivanka could have sworn she saw Grigori's outstretched arms in the flames as the pyre's remnants rained down over Oksana's supine body.

The next afternoon, the remains of the bones were gathered and placed in a large urn to be buried at the crossroads outside of town. Ivanka sat on the hillside and watched this last step in the removal of the taint from the town. In the night, someone had set fire to the fine house by the stream, not even removing any of the expensive furnishings first. That alone hinted how much they feared the Vasiliyev family's wickedness.

It was difficult to tell from outside a household whether there lived within someone who might seek out a demon's aid. Ivanka had merely seen the family's ways *before* the rest of the townsfolk. She watched as the men placed the lid on the large urn, the very last of the Vasiliyev family sealed away forever.

"Do you still worry?" Li-huan asked in her ear.

She glanced at him. She would be leaving with him in a week's time, and all the trials of the last six months would be behind her. It was *over*. She clutched his hand more tightly and smiled. "No."

Li-huan rose, only wobbling a bit, and led her back toward the house. In the trees around them the robins returned to their singing.

THE END

The Waiting Bride

"I hear your intended has come every fall for the last five years," Mei-lin said, "and he hasn't taken you away with him. Does he not want you as his bride?"

Jia-li bit her tongue, resisting the urge to use her talents to throw Mei-lin across the room. Instead of responding as she wished, Jia-li continued folding Hu-lia's garments down into a wooden chest. Mei-lin was new to Jenli Village, having just married Mrs. Yuan's number one son. Gentle Hu-lia had made an effort to befriend the newcomer, but Jia-li suspected she regretted it now. "He will take me with him when he deems the time proper," she answered.

"I see." Mei-lin cast a pitying glance in Jia-li's direction. "What is his family? Is he a nobleman?"

"I don't know," Jia-li lied. Long most certainly had a nobleman's look. His skin was fair and clear, his features handsome. Only his golden eyes hinted at the truth, one she didn't intend to share with sharp-tongued Mei-lin.

"When was the arrangement made?" Hu-lia asked, fixing Mei-lin with a minatory glance.

"I was nine," Jia-li said. She'd actually made the bargain herself—offering herself as a bride in exchange for Long's protection. At nine her head had been full of folktales. That was what had given Jia-li the idea, what had made her think the dragon might want a human wife—it happened in stories. She had no assurance it would work in truth.

"And how old was he?" Mei-lin handed her another tunic to fold.

Jia-li bit her lip. She had *no* idea. She'd never had the nerve to ask him that. A thousand years old? More? "I don't know," she answered again, all too aware of the other girl's mocking expression.

"Well, what *do* you know about him?" Mei-lin pursued.

"That he's kind and very reserved," Jia-li answered honestly.

Mei-lin glanced up from under a lowered brow. "But does he want you?"

"Do not speak of such things," Hu-lia snapped, rapping Mei-lin's fingers with a fan. "She is not married yet."

Jia-li felt a flush staining her cheeks. She knew exactly what the other girl meant, but Long had never shown the slightest interest in kissing her. For the first time, she wished he had.

Mei-lin laid the last tunic in the trunk and closed it. "Well, I know *my* husband didn't want to wait to claim me."

Hu-lia bowed and faced her squarely. "Thank you for your help, Mei-lin."

It was a flat dismissal, the rudest thing Jia-li had ever seen her gentle friend do. Mei-lin cast a spiteful glance in Jia-li's direction and took her leave, the heavy scent of her perfume departing with her. "You should be glad you're leaving in the morning," Jia-li said. "Mei-lin would never let you forget that."

"I cannot bear for her to be so rude to you," Hu-lia said softly, "particularly after she asked me to introduce you to her. She makes it sound as if your intended does not want you as his wife."

How many of the girls of Jenli Village thought that, but had simply never said it aloud?

"I honestly don't know whether he does or not," Jia-li admitted. "He has never said so." Mostly her own doing. Long had first visited the village when she was twelve, but she'd not wanted a husband at that age. She wasn't certain she wanted one *now*...so much as she wished to see him again. She missed him when he was gone, which was most of the year.

Hu-lia sat on the edge of her bed, her feet tucked up against the platform. She favored Jia-li with a curious expression. "Surely he does. You are pretty and clever, and your family is wealthy. What man would not want such a wife?"

Pretty. Jia-li bit back a sigh. Hu-lia had not called her beautiful because she was not. Her fair skin was too often tanned from going out hunting with her brother and her hair was a pallid brunette. Her brownness didn't compare favorably with Mei-lin's alabaster skin and raven black hair, while Hu-lia had a quiet beauty all her own. Jia-li sat on the edge of the bed next to her, fingering the coverlet. "I have never told anyone else this. You must promise never to tell."

Hu-lia took her nearer hand. "I promise, Jia-li. Never."

"My intended, Long...it is not *just* his name."

Hu-lia's small mouth drew down at the corners. "I don't understand."

"He is a dragon," Jia-li whispered. The word 'long' meant dragon, but many people might claim such a name without it being literal truth.

"I don't understand," her friend repeated.

Jia-li puffed out her cheeks. How could she explain this? "You know I come from a family of wizards?"

"I had heard so," Hu-lia said, her eyes averted.

Although it was rarely spoken in Jenli Village, everyone knew that she and her brother Yun-qi were the dragon wizard's children. Most younger folk barely remembered the wizard and his fire-dragons, but the older villagers never forgot. Jia-li could tell it made Hu-lia nervous just speaking of him...and the other girl didn't yet know that Jia-li had inherited her father's powers. She could speak with dragons, call fire from the air, and move things with her mind. She'd kept that secret from others, fearing their censure. Her father had been despised in this part of the world.

She went on. "When I was a child, I made a deal with a water dragon—that I would become his bride if he would save me and my family. He did, and he is bound by that bargain. He must take me for his bride, whether he wants me or not."

Hu-lia covered her mouth with one elegant hand, her eyes wide. "You made a deal with him? Like a matchmaker?"

Jia-li shrugged. "I was only nine. I didn't truly understand. I sometimes wonder if he accepted only because he sought an excuse to save us. A dragon doesn't need a human wife, does he?"

Hu-lia simply sat for a moment, staring at the wall of her bedchamber. "You're telling the truth, aren't you?"

It sounded impossible, Jia-li knew, but much of her life seemed so. "Yes."

"I always thought he seemed a bit odd." She turned curious eyes on Jia-li. "So, do you want to marry him?"

The answer had been troubling her for some months. Did she? She *missed* him. Long would speak into her mind at times or sing to her, knowing she alone could hear him, but not as often anymore. Things had grown complicated between them in the last few years. She'd begun to dread that he would simply find a way to escape their bargain through *evading* the marriage—not by refusing, but merely putting it off until she was so aged it would not matter. "Not if he doesn't really want me," she said. "I don't want him to come for me only because he must."

A handclap sounded, and Jia-li glanced up to see Mei-lin's servant standing at the edge of the screen. Before Hu-lia could ask what the girl wanted, she pointed to a small silken bag Mei-lin must have left behind. Jia-li picked it up and handed it to the girl, who bowed respectfully and whisked herself away.

"But do you want to marry him?" Hu-lia asked again once the girl had gone.

"Yes," Jia-li whispered. "He suits me well. I *do* wish he would come for me."

"I'm certain he will." Hu-lia patted her hand and smiled. In the morning, she would leave with her intended husband's kinsmen, a delicate veil hiding her face. Hu-lia would not even meet her husband until the wedding.

The very idea of *that* made Jia-li glad she'd made a different way for herself, even as uncertain as it was.

Jia-li never suspected his presence until she felt a warm breeze about her shoulders. She shivered, the chill of the pool's water not the cause. She gasped and crossed her arms over her chest, wishing hard for the tunic and trousers that lay on the rocks by the shore. Unfortunately, her talents wouldn't grant her that. She could push things away, but rarely bring them toward her.

"Is that you?" she called out without turning around.

"I believe it is," Long said, a hint of confusion in his quiet voice.

Jia-li bit back a smile, mentally picturing his expression. He would have that look on his face that suggested that humans rarely made sense. He must not be too far away, she decided, perhaps on the bank. "Um, could you turn around?"

"How many times?" he asked.

"Just face away," she said, getting more desperate to reach the bank and her clothing.

"Very well."

Jia-li peeked over her shoulder. On the bank, Long stood with his back to her. His garments were the same brilliant white as always and his black hair fell in a queue down his back—longer than it had been at his visit last fall. That told her he'd been wearing his human form more often since she had last seen him.

She quickly waded to the bank and grabbed up her clothing. Fingers shaking, she clutched them to her chest, clambered onto the bank and began dressing, lamenting his timing. She had just come down from the high pastures after taking a basket of foodstuffs up to her aunt and uncle there. She had never been able to resist playing with the dogs, which always meant a bath afterwards. Her damp tunic fell to the dirt, but she managed get her trousers on and the drawstring tied. When she looked about for her tunic, she discovered Long holding it out to her.

For several beats of her heart, she could not breathe.

His golden eyes were fixed on her slight breasts, his expression not one of lustfulness but curiosity. He made no effort to hide that as another man might, as if he didn't know it wasn't polite.

A breeze sent gooseflesh creeping along her arms and she jerked the tunic out of his hand. She dragged it on over her head, tugged the hem firmly down about her hips, and tied the tapes at her neck and shoulder. "I asked you to face away."

"I did." He met her eyes, not at all embarrassed.

She sometimes wondered if his tendency to take every word she said literally might be a ruse—if instead he simply was far too clever for her. That wouldn't be too difficult. She wasn't as clever as her aunt Kseniya, didn't judge people as well as her aunt Ivanka, and didn't have the wisdom of ages to temper her actions and words.

"I *meant* for you to stay turned until I'd finished dressing," she protested.

"You did not say that," he reminded her, his tone mild.

The wind blew against her dripping hair, and she shivered. She suspected she'd heard smugness in his voice, but decided she must be mistaken. He was never smug or mean or anything bad. "Why did you come here?"

"Did you not say you wished I would come?" He wore a perplexed expression now, which she took for truth.

When she was with Hu-lia? "How did you hear me?"

He smiled his slight smile. "I always hear when you speak my name. I regret it took so long to get here, but it is fair distance, even for me."

She didn't think he'd ever confessed that ability before. Had he? She clutched her arms about herself and desperately tried to recall exactly what she'd wished for yesterday, but couldn't. "So you came?"

Then she wished *that* unsaid because it was stupid. Of course he'd come; he was standing before her now. She wanted to hide her face. If she wasn't going to be wise, why couldn't she be clever?

A furrow appeared between his brows, and the wind that danced about them died. "Have you changed your mind?"

Jia-li just gazed at him, too indecisive to form an answer.

He nodded and stepped back. Then he bowed. "I shall come again when you wish me to."

"Do you...?" She looked her worst, with her wet hair tangled down her back and her oldest tunic damp now from her skin. Her blood pounded in her temples. Jia-li rushed on before she lost her nerve. "Do you want to kiss me?"

The warm breeze returned. Long reached out and touched her cheek. "Yes."

She couldn't have spoken at that moment. Jia-li simply stood there, mute.

Long came nearer, close enough that she could smell his skin, a scent that made her think of the earth near damp pools and stream banks in shadows. He leaned down and his lips touched hers so gently that it seemed to her like the brush of a feather. When he pulled away, he said, "You taste of fire."

Oh, no. Jia-li felt a flush rising to her face. The wretched smell of her skin lingered even when she'd just bathed. Her flesh bore a sulfurous taint inherited from the fire-dragons with which her wizard father had consorted. "Does it...offend you?" she managed, her voice little more than a squeak.

"I like it," he said softly. "May I kiss you again?"

Jia-li cleared her throat. She was *not* going to behave like a child, and she shouldn't sound like one. "You *are* my intended."

His eyes narrowed. "And what does that mean I may ask?"

"Whatever you wish," she said.

Long raised one eyebrow, much as her brother often did. It made her suspect he'd learned that human expression from Yun-qi. "Am I not supposed to wait until after the wedding?"

Jia-li's face flushed with heat again, but she made herself meet his golden eyes. "I did not mean that. I meant...I meant you might kiss me again, but not more. I just..."

She stopped talking, her eyes shifting to the ground. She *did* sound like an idiot child. Why could she not do better than this?

"You wished to know," he said, "why I have not claimed you as my bride."

"I have no right to question that," she whispered, her eyes fixing on his buff-colored boots. The back of her tunic was sodden now. She desperately wanted her comb, which lay abandoned on the rocks next to the pool. "I will wait until you deem the time appropriate."

"There is one more," he said.

One more. This was her fault then. His battle with the fire-dragon years and years ago, while it had saved her and her family, had brought down on him the vengeance of that creature's hatchlings, a dozen of them. Since that day they had hunted Long. One had even pursued him to Jenli Village when she was twelve. If she'd not asked him to intervene, none of this would have happened.

"I located it on the steppes," he continued, "but then I lost track of it. I do not know where it has gone. Until I have destroyed the last of them, you would not be safe in my home. Only I cannot find it." Jia-li hung her head, but his hand touched her cheek again like a warm breeze. "And your brother once did say he would prefer I wait until you are thirty."

Her eyes jumped up to his face. "Well, I don't care *what* Yun-qi prefers, I..."

Long raised one eyebrow.

"He didn't ever say that, did he?" Torn between irritation with her brother and discomfort from Long's teasing, Jia-li did the only thing that presented itself as a feasible reaction. She ran.

The dragon followed at his own pace.

The sight that greeted Jia-li at the Zheng household surprised her. *What happened*? She stepped over the threshold of the inner hall only to see the contents of the shelves thrown onto the floors. The pots that held incense and rice had been emptied onto the reed mats, brushes and paints dumped haphazardly atop the mess. Broken crockery littered the floor as if someone had taken everything and smashed it merely to see the contents.

Jia-li stopped, all too aware she'd left her slippers back at the pool. "Is anyone here?"

"Be careful," her aunt called from the second courtyard. "There are broken pots in the hall."

Jia-li craned about, trying to spot her. "I see that. What happened? Did someone set a goat loose in here?"

A moment later her aunt came up from courtyard and into the hall. Even with her reddish hair braided back, her tall aunt had a strikingly foreign appearance. Kseniya Ilyevna wiped dusty hands on the hem of her tunic and came over to where

Jia-li waited. "Dearest, where are your shoes?"

Jia-li felt eight years old again. "I left them at the pool, Aunt. What happened?"

Her aunt gave her a careful perusal. "Someone was evidently in the house while we were at market. Are you all right?"

"What happened?" Jia-li asked again, unsatisfied.

"I don't know," her aunt said in a tone meant to calm her. "I wasn't here. I've just put the children down to nap and hoped I could get the mess cleaned up before your grandmother and step-mother get back from their visits. Let me sweep a path for you. Then you go and straighten you own chamber. They went there, too." Crunching across bits of pottery, she retrieved a broom and cleared a space for Jia-li to get past. "And please comb out your hair, dearest. Your brother warned me we have a special visitor coming."

Her brother's occasional moments of prescience always seemed to warn them too late. "He's already here," Jia-li grumped as she slipped by. "I wish Yun-qi would have warned me before. Long found me at the bathing pool."

Her aunt's blue eyes brimmed with laughter, but she held it in. "I see."

Flushing again, Jia-li walked out into the courtyard and down to her bedchamber. When she opened the door, it looked almost as bad as the hall. Down from her favorite pillow coated the room in white. Her mattress was cut open, the contents turned out. The bed-curtains had been yanked down and the contents of her tall cabinet dumped onto the floor.

Jia-li groaned and covered her face with her hands. Of all the days for some malicious spirit to visit their home. Why did she always meet with Long when she was at her very worst? It seemed this visit would go no more smoothly than the previous ones.

"Well, at least he can't claim he expects me to be perfect," Jia-li mumbled under her breath as she set about straightening things.

Some time later, Long showed up at the door to her bedchamber. Jia-li groaned inwardly. She hadn't combed out her hair yet and had managed to get down tangled into it as well. She still wore the same clothes. They had dried, but she didn't look any better than she had before.

"So this is your bedchamber," Long said, his eyes making a survey of the room. "I have never seen it before. I imagined it would be....tidier."

The expression he turned on her was bland. His golden eyes remained politely averted from hers now, possibly focused on the piece of down she could feel clinging to her cheek. She brushed it away. "Um, someone was looking for something, I think. They turned everything out. Where have you been?"

"Helping Mistress Kseniya clean the hall," he said, politely ignoring her sharp tone. "I am good at sweeping, although I don't think that would help here."

Good at sweeping. He could control the winds, so Jia-li expected it was little more than the matter of his puffing his cheeks out. The scattered rice would simply blow out the front door if he wished. Jia-li took a deep breath to calm herself and said, "The down is inclined to stick to everything."

He nodded. "I see. May I smell it?"

"The down?" She didn't think down actually had a smell.

"No. I meant the room. If you come outside for a moment, I might be able to smell who did this."

Jia-li stepped outside her room and watched him as he entered and walked about her bed. For a long time, he stood with his eyes closed, scenting the air. He looked at ease, just as he had at the pool. She envied his calm. Clearly he hadn't found that interlude nearly as disquieting as she had.

"It was a jest," he said without opening his eyes.

"Someone did this as a jest?" she asked.

"Ah, no," he said, glancing over at her. "What your brother said, about waiting until you are thirty. I believe he said that as a jest."

She couldn't think of a clever reply, so she kept her mouth shut.

He came back to the threshold and stepped down into the courtyard. "I begin to think my absence has not served to protect you after all. Whoever did this was human, but I suspect they were working for the last fire-dragon. Your room is full of curses."

"Curses?" Jia-li glanced inside, but saw nothing she would consider cursed. Her clothes were folded neatly away. As much of the stuffing as she could gather had been restored to the mattress so she could sew it up again. The curtains lay folded atop a chest. The one thing she hadn't managed to clean up was the down.

"Yes, although the wizard who made them did a poor job of it. I would not let anyone else here." Long surveyed her bedroom one last time. "You would not be harmed by them, but I suspect the sender didn't know that. It might be wise to discuss this with your...aunt and brother."

She managed not to giggle at his baffled tone. Despite his wisdom, Long struggled to grasp how all the members of the Zheng household were related. Since her aunt Kseniya had married her half-brother Yun-qi, Jia-li could well understand his confusion. It made their children both her cousins and her nephews at the same time. Kseniya's youngest sister Ivanka had later married Yun-qi's youngest brother Li-huan, compounding the problem. Jia-li herself had trouble keeping track of how she was related to each of them. She grabbed up her wooden comb from the table next to the door. "Then let's go find them."

Yun-qi had returned from his visit to one of the tenant farmer's households and looked extremely displeased to discover that someone had come into their home during his absence.

"And they went through Jia-li's bedchamber as well?" he asked just as Jia-li entered the main room with Long close behind her. He wore a scowl, which he rarely did.

"Just there and here," her aunt said in that same calming

tone she'd used on Jia-li. "I suspect they must have heard me coming in the front gate and fled through the courtyards and out the back." She bowed her head when she spotted the dragon entering. "And our visitor has arrived."

Yun-qi turned to face them and bowed to their guest. "I apologize, my lord. You have found our house in a shambles again."

The dragon returned the bow, his hands pressed respectfully together. "And once again, it may be my fault, Master Yun-qi." He turned to Kseniya. "Mistress, I believe there were only two of them, but one was a wizard, for they left many curses in Jia-li's bedchamber."

Her aunt's face took on a shrewd expression. "I can guess what they were searching for, but why the curses? Of what sort were they, I wonder?"

Long stayed with his hands folded together. "Sicknesses, which would not affect her. Sadness, which she could have easily overcome. And Spots." A smile tugged at the corner of his lips. "I have no explanation for that one."

Spots? Jia-li cringed. Her clear skin was one of her few beauties.

"That sounds spiteful," her aunt said. "Can we do anything to remove them?"

"If you will let me," Long said, "I believe I can do so before they cause harm to the household. The curses were poorly made, so it should not be too difficult."

Yun-qi bowed again. "We would be most grateful, my lord."

Her brother always started off that way. He would treat Long like a lord for the first day of his visit, but by the end of a week, he would act as comfortable with the dragon as he was with his younger brothers. Jia-li watched the dragon head back toward her bedchamber and turned to gaze at her aunt. "What were they looking for?"

"I am not completely certain, dearest," her aunt said. Her eyes slid in Yun-qi's direction as if seeking permission. When he nodded, she added, "But I believe they are looking for his pearl."

"Pearl?" Legend claimed that each dragon possessed a pearl which held much of his magical powers. The first time Long had visited their house, a wizard had been seeking that pearl back on Long's mountain. The man had even worked with one of the fire-dragons that sought to destroy Long, although in the end Long had vanquished that wizard. Jia-li frowned. "I thought he said he didn't actually have a pearl."

"He did," Yun-qi answered her. "How could a pearl hold his magic? It would have to be the size of a house."

"But someone thinks it's here? And they're looking for it in my bedroom?"

Her aunt gave her an inscrutable look. "It appears so. Or do you know of something else they might have been searching for?"

"Of course not. But why come here?" The answer occurred to her before the last word left her mouth. "Oh, they must know of the...arrangement. How would they know that? I haven't told..."

Yun-qi raised one hand to stop her. "Someone must have discovered that he visits here every year after the harvest. Easy enough to figure out why."

Jia-li's shoulders slumped. Hu-lia, of course, would never have told anyone once she gave her word, but perhaps someone had overheard. "So what should I do?"

Yun-qi reached over and plucked a bit of down from behind her ear. His dark eyes danced with laughter. "I suppose you could start with combing out your hair, little sister."

Dinner that evening passed in the normal jumble the Zheng household experienced. Nagged into it by her grandmother, Jia-li wore her best tunic. Old Bao-yu had lovingly embroidered the bright blue fabric with silken flowers and vines, and Jia-li lived in terror of soiling it.

With the entire family gathered in the main room, the house was overly warm, but they opened the doors in hopes that a breeze would cool them. The wind complied, no great surprise when the winds' master sat inside.

Afterwards, the men went out to the second courtyard to admire Yun-qi's newest sword in the failing light, leaving the womenfolk to clear the tables. Jia-li had just carried all the bowls out to the front courtyard to be cleaned when a brisk knock came at the gate. They expected no visitors that night, but it would not be unheard of for one of the tenant farmers to come by to speak with Yun-qi in the evening, so Jia-li went to the gate and found a disagreeable surprise there.

Mei-lin stood in the gateway, a fine embroidered wrap clutched about her shoulders as if she were on the way to a temple. Her servant girl waited outside with the donkey-cart, which didn't surprise Jia-li at all. Mei-lin dragged the poor girl everywhere with her, merely to display her consequence.

"Mei-lin, I am honored by your visit." Jia-li tried to make it sound convincing, but suspected it fell flat. She escorted her through the courtyard and toward the inner hall.

The other girl sighed and asked, "Did Hu-lia give you anything to give to me?"

Well, at least her directness would get her out of the way faster, Jia-li reckoned. "No. I don't know what you mean."

"One of my hair combs is missing," Mei-lin said. "I was wearing it when I went to Hu-lia's house. Could you have picked it up and slipped it into your shirt, perhaps?"

For a moment, Jia-li wondered if she'd heard correctly. Had Mei-lin just accused her of theft? "Why would I do so?"

"For the pearls, of course," Mei-lin snapped. "The set was a gift from my father."

Jia-li made herself be patient as she opened the door to the main hall. "I have not seen any comb, Mei-lin. I'm sorry you have come so far for nothing..."

Over Mei-lin's shoulder, Jia-li spotted a dark haze filling the lower part of the sky. It was definitely not normal. Only a heartbeat later, the haze resolved into hundreds of moving shapes, all coming toward the house. Birds, she decided, approaching fast.

"*Aunt*," she called back into the house, her voice sounding panicky to her own ears.

Her aunt Kseniya came running to the doorway, the three young boys behind her. She stared out past Jia-li, then cursed quietly in her own tongue and touched Jia-li's arm. "Bats. They must be be-spelled."

Mei-lin turned around, spotted the dark forms whirling in the direction of the house and shrieked. She pushed her way past Jia-li into the main room in a cloud of heavy perfume. She hid behind the door, tears running down her beautiful face. "They will kill us all!"

Her aunt calmly closed the door, and cast a disdainful look at the cowering Mei-lin. The three boys ran to the screens at the front and stared out wistfully at the flying creatures. The sound of wings grew until they could hear the chittering of the creatures all about, but none entered through the windows or open doors.

Mei-lin continued to whimper, her hands pressed over her delicate ears. The tears had traced a path in the rice powder that whitened her skin, revealing a smattering of blemishes on her cheek.

Jia-li looked to her aunt, who seemed unconcerned by the sudden onslaught. Kseniya folded her arms across her chest and frowned. After a couple of minutes, the sounds of the myriad wings faded and the boys slumped down from the windows, deprived of the spectacle.

"Boys," Kseniya said then, "go on out to the second courtyard and see if your fathers saw them." The trio ran out the door in search of the men. Kseniya turned and fixed Mei-lin with a frost-laden stare. "Exactly *why* are you here?"

That made Mei-lin stop crying. Her eyes narrowed and for a brief moment, Jia-li suspected the girl might actually speak to Kseniya in the insulting way she'd spoken to her. Most people wouldn't dare. But Mei-lin seemed stricken dumb.

"She came looking for a pearl hair comb," Jia-li answered for her. She turned back to Mei-lin. "Why would Hu-lia have given it to me?"

"Well, I assumed that if I left it there and she found it, she would have instructed you to give it back to me." Mei-lin rose, wiped a hand over her smudged cheek, and fussed with her wrap. "I suppose I'll have to visit her tiresome mother myself now."

She headed for the door without any of the normal courtesies to the women of the household, and Kseniya opened it for her. Mei-lin strode out, shrieking for her servant to hurry. Once the door had shut behind Mei-lin's silk-clad back, Jia-li felt her aunt's disapproving stare settle on her. "Why did you answer *for* her? I wanted to see what she said."

Jia-li waved her hand to get the smell of the other girl's perfume out of her nose. "Why? She never has anything good to say."

"She didn't look around," her aunt said. "Did you not notice that?"

Jia-li shook her head. "I don't understand."

"Did she *touch* you? Touch anything?"

"What are you talking about?"

Li-huan's wife, Ivanka, spoke up for the first time. "She didn't look around the room, Jia-li. Not even at the icon corner. *Everyone* looks at that."

Jia-li glanced at the icon corner, where her aunts kept a gilded wooden icon from their homeland on a shelf next to a small lamp. With red paint on the wall surrounding the carving, that foreign shrine drew the eye of every visitor to the main room of the Zheng household. Despite facing in that direction, Mei-lin hadn't seemed to notice it. "You mean that she's seen it before."

"Precisely," Kseniya said. "I doubt there ever was a pearl comb."

"She is a bit self-centered," Jia-li felt bound to point out. "I think it more likely that she doesn't consider anything we own worth her time to view." It was ironic, since the Zheng family was far wealthier than the Yuan family. Jia-li's family simply didn't spend their money on fine silk wraps and unnecessary servants.

"She doesn't like you, Jia-li," Ivanka said. "I could tell. Something personal."

"I hardly know her." If there was one thing Ivanka understood too well, it was spiteful women. Jia-li considered Ivanka's assertion, and recalled what Hu-lia had said that last day. "She *asked* Hu-lia to introduce her to me."

"I definitely think she was the one who came here this morning," Kseniya said. "But knowing *that* still leaves many questions unanswered."

"She is *not* a fire-dragon," Jia-li said without doubt. Mei-lin could not have hidden that. She would have felt it in her bones—that distant kinship to one of them. And fire-dragons smelled even in human form, their sulfurous scent stronger than that of Jia-li's skin.

"No," her aunt agreed. "Which just makes me wonder where that missing fire-dragon is."

Long must have told her aunt of the one he'd misplaced. The men returned from the courtyard, towing the children behind them. Jia-li's grandmother gathered the boys and led them away toward their bedchamber.

"The boys claimed we had a guest," Yun-qi said.

"Yes," her aunt said. "One who raised more questions in my mind than I like."

Her aunt had a gift for plotting, a cleverness which Jia-li had not inherited. She'd been trained like a soldier, and thought like one. Jia-li waited a moment while Kseniya considered the ramifications of the visit.

"I wonder if this guest did not know I would be here," Long said softly. "I realize you cannot see it, but there is a curse left behind the door."

Jia-li felt ill. That was where Mei-lin had cowered. "So she did leave the curses here before."

"They are of the same craftsmanship," Long said. He went

to the wall behind the door and crouched gracefully, gazing at the unmarked stone. "I believe this one is intended to call rats."

"Could the same person have also called the bats?" Kseniya asked him.

Long glanced up at her over his shoulder. "Yes, mistress. Perhaps as a distraction?"

Jia-li shook her head. "Why would she do that?"

Ivanka rose and gazed down at the dragon where he crouched with one hand now touching the wall. "You have something she wants."

Jia-li lay down that night on her hastily stitched-up mattress, reassured that their house wouldn't be overrun by rats. She wasn't reassured about anything else.

Long had readily disposed of the curse captured in a single strand of black hair pressed into a crevice between two stones. Her aunt had asked Jia-li numerous questions about Mei-lin, trying to determine exactly what their unwanted visitor knew about the Zheng family. Her brother questioned the dragon with equal long-windedness about the nature of the curses left behind. The exercise only left them with more questions.

She hadn't had much chance to speak with Long during what remained of the evening, but it seemed that kiss by the pool had already been forgotten, pushed aside by all the havoc around them. Perhaps he had changed his mind, she worried, and didn't want her after all. That troubled her far more than

Mei-lin and her petty tricks.

He had good ears, she recalled, and didn't sleep. Or at least he'd not learned how to sleep the last time she asked him. Hardly more than a whisper, she dared to ask, "Long, do you still want to marry me?"

"I did not realize that was in question," he said from only a few feet away.

Fire blazed momentarily around her hands in a panicked response, and Jia-li jumped from her bed. The smell of singed cotton filled her room. "What are you doing here?" she squeaked, calling fire to one hand to see better.

Long sat in the chair in the corner of her bedchamber. His garb had gone from the pure white of a summer cloud to the deep grays of the thunderstorm. He regarded her with a concerned expression. "Do you always burn things when startled?"

To cover her embarrassment, Jia-li busied herself with lighting her lamp. Then she let the fire gathered to her hand flicker out. When she had control of her voice again, she said, "I sometimes do. Why are you in my bedchamber?"

"I am concerned," he said.

She stared at him, his handsome face lit by the sputtering lamp. He seemed unconcerned about being in an unmarried girl's bedroom in the middle of the night, and for the very first time she wondered if he might be unmoved because he had done the like many times before. Jia-li caught her lower lip between her teeth. She had no way to know what he did when back on his mountain. Perhaps there had been dozens of human girls willing to entertain a handsome dragon in their bedrooms. She swallowed. "Um, how did you get in?"

"I came through the door."

Jia-li picked the singed sheet from her bed and wrapped it around her shoulders. "I didn't see it open."

"I didn't open it. I came between the panels."

Jia-li surveyed the door and glanced back at him. "Were you a cloud?"

He smiled. "Yes. It is the easiest way to get in somewhere when I wish not to be noticed."

When he took human form, she tended to forget he wore any other. "But why?"

"I am concerned," he said again.

"About what?"

A furrow appeared between his brows. "Too many things. The curses were trifles, so I wonder if they were a ruse, left to obscure some greater danger. Or if, on the other hand, they were indeed meant to hurt you, and the maker simply could do no better." He frowned, and added, "A dragon is more direct. Their threats and attacks I understand. A wizard is a creature with a convoluted mind, though. I do not think I grasp their designs."

Jia-li sat down on the edge of the bed. Her own father had been such a man, and the twists and turn of his mind had always eluded her as well. "My aunt and my brother are much better at that kind of thing."

"I will let myself be swayed by their counsel," Long said, "but for now I prefer to be certain you remain unharmed."

"Do you intend to sit and watch me all night?"

"Yes," he said without hesitation.

Jia-li doubted she would be able to sleep with him sitting in the room. The memory of his feathery kiss raised inappropriate thoughts in her mind. "It isn't proper."

"I had not thought you overly concerned about propriety."

She felt the blood rush to her face. She lay down and tucked the singed sheet about her, saying, "Oh, do what you want. You were easier to talk to when you were a dragon."

She turned toward the wall, but his voice drifted to her ears anyway. "Yes, things were simpler then," he said. "This body makes demands of its own. Ones I did not know in my other form. It makes me question my path, and I find no easy answers."

She fixed her eyes on the wall, considering the wistful sound of his voice. The lamp fluttered out, when she knew he had not come near it. A cool breeze touched her cheek. Despite her doubts, she slept.

Jia-li lay in bed for some time before she had the nerve to admit she'd woken. The sun sent a dim light into her room, and the smell of the scorched sheet had begun to tickle her nose. "Are you still here?" she asked timidly.

I am elsewhere, he answered, his voice floating into her mind in the way that dragons had.

She let out a sigh, got up and dressed quickly. She found her grandmother at the oven in the courtyard preparing steamed buns, but saw no sign of their guest. "Is he here?"

"Second courtyard," her grandmother said as she lifted the lid to check the buns.

Of course. Jia-li found them all there, the men and her aunt Kseniya going through their exercises like any other morning, Long among them. His garments had returned to the white he normally wore. Had she imagined his appearance the night before?

At the moment, he was turned away from her, and she watched him as he went through the motions. He was the most graceful by far, an ease to his movements that suggested the flow of the wind. *Not human*, she reminded herself. For the thousandth time, she wondered what evil she'd unknowingly done as a child when she'd provoked him to take human form so he could marry her.

The pattern of the exercises caused him to turn just then and, catching sight of her, he smiled. Her heart lifted and her worries drifted away.

"Come sit with me," Ivanka said, patting the bench on which she sat.

Ivanka clutched her embroidery in her other hand, but Jia-li doubted she'd made more than a couple of stitches in the last week. Ivanka generally came out to the courtyard only to watch her husband with adoring eyes. Jia-li sat down next to Li-huan's wife, wondering if she had been looking at Long in the smitten way that Ivanka gazed at Li-huan.

"Kseniya says it's a trap," Ivanka said. "She doesn't think your friend could be such a poor wizard save by intention."

"She isn't my friend," Jia-li protested.

"Acquaintance, then." Ivanka shook her head. "People often tinker with power they don't truly understand and mistake their occasional successes for control. I think she's as weak as her mistakes suggest...and she's taunting a creature who's far beyond her strength."

"I don't know that anyone could defeat Long," Jia-li admitted.

"I meant *you*, actually," Ivanka said, nudging Jia-li's shoulder with her own. "No one here truly knows what you can do and therefore neither does she."

Jia-li suppressed a smile. "But why is she taunting *me*?"

"You have something she wants," Ivanka repeated. "You need to figure out what that is, and decide whether you intend to surrender it to her."

Her brother and Kseniya both shared a gift for understanding the plots and strategies of men, but Ivanka understood women. Jia-li let her eyes slide back to Long's moving form. She had a very good idea what Mei-lin wanted. "I'm going to go help Grandmother with the breakfast," she said, and slipped out of the courtyard.

The path was dusty, and Jia-li accumulated a coating of

grime by the time she reached the village. Added to the fact that she still bore the faint scent of scorched sheet about her, Jia-li wore clothes she'd meant to wear only to the pool where she could bathe, so she doubted she would make a favorable impression. But that wasn't her concern right now. She squared her shoulders and knocked on the gate of the Yuan household.

The servant girl opened the gate, her eyes averted politely. She bowed.

"She's a mute," Mei-lin said harshly from behind her. "You needn't bother with her."

Mei-lin wore the plainest costume Jia-li had ever seen on her, a solid serge that one might wear to work in the garden or to travel. Even so, she carried a fan in her hand as if she intended to dance about the courtyard.

Jia-li turned back and gave the girl a half bow anyway. The girl smiled hesitantly before walking around the spirit wall and disappearing into the courtyard. Jia-li turned her attention back to Mei-lin. "I don't know what you want from us, but I want you to leave my family alone."

Mei-lin gave her a coy smile, lifted her fan and blew. Dust flew glittering through the air, spraying Jia-li's face.

The world spun, and Jia-li clutched at the gate. For a moment that seemed to stretch on and on, she blinked at a simpering Mei-lin, wondering where Mrs. Yuan and the rest of her children had gone. Then she lay dazed on the flagstones as Mei-lin closed the gate behind her.

"She shouldn't be awake yet," Mei-lin said in an irritated voice. "Doesn't *anything* you make work?"

Jia-li tried to reach up to wipe her gummy eyes but her hand wouldn't move. She forced her eyes to focus and took stock of where she was: in a chair in the Yuan's inner hall. Unfortunately, her hands were tied behind her back.

"Don't bother," Mei-lin said, speaking this time from behind her. "I, at least, know how to tie a knot."

Jia-li blinked madly, trying to get the last of the dust from her eyes. Ivanka had been right—clearly Mei-lin didn't know she could call fire to burn the ropes. Jia-li wished Mei-lin would come where she could see her. Surely she could judge her situation better then. "Where are Mrs. Yuan and her sons?"

"Asleep," Mei-lin said disdainfully. "The less I have to put up with my husband the better. I will wake them when I have need."

Out of the corner of her eye, Jia-li spotted the servant girl crouching at the edge of the room near the door as if waiting to fetch anything her mistress required. The girl watched Jia-li with a curious expression caught halfway between admiration and dislike. Jia-li wondered if she might be that missing fire-dragon hidden in human form, but fire-dragons never managed human shape well unless reborn into one as Jia-li's grandfather had been. She would have smelled it on the girl if that had been the case.

But she felt certain now that the servant girl was her true adversary. "Who are you," Jia-li asked her. "What do you want?"

The girl rose from her crouch and came closer, her eyes locked with Jia-li's streaming ones.

"I want the pearl," Mei-lin answered.

"I don't have a pearl," Jia-li snapped at her. "And I wasn't talking to you."

"You don't have his pearl," the servant girl agreed softly.

Mei-lin darted around Jia-li's chair and grabbed the serving girl's arm. "You *said* she had the pearl."

The girl gave Mei-lin an apologetic look. "No. I said the pearl was in that house, mistress."

Mei-lin's beautiful face twisted into a scowl. "It's still there? How do I get it?"

The girl's dark eyes turned on Jia-li, a considering glance that Jia-li didn't believe at all. "If she calls the dragon, perhaps he will come to free her."

"And bring the pearl?" Mei-lin asked.

One corner of the servant's lips twisted upward, a secret smile that belied her soft words. "I think it possible, mistress."

Ivanka and Kseniya had *both* been right, Jia-li decided. Mei-lin was as incompetent as Ivanka suspected—but the servant girl wasn't. "What exactly did she promise you, Mei-lin?"

Mei-lin's delicate eyebrows rose. "Do you think I am a fool? The only reason a dragon would have agreed to wed such a drab girl as you was that you have stolen his pearl."

No, Mei-lin had no idea as to the truth. Incompetent *and* stupid. "And you think that if you have his pearl," Jia-li asked, "he'll marry you instead?"

"Any man would be pleased to escape you for me," Mei-lin preened.

Of course she would think that. "Need I say that you already have a husband?"

Mei-lin shrugged eloquently. "A problem easily disposed of."

Jia-li shook her head and laughed. "She's lied to you, Mei-lin. I have no pearl. I never did."

Mei-lin gave the servant girl a sharp glance. The girl gazed back at her and, when Mei-lin opened her mouth to castigate her, threw a handful of dust into Mei-lin's face. Mei-lin gasped, coughed, and sat on the floor quite abruptly in a poof of serge skirts. She fell back to lie on the floor. Then she began to snore.

The servant girl turned back to Jia-li. "Call him."

Now she was dealing with her true adversary. "Why do you want him here? Who are you?"

The girl prodded Mei-lin casually with one foot. "I hardly matter. Call him."

"Why would I help you?"

The girl crouched in front of Jia-li's chair and drew a slender knife from inside her tunic. "They're all sleeping. They wouldn't even put up a fight. I will start with the youngest boy." She paused as if to see whether Jia-li understood the threat. "If you want the Yuan to live, call him."

Jia-li wished she intended to start with Mei-lin instead, but Mrs. Yuan and her sons were kind people. She kept her eyes on the girl and said, "Long, do you hear me?"

His voice whispered into her mind. *Where have you gone?*

"The Yuan household. I'm a prisoner, and my captor wants you to come here," Jia-li said.

The girl stood up and backed away, a dry smile twisting her lips.

I will come.

Jia-li returned the girl's smile. "He is coming."

"I suspected he would," she said. "I have his pearl, after all, that thing beyond all price to him."

The absolute certainty in the girl's voice gave Jia-li pause. She could only think of one thing in the Yuan household that could be the missing object—herself.

And her aunt and brother had known all along. At some point, Long had invested some of his power in her. Her own abilities had improved greatly since his first visit, but she'd believed that a factor of aging. Clearly she'd been blind. It explained Long's confidence that the curses left in her room wouldn't hurt her.

"You didn't even know, did you?" the girl asked. "I studied my father's papers and found an obscure reference that suggested such a thing was possible. My father spent years searching for the pearl, all in vain, for it already hid in this village far from the dragon's mountain."

"The wizard who tried to steal Long's pearl. You are his daughter?"

The girl bowed and turned angry eyes back on Jia-li. "The dragon killed my father for trespassing in his lair."

That same wizard had offered his daughter to Long in return for knowledge, a bargain Long had refused. "Then your father was no more than a thief," Jia-li said, hoping to goad the girl.

"My father was a great wizard." She came closer and stared into Jia-li's face. "Are you not the dragon wizard's daughter? You know what power it takes to enslave fire-dragons as my father did. To give them human form and send them to do his bidding. Only the one that he sent here five years ago didn't know about you. You killed it too soon, and your dragon returned to his mountain before my father was prepared. My father's death is on your head as well."

A mist seeped into the room through the screens that closed off the main doors. Jia-li forced herself to keep her eyes on the girl instead. "If you are a wizard, then why all the petty curses? Why make Mei-lin plant them in my house?"

The girl glanced down at Mei-lin's supine form. "An easy accomplice. I let her think she worked to her ends rather than mine. The curses got you here, did they not?"

Jia-li took a careful breath. She needed to think, not just react. "So what do you intend with me?"

"I would like to see your intended husband dead," the servant girl said, "but I am not fool enough to think I can kill a dragon. He *will* bargain with me...or he will watch you die."

Faint at first, almost transparent, the mist coalesced into Long's familiar form. He gained solidity with every moment she stalled.

"Bargain with you?" Jia-li asked. "For what?"

"I learned from my father's mistakes," the girl said softly. She turned to face Long and pressed her knife against Jia-li's neck. "Well, my lord dragon, you came for her readily enough. I *am* impressed."

Jia-li's first impulse was to force the knife away from her neck with her mind, but Long spoke into her head, warning her to be still. *Think*, she reminded herself.

"I am here," Long said aloud to the other girl.

Wind teased about the room, tugging at Jia-li's tunic. Seizing the opportunity afforded by the girl's distraction, she called fire into her hand, only a spark. She twisted her fingers around and grasped the rope. The faint scent of fresh burning tickled her nostrils, but the wind blew the smoke away into the depths of the house.

"Do you know who I am?" the servant girl asked Long, her humble demeanor gone. "Do you see my father's face in mine?"

A furrow appeared between Long's dark brows. "I have difficulty telling humans one from another. If I know your father, I am not aware of it."

Jia-li bit her lips, trying to keep from crying out. She couldn't see what she was doing with the flame she held and she'd just burned herself. The girl's hand trembled as she spoke to Long, and Jia-li felt another sting as the knife's edge broke skin. She tugged on the rope discreetly, hoping it would snap. It didn't.

"Five years ago," the girl said, "you killed the wizard Chen

Ming-li. I am Ming-hua, his daughter. Did you think no one would seek vengeance for his death?"

Long sighed. "I am exhausted with vengeance. What do you want?"

"I will let this girl live," Ming-hua said, inclining her head toward Jia-li, "provided you give over to me that portion of your powers you gave to her. I will have a dragon's power one day, one way or another."

That was the same ambition that had gotten her own ancestor exiled from the Imperial court, Jia-li knew. Her family had since been tangled in that quest to control dragons and their powers. She and her brother had been the first ones to choose *not* to use their talents that way. But another family was already seeking to assume that power in their place.

Could you dispose of that knife now? Long asked her without speaking.

Jia-li allowed the flame to die, and centered her mind on the knife instead.

Long shook his head sadly at Ming-hua. "What makes you think Jia-li needs my protection?"

Just as the girl bent the blade toward her, Jia-li gathered her will and forced it *away*. It jerked out of the girl's hand, flew across the room and buried itself in a rafter.

The doors blew open and wind roared through the room. It caught the girl's tunic and full sleeves, dragging her off balance. Jia-li jerked hard on the weakened rope and it gave. She spilled onto the floor, clutching her burned hand against her chest. Her legs, stiff from sitting so long, didn't cooperate when she tried to rise. A heartbeat later, Long was there, one arm under her shoulders to help her.

Jia-li buried her head against his chest, too embarrassed by her weak knees to face him. But his arms settled about her, setting her heart to pounding for a different reason and making her forget about her wobbly legs.

"Are you hurt, Jia-li?" he asked, his voice very close to her ear.

The wind still whipped about them, and Jia-li managed to draw back enough to answer. "My hand is burned, no more."

Long touched fingertips to her neck and they came away bloody. He wiped the blood onto his sleeve, where it disappeared. "I am now ill disposed toward this woman."

Jia-li didn't know how to answer that. There was anger in his eyes, something she'd never seen before. Angering a dragon could not be wise. Still clutching her hand, she looked about for the girl, but didn't see her anywhere. "Where did she go?"

Long ignored that. Instead he opened her blistered palm to inspect it. "Can you heal this?"

She glanced down, but saw nothing worse than she'd endured in her childhood days of learning to control fire. "It's not bad."

"I dislike burns." He let her hand slip from his grasp. He stepped away from Jia-li, leaving her feeling chilled. "She went out the door. I need to follow."

Jia-li glanced at Mei-lin slumped on the floor and felt a

moment of pity. "We can't just leave her."

Long raised one eyebrow. He opened his mouth to speak, but the sound of the footsteps at the door caused him to turn about. Looking past him, Jia-li saw her aunt and brother entering the main room, both armed to do battle.

Her brother's expression revealed his disappointment in being cheated of a fight. "What happened?"

"We need to go after her," Jia-li told him. "Can you look after the Yuans?"

"Go after *her*?" Yun-qi asked with a pointed glance at Mei-lin.

"The servant girl," Jia-li explained. "She is the wizard's daughter."

"I will go alone," Long told Yun-qi. "I could smell fire on her, so I suspect she has worked with the fire-dragon."

Jia-li recalled the girl's words, then. "She said her father had transformed fire-dragons into human form, including that one who come here after you five years ago."

"I heard," Long said. "The last fire-dragon must still be alive somewhere. She will flee to its protection. I will go after her. It is time to end this." His eyes fixed on Jia-li's face, and what she saw in them made her flush.

"I want to go with you."

Jia-li's aunt handed over her favored bow and quiver, but Long said, "I will go faster alone."

"I can run," she protested.

"I can *fly*," he reminded her.

Jia-li had no good argument to battle that, so she bit her

lips.

Long gave her an appraising look. "But I think I can carry you."

The winds lifted them, Jia-li with one arm around Long's shoulders and he with one across her back. As the Yuan's courtyard grew more distant in her eyes, her heart leapt into her throat and she couldn't breathe.

Then she saw the sky about her and felt the wind holding her. Her fright fled in wonder. A giddy laugh spilled from her lips. The village spread beneath them, and she could see into the courtyards where laundry dried and men did their morning exercises. "Can they see us?" she asked.

"No, I have made a cloud about us." Long's voice boomed about them, as loud as the sound of thunder. "I hear her below."

They flew so high that the people in the town looked like ants in their tiny courtyards. He pointed with his free hand to the road leading from the village, where a dark form moved swiftly toward the plains. The winds carried them in pursuit. Jia-li clung more tightly to Long as they sped faster.

"Do not be concerned," he said with a smile. "I will not drop you."

They swooped down lower over the failing mountain range, coming ever closer to that fast-moving figure. For a moment Jia-li thought her stomach would empty itself, but the sensation passed and she could finally see that it was indeed Ming-hua below, riding Mr. Yuan's fine black mare into a lather. "Where is she going?"

"There, in the last of the mountains. I smell it," he said. "The fire-dragon."

"Are you certain it's not me you smell?"

He flashed a grin, showing teeth. "I know the difference."

The figure below drove the horse into a narrow canyon and jumped from its back. She sprinted in the directions of the mountainside and climbed up among the rocks.

"Where is she going?" Jia-li asked, and then saw the ground was rapidly approaching—too rapidly. She clutched her bow against her side and buried her face against Long's shoulder.

He wrapped himself around her and hit the ground with a surprised cry. They rolled over and over, dirt flying about them. Then they stopped moving. Jia-li found herself resting on his chest, staring down into his startled golden eyes. She was bruised and scraped, but not seriously hurt.

Long blinked up at her in a bemused fashion. "I must rethink the landing."

Jia-li rolled away from him and rose, only a bit stiffly. Her tunic had torn, the sleeve hanging loose, and her shoulder did indeed have a nasty scrape. She was covered with grit from the road. All in all, she decided she was glad he hadn't actually tried to land on the mountain.

Still looking dazed, Long sat up and dusted off his pristine white tunic. His queue didn't even have dirt in it, Jia-li noted. "Rethink?"

"I did not allow for the added weight," he said. "I will do better next time."

"I see," Jia-li lied. Even so, he knew far more about flying than she did. She settled for stringing her bow, and then slid the quiver over her other shoulder. "What do we do?"

He shielded his eyes and gazed up at the mountainside. "We go up there."

Ming-hua had disappeared. Jia-li spotted a path leading up to a cave not high on the side of the mountain. The wind carried the familiar scent of sulfur to her nose. "If the fire-dragon is in there, why does it not come out after us?"

"I do not know," Long said, and began to climb the pathway. Jia-li followed. The path was not too steep, and in those spots where it grew so, Long reached back to help her up, speeding them both. When they finally reached the mouth of the cave, the stink of sulfur was unmistakable. Jia-li called fire to one hand to light their steps.

"You are too late," a voice called from the depth of the cave. "It is dead."

Jia-li made the light flare in her hand, illuminating the small cave. Ming-hua crouched in the shadows next to a pile of coppery-colored rock—rock not native to these mountains which lay in the shape of a man. Jia-li had seen the like before, when Long had killed that dragon's parent in her aunts' homeland, and again a few year later when she had killed a fire-dragon in Jenli Village. Fire-dragons were no more than stone from the depths of the earth, animated by spirits of fire, and when the spirit turned loose of the body, it returned to the stone it had once been. Robbed of her quarry, Jia-li let the light die down, leaving Ming-hua to the shadows.

Long stepped back from the mouth of the cave, a rare frown on his face. He drew Jia-li a short distance away. "What would humans do about this?"

Jia-li weighed the circumstances. In the end, the girl had proven no more than a nuisance, but only because she had underestimated her opponents. In the future Ming-hua would be less likely to do so. But what crime could she be said to have committed? "She helped Mei-lin entrap the whole Yuan family. Although they escaped unharmed."

Long nodded. "Can the elders of Jenli Village hold her forever for such a crime?"

"No," Jia-li admitted.

Long-s nostrils flared and he cast a glance back at the dark cave. "She is a wizard, even if poorly trained. If she could enspell an entire family, she is more dangerous than they can handle. I do not have the power to take those arts away from her."

"What do you propose, then?" Jia-li yanked her torn sleeve up and dusted some of the grit from her elbow. "Let a wizard run loose?"

"It would be simplest to kill her," Long said softly.

Jia-li raised her eyes to his. She had hunted and killed before. She had knowingly freed the fire-dragons who killed her father. She had killed a fire-dragon herself five years before. But Ming-hua was human and...

Without glancing away, Long asked, "Do you not agree, little wizard?"

He wasn't talking to her.

Jia-li turned and saw that Ming-hua stood at the mouth of the cave now, close enough to hear them speak. She could not get past them to escape down the path and apparently stood awaiting their decision. "You will not kill me," Ming-hua said to Long, "and I will not fight you, my lord dragon. Take me back to the village. I will suffer the punishment allotted to me."

Jia-li gave Ming-hua a sharp look. The girl must have some hidden advantage to capitulate so readily. Before Ming-hua could move away, Jia-li grabbed her arm and thrust the girl's tunic aside. She placed her hand on the girl's flat belly, using her healer's talent to read the girl's health. She found what she feared and turned the girl loose with a grimace of distaste. "She is carrying its child," she told Long.

Ming-hua gave her a disdainful look. "I am blessed, am I not?"

"I feared this," Long said. "The last fire-dragon allowed its spirit to go into the unborn child. It is how the very first dragon wizard was created—your great grandfather. Part human, part dragon."

Jia-li glanced at the girl again, and then back up at Long. "If we let her go, we will always be wondering when she will strike at us—or when her child will."

"Take me back to the village then," Ming-hua said smugly.

Jia-li felt a strong urge to use her talent to throw the girl from the mountain merely to get that smile off her face. Killing the girl *would* be simplest, but she couldn't bring herself to do so, not when Ming-hua offered no resistance.

Her half-dragon child would have the talents of a dragon along with whatever sorcerous arts Ming-hua could teach it, but Jia-li had such blood herself. If she wed Long and bore a child—*that* child would also bear half a dragon's blood, although of a very different sort.

She licked her parched lips and realized that Long was waiting on her decision. "I say we leave her here." She turned back to Ming-hua and said, "Enjoy your victory now. My family carried such a curse as you've invited into yourself, and I think it will not be long before you regret this day."

Ming-hua laid one hand to her belly. "Your family was weak."

Jia-li pressed her lips together. There was no point responding. Ming-hua would never be won over to her side in this. The lust for power had her firmly in its grip. Jia-li turned back to Long. "We can leave now."

Long gave Ming-hua a cautious nod, then slid one arm about Jia-li's back. The wind bore them both into the air. Jia-li watched until Ming-hua was no more than a dark spot against the brown of the mountainside. Then she turned her eyes toward the way ahead.

The grass in the meadow near the bathing pool would have

made for a much easier landing, but Long kept his feet this time, evidently having properly accounted for Jia-li's added weight. He held on to her for a moment after he set her down, and the way he looked at her made her feel more breathless than the flight had. He let her go, though, sooner than she'd expected.

She didn't know what that meant. Jia-li sat down heavily next on one of the stones next to the pool, and laid her bow and quiver to one side. An idea had been troubling her, so she asked, "Would you have let her go if I had not been there?"

"Yes. I would have made the same decision." Long settled on another rock near her. "I intended to kill a dragon, not a human."

"You killed her father," Jia-li pointed out.

Long shook his head. "He was in my home, and had already caused me some grief. I had the right."

"I understand." She pulled off her slippers and set her feet in the pool, and sighed at the touch of the cool water.

Long gave her an odd look. "What are you doing?"

Recalling the last time he'd found her here, she blushed. Did he think she was about the strip off her garments and bathe again? "Only my feet. It feels good." When he continued to gaze at her quizzically, she asked, "Have you never put your feet in the water?"

"There are *many* things I have never done." He regarded the water, then, his golden eyes pensive. Then with hardly a splash, he slid from the rock and into the deepest spot in the pool. He came up from under the water near where she sat, and gave her a sly smile. "Swimming is one thing I know."

Did her eyes look as large as they felt? His white tunic was gone, lost in the water. Had he even been wearing clothing at all? Her cheeks heated at that thought. "I should have guessed that," she heard herself mumble.

He came closer, until he must be standing on the pool's bottom. "Even though all the fire-dragons are dead, with her still free I cannot promise you safety in my house."

Ah, yes. His reason for putting off their wedding. Jia-li shook her head. "I am not afraid of her. I will not spend my whole life worrying about her."

His eyes stayed on her face. "The child could become very powerful."

"So you wish to wait to marry me until the child has grown and you have vanquished it?"

"I admit, I am impatient." His golden eyes turned to the water. He ran a hand over the surface, and Jia-li felt the water tug at her feet almost like a rope wrapped around them. Was he doing that? "Would you be willing to risk my home?" he asked.

Well, my tunic and trousers need washing anyway. Jia-li gave into the water's urging and slid into the pool, still clothed. Long came closer and, when she didn't flinch, drew her into his arms. "If I surprise you," he asked softly, "you cannot burn me here, can you?"

"Do you intend to surprise me?"

One of his wet hands caressed her cheek. "I would like to try."

Jia-li thought she would like that as well.

THE END

Bonus Story:

A time for Every Purpose

A Time for Every Purpose

The screens in the house of Zheng Zhuang didn't block sound. From where she stood, Sofiya could hear them quite clearly—her daughter and Prince Ilya. "So I had marriage lines drawn up," he was saying to Kseniya, "between myself and your mother. The priest dated them so that the arrangement supposedly occurred before you were born, before I was wed to Grushka."

Sofiya grabbed the edge of the screen. She wanted nothing more than to scream at him, at his lack of regard for her wishes in the matter. *How could he do this to me?*

She peered around the edge of the screen, getting her first glimpse of Prince Ilya Vladimirov in decades. He seemed absolutely alien in this house, a tall man with graying blond hair and ruddy cheeks. The prince might wear that red tunic with its colorful embroidery about the neck at his manor, but his trousers and horse boots suggested travel. He looked tired and, for a brief instant, her anger with him lessened. It was in Sofiya's nature to help others and, with a child between them, there was still a tie to this man, no matter how much she wished she didn't feel it.

At the table, Kseniya regarded her father with dismay. "You can't do that, Father. The Church wouldn't allow it. That would be bigamy."

Sofiya knew better. The Church and the princes shared power, a matter of continual negotiation. What they would censure a farmworker for, a prince could do with relative impunity, receiving a quick dispensation and a mild penance.

She calmed herself and took a more careful look at the man who had just claimed to have married her by proxy. Ilya seemed uncomfortable, more likely feeling out of place than enduring uneasiness over this ecclesiastical misstep. He'd come to visit Kseniya at her husband's house, south of the border between the Rus principalities and the Celestial Empire. It was, Sofiya reckoned, the first time the man had traveled so far in his entire life.

He sighed and ruffled a hand through his hair. "Father Petrov was the one who arranged it for me, not long after Grushka's death. The paperwork was intended to remain lost unless your sister didn't return, in which case it would suddenly be found and then *you* would become my legitimate heir."

"Do you realize what you've done?" Kseniya asked. "It makes your other daughters bastards."

He'd had three wives, Sofiya recalled, but only two daughters by them. The older princess had been given as a concubine to the dragon wizard and died bearing a child on a frozen mountaintop. The younger princess had died from influenza about a year ago. That made Sofiya grateful her six children had all survived to adulthood, only now this bit of chicanery threatened them.

The prince shook his head. "Your half-sisters are dead, Kseniya. They are beyond caring."

Sofiya stepped beyond the screen so that Kseniya and the

prince could see her. "My children aren't."

Ilya had the grace to flush, at least. He rose slowly, favoring one knee. "I apologize, madam. I thought it necessary at the time."

Sofiya came farther into the room, too angry to be intimidated by a nobleman, even this one. "If I was supposedly married to you, that makes all five of *my* other children bastards. How could you do that?"

"It makes your first child legitimate, though," the prince pointed out, gesturing to where Kseniya still sat.

Kseniya rolled her eyes. Her husband, Yun-qi, had no interest in her legitimacy or lack of it, and therefore it had little value for Kseniya either. And as Yun-qi needed neither the prince's money nor his goodwill, the inheritance of a distant northern household would only be an inconvenience.

"She is the one least likely to care!" Sofiya closed her eyes and shook her head. "Why is this happening?"

"Mother, why don't you come sit down," Kseniya said. "This may be my fault."

Sofiya hadn't come too close before, in some part fearing ridicule over the manner of her dress. She wore clothing preferred by the people in Jen-li village, a blue tunic that tied at the neck and shoulder over a pair of loose brown trousers. She'd left her hair uncovered in deference to local custom, but neatly pinned up. Even so, her garb would be considered scandalous among the Rus. And the last time Ilya had seen her she'd been a slender girl of sixteen, with hair redder than

Kseniya's. Now she was a matron, a mother of six children...and her hair had gone mostly gray.

She did her best to walk serenely to the table and there she settled on a cushion with far more ease than Ilya had shown. The prince wisely said nothing to her of her costume.

"I wrote to him," Kseniya said, placing a hand atop hers. Of her five daughters, Kseniya looked most like her, only her hair was still red, and her hands were those of a young mother. "After you left Petrivka and came here, Mother. To let him know the new priest was making things uncomfortable for the healers there."

The new priest lacked respect for the healers and wise-women of the common folk, calling them witches instead. A mistake, since the ruling family of the princedom also had healers among its womenfolk.

Ilya settled on his cushion again, grunting as he did so—he was no longer a slender stripling, either. "I had an altercation with the bishop. He gave into my demand that healers not be persecuted, but exposed this particular bit of foolishness as my punishment for defying him."

"*You* are being punished?" Sofiya said, allowing her disbelief to show in her voice. "You? It's my children who are punished by this."

"I am aware of that." He splayed both hands on the table's rosewood surface. "The bishop intended it for me, I assure you."

"Your children are dead. Your wives are dead. How are you punished by this?"

"Because he has no heir now, save me," Kseniya pointed out, her fingers squeezing Sofiya's hand. "And I don't want to be his heir."

Sofiya turned to Kseniya. "This makes you a princess, does it not?"

Kseniya shuddered. "Yes, mother. I should point out that because your marriage by proxy supposedly predates all of his other marriages, his other wives have been relegated to the status of mistress. You *are* officially his wife in the eyes of the Church."

She had worked that out already. If the bishop enforced the spurious marriage, she would become Ilya's wife—a farm girl thrust upon a prince. "No one actually believes this, do they?"

He sighed. "No, but the bishop holds the power in such matters, and has already declared all my other marriages void. It is done, and there is no going back."

Sofiya leaned back and gazed at Ilya. That night he'd lain with her long ago, he'd been on his way to meet his intended wife. She recalled that quite clearly. She had known then that he wouldn't marry her, but nevertheless had conceived a brief passion for a diffident young prince with pretty eyes and a sad tale. It had been the worst time to form an attachment to a young man. "Surely someone else knew these papers were drawn up *after* your marriage to Grushka?"

"Only myself, Father Petrov, and my uncle knew of it. They're both dead now, so it is my word against...a piece of paper."

"A rather damning piece of paper." Sofiya turned to Kseniya

with narrowed eyes. "He doesn't actually have any authority on this side of the border, does he?"

Kseniya smiled at her father's outraged expression. "No, Mother."

"Good." Sofiya rose, straightened her tunic, and looked down her nose at him. "Ilya Vladimirov, you are an idiot."

Then she gathered her dignity and walked away.

Kseniya came to her bedchamber a short time later, a half-smile lingering on her lips. Although Kseniya had her father's height, in most other ways she'd taken after her mother, which gave Sofiya great pleasure, even though she rarely said so. "He's very embarrassed, Mother, and almost apologetic."

Sofiya had kept her hands busy by refolding every bit of clothing she'd had in her tall cabinet. She set the last tunic back inside and shut the doors. "*Almost*. I believe that."

Kseniya sat down on the edge of her bed. "Mother, I sincerely doubt he intended for you to be bothered by this."

"I doubt he thought of me in any way at all." Sofiya sat next to her daughter and took her hand. "He figured I would never know, and he would never have to face up to it."

Kseniya bit her lips, and then said, "He says he wrote to you, some months after your husband died."

Sofiya felt a guilty flush heat her cheeks. *The letter*.

She sighed, got up, and opened the cabinet again. After

digging under a couple of spare quilts, she pulled out the wooden box that held her personal treasures. They were laughable things by the standards of a prince, a pair of earrings her parents had given to her, a sting of copper coins gifted by her husband, beads taken from an old headdress that had belonged to her grandmother. Selling them would probably bring no more than a few days' wages, so she'd kept them. Underneath it all lay two folded pieces of beige paper, yellowed with age yet still sealed with wax.

She handed it to Kseniya. "I didn't know who'd sent it, but even so, I wasn't eager to share it with Father Ivanoff."

The priest had been the only person in the village who would have learned to read. The skill was forbidden to commoners.

Kseniya turned the letter over and glanced at the seal. "This is Father's seal."

"How was I to know?" Sofiya tucked a strand of loose hair behind her ear.

"Why have you never shown me this before?"

Because it had been *her* secret, a precious thing. She had long believed it had come from her prince, most likely a polite letter of condolence on her becoming a widow. It had passed through many hands to reach her; someone had—*he* had—thought her worth that effort. That was enough. "I never needed to know what it said." She gazed down at her hands. "I don't suppose the prince realizes that I don't read."

Kseniya smiled gently. "I didn't mention that to him. May

I read it to you?"

Sofiya nodded, and cringed as her daughter broke the seal. It had been there for so long. It seemed as if opening the thing would release whatever tidings it had held for so many years.

Perhaps it's time.

Kseniya opened it with careful fingers, but the brown paper rattled, dry with age. For a moment, she gazed at the faded ink that cluttered the paper. Her eyes darted across the page. "He starts off with his usual salutations, and then he says, 'I cannot know if you have heard that my daughter Anushka has been taken as a concubine by the wizard of the southern mountains. Grim news, but even worse, I must also tell you that Kseniya went with her to that place. I cannot promise they will ever return. I have served our daughter very ill in this, and failed your trust.'"

"I knew that," Sofiya said. News did trickle out to the villages eventually.

Kseniya nodded and waved one hand. "He goes on to talk about his reason for sending us, mostly that he feared eradication of our people such as the wizard's actions toward the Mongols and Tatars. Then he says, 'My household has been in flight since that time, and thus I cannot come to you to speak of this in person. I fear Anushka will never return, but in my heart I know Kseniya will. She has twice the intelligence of her sister, three times the resourcefulness, and four times the stubbornness. The first two qualities I believe she must have inherited from you.'"

Sofiya smiled at the backhanded compliment. "I would have to agree."

"Here it is," Kseniya said. "'This belief has driven me to take a step you might find objectionable, but I feel it necessary for the stability of the princedom.' Then he goes on to describe the whole scheme."

For a moment Kseniya read in silence, turning to the second page of the letter, her lips moving while her eyes remained fixed. Then she glanced up. "I don't know a good way to say this, Mother. He asked you to come to him."

"Why?"

Kseniya raised her eyebrows, a smile tugging at the corner of her lips. "To become his wife. He felt bad about this even then, it seems, and hoped you might come and make a truth out of his lie."

Sofiya laughed, too startled to guard her reaction. "What must he have been thinking? His family would never have accepted me."

But I was not married at that time. If the prince had simply put that date on the marriage lines, it would have been legal, if not wise. Then again, it would have failed to make Kseniya his heir.

Kseniya touched her shoulder. "Mother, I always felt he chose better for himself than his family did for him."

Sofiya stroked her daughter's hair. "You might be biased, child."

"I'm not." Kseniya cast a sheepish glance toward her. "I

didn't know you at all then, but I thought that."

She had handed Kseniya over to Ilya when she was only a baby, thinking the prince could better care for his daughter than a country girl without a husband. She'd not seen Kseniya again until she was full grown, standing in her herbalist's shop in Petrivka, her foreign husband with her and her belly showing that she would soon have a child. Although most Rus women never spoke of a child until after it was born, Kseniya feared that her coming child—now a healthy boy—might be endangered by the magic she and Yun-qi both carried. And thus, she had come to her own mother for a healer's help.

Kseniya rose. "Would you be willing to look at his knee, Mother? He twisted it a couple of days ago, he says, getting off his horse. You would do it better than I."

Sofiya sighed. "That's how I got into this trouble in the first place."

"Why are the tables this low?" Ilya groused under his breath. "I'd do better if I didn't have to sit on the damned ground."

Sofiya folded her arms over her chest. "Do you want me to heal your knee or not?"

"Of course, I want you to heal my knee," he said. "And I am not an idiot."

Sofiya decided not to answer that. She glanced about the main room of the inner hall, and saw the tables, all either too tall or short to suit his height. "I think one of the bedchambers would be better for this. You can lie down and keep your weight off it."

He raised his eyebrows.

"Don't bother to think it, Ilya," she told him sternly. "I am older, and experienced enough that my head won't be turned by a simple healing."

That had been the start of their troubles. Healing a man often left the healer with a strong attraction to him. She had healed a cut on the hand of a passing traveler, a prince on the way to meet his intended bride. He'd been handsome, and young, and unhappy with that upcoming marriage, and her sympathy for him had only fueled her attraction. A few hours later, she'd found herself in the hay in her father's stable with him. A few weeks later realized she was carrying his child. At fifteen, she hadn't given that possibility the proper consideration.

He rose stiffly and followed her to the bedchamber generally used for guests of the Zheng household. She pulled back the bed-curtains, revealing delicately embroidered cotton—old Bao-yu's work. Ilya shot her a doubtful look. "I can't lie on that."

"Why not?"

"I stink of horse," he said.

"Yes, you do." She drew the coverlet down and folded it up. Once she'd revealed the plain sheets, she bade him sit on the bed's platform and remove his boots. "Lie back."

He complied, surprising her. He lay with his hands at his side and gazed at her with a furrowed brow. Sofiya came and sat next to him. She laid one hand on the crown of his head, just to get a feel for the flow of energies in his body.

"I would make you a good husband," he said, a new attack.

"I have no need of a husband." She moved her hand to his forehead. "Try to be calm."

He closed his eyes. "I would like to have you for my wife."

"Your family would never allow it." When she decided that his energies flowed properly through his mind, she placed her hand to his throat. “A simple village herbalist? I think not.”

"It's not a matter of allowing it. The bishop has already said it is fact, therefore they cannot complain."

Sofiya drew her hand away and looked at him. "Do you think I’m a fool? They would do their best to make me miserable. How many sisters do you have? And aunts and nieces? "

He rose up on his elbows to argue with her. "I do control who resides within my household. If any were to give you difficulty, I would send them away."

And so it went, with him giving a promise to combat her every argument, save the first—that she had no need for a husband. When she laid her hands against his swollen knee, she willed the energy to flow more slowly there to bring the swelling down. "I cannot simply heal this, Ilya. There are tissues that need to heal, and that will take time."

He didn't argue that time.

Sofiya glanced up at his face. He'd fallen asleep when she

called for his energies to slow. So she took advantage of the time to inspect his health—as would only be proper—she told herself. She began with one hand laid against the top of his head and felt the energy flowing through the power center there. Like many older men, his blood flowed sluggish through tightened portals, so she began the process of setting that to rights. She moved her hand to his throat, and then to the next power center and next until her hand lay at his groin, where the restrictions of the body's flows had become problematic. But she knew how to ease that as well.

These were simple things, things a healer could easily set right. That told her he'd refused to let the women of his family examine him. So he was not as compliant as she'd always thought.

When she was done, he still had the inflamed knee, but would feel far better, she suspected. Sofiya gazed down at him for a time. Her heart still raced, the flow of life in her body wishing to be matched to his. She willed herself to be calm instead, breathing in and out slowly.

I hardly know this man.

Certainly not any better than she'd known him that night long ago when they'd made a daughter between them. His face had aged well, his neat beard hiding a bit of excess flesh at the throat. The gray in his hair blended in with pale blond, making him look deceptively young. Sofiya thought ruefully of her own gray hair, only hints of red left in it now, and sighed.

The Church taught that marriage beyond the age of forty was inappropriate. At that age, one should begin thinking of eternal reward and service to God rather than bodily desires. In her life, though, she'd known plenty of husbands and wives beyond that age who still craved their partner's touch. She'd helped deliver children to women older than she was.

She'd never understood that quite as well as she did now.

Ilya snorted softly in his sleep and shifted on the bed. Sofiya turned and walked out of the room before she did anything foolish.

"He was tried already from the travel," she told Kseniya when she found her daughter in the back courtyard. "He fell asleep in the first empty bedchamber."

Kseniya caught her husband's eye and gestured for Yun-qi to join them. "That's good enough. He can stay there till he wakes up. I've told his men to make themselves comfortable in the front courtyard, although if he plans to stay more than a day I'll need to make better arrangements for them."

Yun-qi arrived at his wife's side, his dark eyes amused—as they often were. He made a half-bow in Sofiya's direction. "Am I to call you Princess now, Mother?"

Sofiya favored him with a dry look. "You are to call me Mother. The other is simply foolishness."

"It cannot so easily be waved away," Kseniya said.

Sofiya set her hands on her hips. "And he cannot force me to be his wife, can he?"

The morning breeze in the courtyard was cool, making the

summer heat light. Sofiya sat with a wide basket on her lap, bundling herbs picked at the sunrise. Usually her youngest daughter, Ivanka—who had married Yun-qi's younger brother, Li-huan—joined her, but Ivanka was in her confinement now, leaving Sofiya to watch alone.

Then she heard Ilya's footsteps approaching. His heavy boots made a distinctive sound on the flagstones of the courtyard, one dragging slightly. "Still sore?"

"What are they doing?" he asked in turn.

He stood behind where she sat, evidently caught by the slow movements of the men of the household—plus Kseniya and her niece Jia-li—going through their morning exercises. Today they worked through a set of figures that had something to do with wind, although Sofiya couldn't recall the exact name. "It is about discipline," she said. "Doing the right thing at the right moment."

Ilya made a harrumphing sound. "Is that meant to be a slur on my behavior?"

She half-turned to gaze up at him. "No, it's the answer to your question. If you want to read an insult into it, you may."

Ilya came closer and lowered himself to sit on the first step. Not as slowly as yesterday, she noticed, but still stiffly. "Do they do this every day?"

"As I said, it's a discipline." She kept her eyes on the moving figures, aware that he carefully did the same. "I want an answer from you."

He glanced in her direction, although she didn't meet his

eyes. "To what question?"

She pointed toward her daughter with her chin. "Why did you choose to have my daughter trained as a boy? To the sword? Surely you knew it would make her an outcast among the women."

"She is good, isn't she?" Pride leaked into his voice.

"I think she would say she is not as proficient as Zhuang or Yun-qi, but more so than Li-huan."

Ilya nodded. "Not long after you gave her to me—she must have been three by then—I met a traveler in a small village. He was a Condara, one of their mystics. And he told me things about myself that gave me no doubt he had some gift. Then he told me of the dragon wizard, how the man could only be defeated by one of his own blood."

The Condara had seers among them, a gift that passed to many of their men. Sofiya could not know whether Ilya knew that Yun-qi's mother was of the Condara people, and through her, Kseniya's husband possessed a hint of that same gift. "That would have been long before the Rus had trouble with the dragon wizard," she only noted.

"Yes, but I recalled what the wizard's dragons had done to the Mongols and the Tatars in my grandfather's day, how those peoples are all but extinct, so I listened to the seer's words. He told me my eldest daughter would go into great danger, and the only thing that would save her was her courage and valor."

Sofiya squared her shoulders. "One need not hold a sword to have courage, Ilya."

He turned on the step to face her. "And if you had raised

her, I likely would not have found it necessary. But she was being raised by my aunts, and all I could see that would come of that was fussiness and pettiness. So I removed her from the women's household and gave her to the man who'd trained *me* as a boy. I asked him to train her as he would one of the boyars' sons."

Sofiya wrapped string about a bundle of astralgus with more vigor than needed. "Knowing it would make her an outcast."

"Knowing that it would, among other things, keep her out of Grushka's hands. That woman hated Kseniya and all she represented, and would have always treated her like a bastard anyway."

In some ways, that made sense. "Kseniya has never complained of it to me," Sofiya admitted. "So that you know. She has never complained."

His gaze returned to the courtyard and his daughter, and a fond smile stole over his face. "No, she's not given to complaint, is she? She has every good quality I could have wished for in a son—save not being a son. I have no fear of leaving my properties in her hands."

"She will not take them, Ilya, and I do not think your people would accept one of her sons, given they all look so much like their father." No matter the bloodlines, the appearance of foreignness would be enough to cause trouble.

"You must help me convince her," Ilya said.

She considered that, and asked, "Are you staying?"

"If her husband's father will allow me," he said. "I didn't

intend to stay the night without his permission, but I seem to have slept the evening and night through."

"You were very tired," she reminded him.

"I wonder if I could learn to do that?" he asked, more to himself than her.

Sofiya bit her lips to keep from laughing. Ilya was closer to her age, not much past fifty, but Zhuang was near seventy. "Perhaps you should speak to Zhuang. He might be willing to teach you. It would be good for you."

Ilya nodded, as if willing to take her advice, which surprised her.

If there was anything Ilya did know, it was how to sweeten others toward him. For the next few days, he *tried.* He arranged for his men to board with the Liu family, who took in guests. He bade them severely to be respectful of the local people.

In the mornings, he copied the figures Zhuang tried to teach him, although clumsily. There was more laughter than Ilya liked, she was sure, but he kept his temper.

He spoke with all the members of the Zheng family as if they were equals, played with his grandsons by Kseniya, and talked with young Jia-li, the daughter of his daughter Anushka. And when he found time with Sofiya alone, he pressed his case again.

"I have no reason to go with you, Ilya," she told him finally, when he came on her in the workroom grinding down the roots of red sage. "I am happy here."

For a moment, he looked shocked—almost as if he'd never once considered that she might continue to refuse his importuning. "How could you not want to return home?"

"I have two daughters here," she said. "I have friends here, who value my learning and experience. Rahime and Yun-qi are both herbalists, so we have much in common. What would I have should I go with you? Do you want me to believe that my children would be welcome there? Or that the women of your household would even speak with me? I heard how they treated Kseniya the last time she visited there."

His jaw clenched, and he had the grace to look ashamed of himself. "I made the mistake in the past of not ruling adequately over the women of my family. At present, I have sent my sisters to live with their own children."

From what she'd heard, he'd been under the thumb of sisters and aunts for his entire life. "Why?"

"That is what started this." He sighed heavily and sat down next to her. "My eldest sister decided that I should marry again almost the day Ludmilla died."

"Another twenty-year-old bride? You are too old," Sofiya said with a mild laugh.

"Thank you," he said in a dry voice. "I had no use for yet another bride that they chose for me. My refusal to consider another alliance—or rather their refusal to accept my refusal—caused discord in my household, so I sent them away."

"I am surprised," she admitted, settling her pestle aside.

“But now I understand why you need a wife so badly. There is no one to run your household."

He remained silent for a moment, and then finally said, "I want a *wife*, Sofiya. I want a woman to keep me warm at night, not a housekeeper. I can hire someone to do that."

She considered her calloused hands. She kept the spots at bay with a poultice of fenugreek, honey, and lemon, but there was no doubt that they were *not* the hands of a princess. "You can hire a woman to keep you warm at night, I imagine."

He made a scoffing sound. "Whether you believe me nor not, I don't care for the idea of a mistress. I've not had one since I was in my early twenties. I prefer to seek my comfort at home."

Despite what she thought of noblemen in general and her own past experience with him, that didn't surprise her. Kseniya had never mentioned her father having a mistress. She tried something else. "Ilya, you hardly know me."

"Better than I did any of the others when I wed them," he pointed out. "And I do know you, Sofiya, far better than you think. I saw you every day as I watched Kseniya grow up. In so many things she did, I thought ‘she must have gotten that from her mother.’ Clever, prideful, resourceful—Kseniya has strengths I cannot attribute to myself."

He'd said as much in his letter. She particularly recalled the mention of stubbornness. That was the gift *he'd* passed on to their daughter. "I will consider it, Ilya. That is all I will promise."

He glanced up at her, his blue eyes full of hope. "That is all

I can ask."

That night, Sofiya gazed up at the canopy of her bed. The curtains were not drawn, and a breeze came in through the screens. She liked it here, in this house. She liked her life here. Yun-qi's family had made her welcome and comfortable here.

But what if there is more? At fifty, she had a life of contemplation and work ahead of her. Back in Rus she was considered too old to marry, too old for a man.

But I already am married, in the Church's eyes, even if falsely so.

She pushed away her quilt, rose, and made her way down to the guest room. The door opened quietly, and Sofiya stepped inside, her feet whispering on the reed mats. She heard him snoring softly and, for a time she considered not waking him. But she sat on the edge of the platform and touched his forehead.

He jerked awake with a strangled sound. "What?"

Sofiya gave him time to calm. "It is still not a *yes*, Ilya. But you have my permission to try to convince me."

"What?"

She waited. The sheet had fallen when he sat up, revealing that he'd lain down to sleep without any tunic.

"Oh," he finally said. His fingers touched her cheek, and then he grasped her braid. "Come closer."

Sofiya lay in the pre-dawn darkness and listened to his snoring. It was overly warm in that room with the screens closed, but she didn't think she could get away from him to open them. Ilya lay behind her with one arm around her waist and a leg over her hips, a possessiveness even in sleep that surprised her.

It was pleasant to have a lover.

She had missed this from her married days, although that had been long ago. She'd missed the sense of belonging somewhere, or rather, *with* someone. She could almost believe his promises to keep his womenfolk from belittling her.

And he had been unusually considerate of her wishes in the last few days. The temptation to give in increased every hour.

Temptation only, though. Sofiya knew better than to think that a nobleman would not tire of a low-born wife quickly. Once the passion of getting his way died out, he would be saddled with a wife who embarrassed him.

The gentle snoring had stopped, and the arm around her waist tightened. "You're awake, are you not?" he asked.

"Yes, Ilya."

"But you still say no."

She felt his forehead touch the back of her neck, resting there. "Ilya, surely you see what you're asking is impossible. I'm a commoner. I will never be accepted as your wife."

"You will be accepted because I say you will," he snapped. "Damnation, woman. You *are* my wife. There is nothing for anyone to question."

"Save your sanity, Ilya. Or they will say I bewitched you."

"Why are you so afraid of this?" he whispered. "Do I not please you in at least one or two ways?"

She chuckled at his desperate tone. "Ilya, you please me in many ways, but I fear the day you will tire of me."

"Sofiya, yes, I did have a mistress when I was young, for a few years. But after that, I was never unfaithful to any of my wives again."

"I do not think you would be unfaithful." She pulled away from him. "You are nothing if not dutiful, Ilya. You would stick with me whether you came to hate me or not. And I wouldn't be able to bear that."

He said nothing as she struggled free of the bedding and gathered her tunic and shirt and trousers. She dressed in silence.

"Do you think I am so petty?" he asked. "That I am so easily swayed by others that I cannot form my own opinions? Make up my own mind? "

She paused with on hand on the door. She owed him an answer, but couldn't look back at him. "I don't know that you ever *have* before, Ilya. You might be able to, but I don't want to be the one who is hurt and humiliated when you find out that you can't."

Sofiya managed not to be alone with Ilya again until he left that day, taking his men away with him. And every night after that, she lay and stared up at her canopy far longer than she should, waking in the mornings with dry and bitter eyes and wondering if she'd not made a mistake.

Is this all there is?

She had, once and long ago, thrown caution away for a man. Of that she had a daughter, and the disapproval of the town for being an unmarried mother. *I was fifteen then, not fifty.*

The days sped on, and she could not seem to escape her tiredness. Kseniya tried to cheer her, and for her daughter's sake, Sofiya did her best to return to her normal cheerfulness. But the question dragged at her mind as she bound herbs and hung them in the rafters to dry.

When Ivanka emerged from her seclusion, many of the Zheng family's friends gathered to host a party for the new baby, a pretty infant with dark red curls that pleased her father immensely. Li-huan enjoyed the congratulations of his friends, while Yun-qi was teased about his failure to produce a single red-haired child.

Sofiya sat with Rahime, who occasionally provided a translation when the talk went too quickly for her to follow. Like her, Rahime came from another people, and even after almost four decades, still found the local customs bemusing. Then Rahime spotted Li-huan's eldest about to fall into the pool and dashed away to catch the boy.

Kseniya joined her there after a moment, settling at the table. "It is difficult to keep up. Sometimes even *my* head tires of translating."

Sofiya nodded. "Mine aches, I must confess. But this is something I would never tire of watching, I think. It pleases me to see the three peoples getting along, how willing they are to accept us here. If we are to share a border, this is how it should be."

"We have been fortunate," Kseniya said. "The priest here is open-minded enough to understand that the traditions of different peoples will not always agree. He urges a tolerance that many of his station might not. And you know yourself how much difference the priest can make in a town."

She nodded—she had fled Petrivka because of an intolerant priest. "I will do my best to convince your father to try to emulate this on the other side of the border."

Kseniya's eyes met hers, her red brows drawn together. "From this distance?"

"No," Sofiya admitted with a sigh.

What is it, Mother?"

"I need you to write to your father for me," she said before her nerve flowed away. She didn't know how long she had known and denied it to herself, but the question had been answered for her.

Kseniya regarded her with brows drawn together. "Do you regret your decision, Mother?"

"It's not a matter of regret," she said, laying one hand atop her daughter's. "But I've changed my mind, and I should go to him." The time to act was now, before she was further along.

Kseniya seemed as surprised as Sofiya suspected Ilya would be. "What brought this on?"

She would have to say it aloud when Kseniya wrote the

letter anyway, no matter that it was considered ill luck. She took a deep breath. "I am with child."

Kseniya's eyes stayed on the table, but the corners of her mouth twisted up as if she fought not to laugh.

"Oh, go ahead," Sofiya said. "Yun-qi is an evil influence on you."

Kseniya covered her mouth, but didn't laugh aloud. "I'm amused at my father. He was always frustrated because he didn't have more children. Apparently, all he must do is reside in the same house with you and you become pregnant—for surely nothing happened between the two of you while he was here, did it?"

Sofiya gave her daughter a dry look. She didn't intend to explain why Ilya had always had such a difficult time fathering children, that constriction in his groin that she'd healed away. In retrospect, healing him might have been a foolish choice. "Yes, of course, that's it. We'll call it a miracle, and that will make everything work out."

"I see," Kseniya said.

"It was only the one night," she insisted. "The night before he left."

"Ah, now I understand why he left so suddenly. His feelings were hurt."

Sofiya shook her head. "Men believe that lying with a woman completely melts her will."

"Mother, why did you refuse him if you had such...interest in him?"

"Your father is a prince. How humiliating must it be for him to be forced to take a wife like me? How long before he hates me?"

Kseniya regarded her with a worried brow. "Mother, if you believe that, why even consider going to him? You and I both know you need not bear his child. Or bear the child and stay here. He would never need to know."

She had considered that option. And the other. "It is important to him, Kseniya. That much I know. He might tire of me, but never his children."

"Children?" Kseniya asked softly.

Sofiya touched her daughter's brow, brushing back a tendril of red hair. "Yes, you'll have a brother and a sister of this, I'm afraid."

"An heir," Kseniya said softly, and then straightened in her chair. "Shall I go get paper and ink?"

"It can wait until tomorrow, I think."

The celebration went on about them, while her daughter clung to her hand. "It will be fine, Mother."

"I know."

Sofiya had come up on the mountain to calm herself after a hectic morning with the children. The boys had far more energy than she did recently, and exhausted her quickly. She had better get accustomed to that. While older women bore children regularly, two at once promised twice as many challenges.

Even so, it was a pleasant day for gathering herbs. She worked her way along the stream and carefully selected greens to put in her basket. A lone rider approaching the household along the path from town caught her eye. Not a local man—the rider had light hair, and wore clothes from her homeland.

My husband. A title for him she hardly dared to think.

Ilya was days sooner than they'd expected, surely. Kseniya had said eight to ten days just for the message to reach his household, and at least as much for them to hear back. Sofiya had counted on having several more days. She laid a hand over her belly, her breath short.

The rider on the road waved to her and, resigned to being caught unprepared, Sofiya began the long walk down the hillside to the house. She'd only gone a third of the way when she saw that he was coming up the path toward her. At least they would be able to get any embarrassing questions out of the way here, rather than taking anger or embarrassment into the household.

If he'd looked road-worn the first time he'd come for a visit, then this time he looked a wreck. But she noticed he didn't limp, and his color appeared good. Her healing had granted some long-term effect, it seemed. She stopped a few feet from him, uncertain what to expect.

Ilya bowed, and came to take her hands. "I left in anger the last time I was here, Sofiya, and I have come to beg your forgiveness."

The words sounded rehearsed, but they weren't the ones

she'd expected. "Of course."

"And I hope you will grant me another chance to convince you to return with me."

His face seemed perfectly earnest when he said that.

Sofiya regarded him warily. "I have already said I would go with you." When he looked confused, she added, "In the letter Kseniya wrote for me."

He glanced back toward the house, the sun glinting on the silver in his hair. When he faced her again, his brows were drawn together. "The one she wrote before I came?"

Sofiya felt her face warming. She would have to explain it all herself. "Ah. You never got the letter. A couple of weeks ago, that she wrote to you?"

"No, I never got such a letter." And a smile touched his face, making him seem younger. He reached over and took her hands. "Then you have reconsidered?"

It will be obvious soon. The pregnancy, almost a month gone, had already caused her breasts to swell, although the loose clothes she wore hid that. She let him hold her hands, took a deep breath, and said, "Ilya, I will return with you, but I want you to make me a promise first."

"Anything," he said rashly.

"Be practical, Ilya. I am willing to be your wife, but you must promise me that I will have control of the household, and that none of your family will wrest it from me."

He sighed. "I have already said so, Sofiya. You have my word."

"And that includes any children we have," she said firmly.

He laughed shortly. "I doubt that will be a problem, Sofiya."

She stared up at him.

"Agreed," he finally said, shaking his head. "Sofiya, I want you for my wife. These other things will work out in time, will they not?"

"A little more than eight months," she told him. "Which you would know if you'd received that letter."

"What did Kseniya write to me?" he asked, and then, "Eight months?"

It was unlucky to speak of it, but the man was to be her husband. Or rather, he already was. "Yes, it's been almost a month since you left, Ilya, and eight more than that makes nine. I may not be able to read, but I can cipher."

“Nine months?” His eyes went wide, and then shifted to her belly. "You're...?"

He didn’t want to speak the word, for fear of cursing his own children.

She felt a rush of giddy emotion which didn't feel at all matronly. "Yes, you seem to have that effect on me."

He stepped back, the worry line between his fair brows returning. "Is this safe for you? Because I know women...that healers can...if they must..."

A healer *could* end her own pregnancy, as Kseniya had hinted. "Ilya, I would not have told you if I had reservations. I've borne six children already, although never two at once. It is not difficult for me. I admit I would like to have Kseniya there, though."

In all honesty, she would rather bear the children here, where there were healers and herbalists to help her, but if she did so outside his household, others would use that as reason to question their legitimacy.

"Anything," he promised. "Whatever you need will be provided."

Sofiya shook her head, amused by his awed voice. "You should have expected something like this to happen."

His eyes finally left her belly. "I was not very prolific in the past, Sofiya."

She could explain later the healing she'd done. "Shall we go down to the house? They all know, by the way, so there will not be any surprise."

His expression went serious. "I considered your complaints, Sofiya. I will not allow them to turn me against you. I regret that I lacked the will to stand up to my family earlier. I should have married you when I was seventeen."

"The time was not right," she said, feeling her cheeks go warm. "But yes, you should have."

And surprisingly, he didn't argue.

Ilya kept his promises to her, and even suggested that her children by her first husband—whether or not that marriage was considered legitimate in the eyes of the Church—should move from the villages around Petrivka to New Kiev to be closer to their mother. Her son, Ivan, came first, and built a new smithy in the city.

Not long after, two babes came safely into the world, the prince and princess of New Kiev. Sofiya presented them to her husband not many days later, and in time they were properly christened Mikhail and Nadezhda, with their half-brother Ivan as their godfather.

"I never thought to have a son," Ilya whispered to Sofiya as they carried the babes from the church out into the daylight. "But I have had daughters, and I can only pray that these two will live and thrive as Kseniya has."

He *had* lost two of his three daughters, so Sofiya understood his worry.

Forbidden communion because of her foreign husband, Kseniya had waited outside. "Father, I assure you this little sister of mine will be able to take care of herself."

"She will," Yun-qi promised, with what Sofiya hoped was foreknowledge from his faint seer's gift. "And when it's time for the boy to learn to rule, send *her* over the border to us to learn the sword."

"Sword?" Ilya asked plaintively. "Is it too much to hope for a quiet daughter who will sit in the women's house and embroider felt slippers for her aging father?"

"Perhaps." Sofiya gazed down at her newest daughter. "But your daughters and your granddaughter have fought dragons and wizards and fire-demons. Do not expect this girl to be any different."

THE END

If you enjoyed **The Dragon's Child,** please help other readers enjoy it too.

Review it. Reviews help other readers find the books they love with the themes and characters they're excited about. Let other readers know what you thought of the book by leaving an honest review. It doesn't have to be fancy, just honest. It can be one sentence long! It's a little known fact that for every review a unicorn is saved from destruction. So leave a review on **The Dragon's Child**, save a unicorn.

Recommend it. Help others find the book by recommending it to friends, reading groups, and message boards. If you're a member of Goodreads or another social media site designed especially for book lovers that is a great place to make recommendations (in groups you might be a member of, or voting for this book on the various lists it's on).

Join J. Kathleen Cheney's Newsletter to keep up with new publications and free stories that are available. Just visit her website at www.Jkathleencheney.com

Cast of Characters

In New Kiev:

Kseniya Ilyevna Vladimirova—*illegitimate daughter of Prince Ilya of New Kiev*

Anushka Ilyevna Vladimirova—*daughter of Prince Ilya, mother of Jia-li*

Prince Ilya Vladimirov—*father of Kseniya and Anushka*

Grushka—*first wife of Prince Ilya, Mother of Anushka*

Ludmilla—*third wife of Prince Ilya, mother of Ekaterina*

Ekaterina Ilyenvna Vladimirova—*daughter of Prince Ilya*

Father Petrov—*priest in New Kiev*

On the Dragon's Mountain:

Jia-li—*daughter of the Dragon Wizard, Jiang-long*

Jiang-long—*the emperor's Dragon Wizard*

Bao-yu—*wife of the Dragon Wizard, grandmother of Yun-qi*

Yun-qi—*the wizard's bodyguard*

Long—*the native Water Dragon*

In Petrivka:

Sofiya Lebedeva—*Kseniya's mother*

Ivanka Lebedeva—*Kseniya's youngest half-sister*

Grigori Vasiliyev—*Ivanka's husband (dead six months)*

Bogdan Vasiliyev—*Grigori's younger brother*

Oksana Vasiliyeva—*their sister*

Alexei—*Oksana's son*

In Jenli Village:

Zheng Li-huan—*Yun-qi's youngest half-brother*

Rahime—*concubine of the Dragon Wizard, Turkish princess, mother of Yun-qi and Li-huan*

Zheng Zhuang—*former bodyguard of the wizard, husband of Rahime, father of Li-huan*

Lili—*first wife of Li-huan*

Hu-lia—*Jia-li's best friend*

Mei-lin—*catty girl in the village*

Ming-hua—*servant to Mei-lin, daughter of a wizard*

More Works by J. Kathleen Cheney

The Golden City Series

The Golden City

The Seat of Magic

The Shores of Spain

The Seer's Choice

After the War

Other Works

Dreaming Death: A Palace of Dreams Novel

Iron Shoes: Tales from Hawk's Folly Farm

The Dragon's Child: Six Short Stories

Whatever Else

And Forthcoming Works,

From the world of Dreaming Death,

The Horn:

Oathbreaker

Original

Overseer

Coming 2017

About the Author:

J. Kathleen Cheney taught mathematics ranging from 7th grade to Calculus, but gave it all up for a chance to write stories. Her novella "Iron Shoes" was a 2010 Nebula Award Finalist. Her novel, **The Golden City** was a Finalist for the 2014 Locus Awards (Best First Novel). **Dreaming Death** (Feb 2016) is the first in a new series, the *Palace of Dreams Novels*.

Her website can be found at
www.JKathleenCheney.com

CPSIA information can be obtained
at www.ICGtesting.com
Printed in the USA
LVOW11s2321260318
571286LV00001B/37/P